To Make a Killing

Michael Crawshaw

First published in 2012
This edition published 2018

ISBN 9781481095198

Design and layout by Artsgraphique.com

Published by BroadPen Books, St Albans,
Hertfordshire, UK
An imprint of Batchwood Press

1

"Dear God, save me from this agony!"

Frank's body screamed in protest but he had come too far to stop now. He shut out the pain and pushed on. He entered the death zone, running on empty, legs burning, chest bursting, the only thing driving him on … cast-iron, certifiable madness. Why else would he do it?

He collapsed over the finish line and retched air into his starved lungs.

"Keep coming!" A marshal waved him forward.

Frank drifted into the rope funnel, grateful for something to hang onto. He picked up a place disc: one hundred and twenty seven. Out of a field of two hundred. Seriously, what was the point? With apologies he handed his disc to the team captain, hobbled over to an oak tree and collapsed on the sodden ground beneath.

"Are you all right, Sir?"

He looked up into the concerned gaze of DC Eddie Shore. The young officer's face wasn't quite the last he wanted to see on a day off. But it was a close call.

"Are you all right, Sir?" repeated Eddie.

"I think I'm still alive," said Frank. "But I'm waiting for official confirmation."

"It's best to keep on your feet and keep moving."

"What would you know about it?" asked Frank. But Eddie was right, so he pushed himself up onto his feet anyway.

"If you don't mind me asking, Sir, why do you put yourself through this?"

"I do it for laughs."

Frank hobbled away to the car park with Eddie in tow.

"The answer is no, by the way."

"You don't know what the question is yet, Sir."

"Yes I do," said Frank. "MacIntyre left me a message. But I don't work Sundays and he knows that."

"The Super did mention you might have a problem with it."

"It's not a problem," said Frank. "I just don't work Sundays unless I absolutely have to."

"Religious thing is it?"

"Never you mind, son."

Eddie shuffled his weight from one leg to the other. "He seemed very anxious to get hold of you, Sir."

"Did he now?" Frank opened his car and grabbed some warm clothes from the boot. "So what's got the old man's knickers in a twist then?"

"Some banker from Harpenden. Goes by the name of Daniel Goldcup."

"What about him?"

"Drowned in the Thames, Sir. The Met found his briefcase on Tower Bridge on Friday night. Body turned up this morning. The Super needs a DI for the autopsy and with holidays and sickies you're the only one he's got."

"A big vote of confidence that," said Frank. "Why can't it wait until tomorrow?"

"Apparently the Chief Constable knows the chairman of the bank."

"I don't do nepotism."

"There's something else," said Eddie. "The chairman is worried it wasn't suicide. He thinks it might have been a vigilante killing. Anti-capitalist protestors."

"What makes him think that?"

"There is nothing to suggest a suicide. No note, no history of depression. And this banker was only five weeks away from getting paid his bonus."

"Hmmm. Which bank are we talking about anyway?"

"Royal Shire," said Eddie.

"I thought the government had stopped bonuses at Royal Shire."

"Apparently not. And it was due to be a big one." He checked over both shoulders to make sure nobody was listening. "Many millions of pounds."

Frank pursed his lips. It would be odd for a man to top himself when he was about to land the jackpot. But even though it was true the whole country was angry about bankers' bonuses, he couldn't imagine anyone being mad enough to kill over it.

"What do you think then, Sir? I can run you in to the station if you like." Eddie smiled, almost pleading with Frank to do as the Superintendent asked.

"No you won't," said Frank. "I'll give you three reasons why I'm not going in. First, I don't care if the Chairman is best mates with the Home Secretary, he doesn't get any special treatment from me."

"I don't think anyone's suggesting ..."

"Second," interrupted Frank. "If someone did push this banker in the river then I'm in no desperate hurry to catch him. More likely we should give him a medal for making it one less fat cat paying himself a bonus out of tax-payers' money."

"That's a bit harsh ..."

"But fair," said Frank. He sat in the boot, kicked off his spikes and pulled on his tracksuit bottoms.

"And the third reason, Sir?"

"I don't work Sundays."

2

Mickey Summer paused at the glass doors to Royal Shire's Equities Division. Seven a.m. and there were already a couple of hundred brokers in, skimming papers and screens for news and overnight prices.

The sight of the trading floor always produced a tingle in his spine. He loved the business. Lived for it. However, in just five more weeks, he might have to turn his back on it. It might have to be sacrificed to save the one thing he loved even more.

He hoped not, as he pushed open the doors and walked across the floor. He hoped that Helen would buy into Plan 'A'. But if not ... so be it.

"Good of you to make it in," said his deputy, Glen, as Mickey reached his desk.

"Don't start. You're still in your pyjamas when I normally get in."

Glen blew a kiss. "I don't wear anything in bed darling."

"I really don't want to know." Mickey turned on his screens and computer and scrolled down the financial headlines. "Futures are off, oil price up. I reckon London's going to open down again."

"It was all gloom and doom in the weekend press as well," said Glen. "Mind you, this cold weather doesn't help sentiment."

"Brits and the weather!" shouted Ole from behind his bank of screens. "This would be considered a mild winter in Oslo."

"But we're not in Oslo you noggin." Mickey ripped off the front page of the FT, screwed it into a ball and threw it at Ole.

It was the cue for anyone within range to follow suit and Ole ducked under a shower of paper missiles and coffee cups, most of them empty.

Mickey flicked through the daily pack of research notes, highlighting key phrases to put into his one-minute call to clients. Then he pulled up the stock positions of the first client he was going to ring, grabbed his phone, took a deep breath and punched the autodial. One minute later he was on to the next call. After twenty minutes he'd rung round over a dozen of the biggest money managers in the market.

He put on his jacket and wandered over to the podium to kick off the morning meeting. Other speakers were already waiting, scribbling last-minute changes to whatever they were going to say. Mickey's message was in his head. If you had to write it down, it was too complicated.

He stood on the podium, blew on the microphone in time-honoured fashion, and waited until there was almost silence.

"Morning everyone. Looks like we'll be opening down again. I know the house view is that the recession is behind us but all the big punters are still worried about a triple dip and inflation. You might have spotted the oil price and dollar are both up? So for the time being my best guess is we're heading lower. Have a busy day."

Mickey hurried back to his desk.

The oil analyst took his place on the podium, waffling on about US refining margins, and the floor started to talk over him.

"Want to hear the latest odds on the promotion race?" asked Glen.

"Briefly," said Mickey.

"You are still two-to-one," said Glen. "But Daniel Goldcup has moved in to fours."

"I'd be a seller at fours," said Mickey, who'd never rated Daniel as senior management material. "Who else?"

"Ben's at fives. And then a lot of the chat last night was about how Benaifa's coming up on the rails."

Mickey followed Glen's gaze. The new Head of Sales was scribbling notes as she listened to the oil analyst, her free hand flicking her dark hair from her brown eyes.

"And she's prettier than you, Mickey."

Mickey pictured his bent nose and thinning brown hair. "I've got nicer legs though. Price?"

"Eights."

"Sounds about right. It's too early for Benaifa's next move. Who else?"

"That's it." Glen leaned forward to pick up an incoming call. "So you're still favourite."

"Too right I am. Now I better go check in with control."

He followed the corridor past the banks of desks to 'Overhead Row', as the troops had christened the suite of management offices.

Manita was at her desk outside Mickey's office, jacket buttoned up and black hair clipped back as usual.

"Mornin' darlin'," said Mickey. "How are you?"

"I'm fine, but Ollie has hurt his back again."

Mickey raised an eyebrow. "Having a bit of Posh 'n Becks were you?"

"Actually Ollie was moving the bed …"

"That's what I said."

"That's enough Mickey," she laughed, smiling.

"Sorry. Seriously though, you should send him to that back specialist I saw."

"That cost you three thousand pounds."

"I'll pay for it."

She rolled her head from side to side. "Thanks. But three thousand pounds would pay for ten or twenty operations for my countrymen back in Nepal. I couldn't spend all that on Ollie."

"Right," said Mickey awkwardly.

She picked up her notebook and followed him into his office.

Mickey dropped into the swivel chair and tapped 'four4two' into the computer. As it whirred into life, Manita slid over a typed sheet with his schedule for the day and his on-going 'to-do' list.

One item had been highlighted: *'Budget'*.

"Budget's already done," said Mickey.

"Weil wants you to redo it."

"Not again. While we're making up numbers about what business we might or might not do in the future, I'm missing real business out there on the floor."

"He says he really needs you to do it because you understand the business best."

"Huh," grunted Mickey.

"Plus he did ask nicely."

"Oh really."

"And he is your boss."

Mickey sighed. "I suppose it's nice to be appreciated."

"Is it now?" Manita raised an eyebrow.

"Leave it out. You know I appreciate you."

"Well, I'll find out just how much in five weeks won't I?"

"All depends on your expectations. I hope you won't be disappointed."

Mickey meant it. The way things were shaping up, with all the political pressure on City bonuses, none of the support staff would be getting one this year. Any money that did get into the bonus pot would be going out to pay the front-line bankers and brokers. The simple fact was that they were the ones that would walk if they didn't get paid what they expected. This idea that a bonus was some unexpected extra on top of the salary was bonkers. It was factored in to expectations and if it didn't come there would be trouble.

But Mickey wasn't going to let Manita down. She'd worked as hard over the year as anyone. So he had decided to bung her a bonus out of his own pocket. He'd been trying to get HR to make it look like it was being paid by the firm so that Manita would feel better about it. But they were being difficult about that and were insisting he would have to write her out a cheque. Never mind, she'd get her money, and that was the main point. And Mickey also knew that Manita would give every penny of it to her Nepalese charity.

"You going out on a coffee run?" he asked.

"I will if you ask nicely."

"Please will you go on a coffee run?"

"Gladly."

"I'll have a latte and a doughnut."

Manita folded her arms and looked pointedly at his stomach. "Make it a skinny latte and you can have a croissant."

Mickey pulled in his one-pack. "Pain au chocolat?"

"Dealt."

Manita headed for the doors and Mickey hurried back onto the trading floor.

It was strangely quiet. Everyone was at their desk but hardly anyone was on the phone. A lot of people were just sitting around doing nothing. Others were chatting in huddles. Mickey looked up at the large screen to see if the markets had crashed. The Footsie was down thirty points but that couldn't explain the deathly silence in the room.

He walked up to Glen who was staring at the ceiling. "What's going on?"

"Haven't you heard?"

Mickey cupped a hand round his ear. "Heard what?"

"Daniel Goldcup."

Mickey's stomach sank. Daniel had got it. He'd been promoted over Mickey's head. He'd been a rank outsider. No wonder the floor was in shock. So was Mickey. "Has there been an official announcement?"

"Announcement?" Glen frowned.

"Yes," said Mickey. Then it dawned on him that Glen wasn't talking about promotions. "What is it about Daniel?"

"Mickey, Daniel is dead."

3

The mortuary assistant motioned the widow forward. "Are you able to identify the body as that of your husband Daniel Goldcup?"

Her eyes widened as the cloth was pulled back. She turned away, shaking her head, whether in denial of his death or in answer to the question wasn't entirely clear.

"Is the body that of your husband?" the assistant pressed, her voice soft but firm.

"Yes," whispered Mrs Goldcup.

"Thank you." The assistant stepped back.

"Would you like some time with him on your own?" asked Frank.

She shook her head again, turned and walked to the door of the viewing suite. Frank opened it and she passed through to a police woman who put an arm round her shoulder and led her away down the corridor.

Frank followed at a distance, stopping outside the door to the Post-Mortem room where Eddie stood rattling loose change in his pocket.

"You all right, son?"

Eddie nodded silently.

"You've been to a post-mortem before?"

"Just the one, Sir."

"One too many then."

"Can't say I enjoyed it."

"Just as well," said Frank. "I don't work with necros."

They stood to one side as the assistant wheeled the body past. Frank took the opportunity to stretch out his hamstrings, which were still tight from Sunday's race. He caught the reflection of his curly grey hair in the glass wall and thought about Julie's suggestion that he dye it. She reckoned it would leave him looking more like the young fast-trackers like Eddie who kept getting promoted over his head. But it was a crazy world if a few grey hairs were going to hold him back.

Inside the room, the pathologist smiled when he recognised

Frank. "For a man in his forties you're looking remarkably trim, Frank. Still running marathons?"

"Not that far anymore, Philip. The training takes me away from the kids too much. Just enough to keep the tyre off. Unlike you I see."

"Cheers Frank. Tactless as ever."

"Right as ever 'n all."

Philip introduced himself to Eddie and clairvoyantly honed in on a common interest in cooking. An unfortunate topic it seemed to Frank, given that Philip was about to slice and dice one dead Daniel Goldcup.

Eventually their conversation ran aground and Philip pulled on his surgical mask and switched on the overhead microphone. "Here we go then gents."

Eddie rattled his coins again and Frank thought he looked a little pale. He'd have done the theory in training school, but Frank knew from years of experience that the practical was another thing altogether. Frank sympathised. Truth was he had never been convinced of the need to have the investigators in on the autopsy. It was a bit like the southern fad for having the father in on the birth of a child.

Frank had done as instructed and been there for Billy's birth. Hung around at the end of Julia's bed; doing nothing, feeling awkward, putting up with the blood and strange smells. And Julia didn't seem to want him there at all. So when Grace was born he'd done what blokes back up north do and kept well out of the way, just waiting for the simple facts: mother and baby healthy. Thank the Lord he'd thought. An eight-pound-two-ounce girl for those who needed to know the specifications.

So Frank zoned out of the autopsy and tried to ignore the sawing of bone, snapping of ribs, sucking of the vacuum, dripping of body fluids.

He did however take note when Philip said into the microphone: "Cause of death is ventricular fibrillation, secondary to immersion in fresh water."

Some uncertain portion of an hour later, Daniel Goldcup's body lay emptied of his internal organs, which now stood in stainless-steel dishes on the side, ready, it seemed, for Philip to serve up as a starter before the selection of cold meat steaks.

"So he drowned," said Frank, as Philip washed his hands. "If I understand your Latin correctly."

Philip pushed his glasses up off his nose. "No sign of struggle. And water on the lungs, so he was alive when he went in. It wouldn't have taken long after that. He was in no shape to swim, at his age, in cold water, fully clothed. And of course he'd been drinking. But we'll know more on that after the toxicology report."

"Time of death?" asked Frank.

"Friday night fits the bill," said Philip. "I'll pin it down later."

"A straightforward suicide then," said Eddie.

Frank frowned. "When you've been in this game as long as I have, you'll know there's no such thing as a straightforward suicide."

4

Mickey couldn't believe it. Daniel Goldcup. Hovis. Dead. He sat on his swivel chair, turning slowly from side to side.

"What the hell happened?"

"He never got home Friday night," said Glen. "The police found his briefcase on Tower Bridge. They found the body in the river on Sunday morning."

Mickey scanned the whiter than usual faces nearby then looked over at Daniel's empty desk.

"Suicide then?" he asked.

"Looks like it."

"Friday night you say?"

"Must have been after he left the Dickens Inn. Walked up onto Tower Bridge and then he jumped."

Mickey shook his head. "But Daniel seemed on top form Friday night. Full of himself."

"He was all right early on for sure," said Glen. "But he did seem pretty down later. After you …"

Mickey waited for Glen to finish the sentence before realising he wasn't going to. "After I what?"

"After you had a go at him."

Mickey laughed nervously. "Cobblers. I just pulled him down a peg or two. He was showboating. You were moaning about it yourself."

"I know." Glen shrugged. "It's just that Daniel was a bit quiet after that."

"So what are you saying? That I made him jump?"

"Of course not. Forget it."

Manita called through on the intercom. "Mickey. Have you heard the news about Daniel?"

"Yeah. Unbelievable."

"Terrible. Look, I know this isn't a good time, but Weil wants you to go see him about the budget now. He's waiting for you."

Mickey sighed. "If I have to."

He made his way across the floor to Weil's double-sized corner office overlooking the Millennium Dome. He tapped on the glass door and went in.

"I'll be with you in a second," Weil said, before diving back into the piles that covered the floor behind his chair. He groaned as he stretched for a thin black folder and lifted it onto the desk.

"You've heard about Daniel?" asked Mickey.

"Sir Stanley told us at the Operating Committee Meeting. HR will be sending out an announcement."

"The news is out already," said Mickey. "Not a great way to hear that a colleague is dead. Everyone whispering about it."

Weil shrugged. "I told HR to get a move on. Never mind."

"Did you know if Daniel was ill or anything? Depressed I mean."

Weil shook his head. "Didn't know him well. He always seemed happy enough to me."

Mickey was getting irritated by Weil's blasé tone. "Maybe he was depressed but just hiding it."

"I suppose. Still, I could have done without the extra complications right now. I've got Sir Stanley on my case and half a dozen other balls up in the air."

"Selfish of him."

11

Weil frowned. "Sir Stanley?"

"No. Daniel. Dying like that, without checking your diary."

"You know what I mean, Mickey. Of course I'm sorry about Daniel but there's nothing to be done about it, is there?" Weil opened the folder and pulled out a list of names and numbers. "Whereas there is a lot needs doing about these bonuses."

He handed the list to Mickey.

"Bonuses?" Mickey took a seat. "Manita said you wanted to talk about next year's budget."

"That was just a pretext. So that lot …" Weil nodded to the floor, "… don't know we're talking about bonuses."

"They're all worried the Government is going to screw them to keep the public sweet."

"They're right. Sir Stanley's been told to slash the numbers he put forward provisionally."

"How much?" asked Mickey.

"We're to get as close to zero as we can."

"Zero! What the hell? There'll be a riot."

"I know," said Weil. "Tin helmets on."

"But all the good people will walk."

"I know that as well. But there's nothing we can do." Weil handed Mickey a copy of the provisional bonus estimates for all three-hundred staff in the department. "I want to know the absolute bare minimum we can get away with for each person without them reaching for a gun, or worse a lawyer."

They set about the exercise top down, starting with the big hitters who had been pencilled in for seven figures. There was no great rhyme or reason to the numbers they arrived at. It was mostly based on Mickey's gut feel with the odd input from Weil. Later, someone would make up an audit trail using performance metrics and cross-appraisal feedback, to justify the awards in case they ever had to do so in court.

After an hour they had managed to slash the bonus pool from three hundred million pounds to sixty million.

Weil placed the revised sheet back in its pile. "Now, Sir Stanley also wants us to consider our own lock-in money."

"What about it?"

"Well, obviously, given the political climate on bonuses, we need to think carefully about whether we should give up a part of our lock-ins."

Mickey laughed. "You're having a giraffe aren't you? They're not bonuses. They are hard-earned, straight-cash lock-ins."

"You read the papers, Mickey. The Government is on record as saying it will not reward bankers for failure."

"Bollocks to that, Zac. The lock-ins ain't Government money and they ain't payment for failure. That's money given to us by the Yanks when they took a stake in the bank. It was a reward for our success in building the franchise. They wanted to stop the real assets walking out the door. It's State Financial's bribe money. It's ours fair and square. Got nothing to do with the credit crunch."

"I know, I know." Weil held up both hands. "But in the meantime the UK Government has had to pump in fifteen billion pounds to save Royal Shire Bank. Sir Stanley is worried that the politicians and the public won't get the subtle nuances between lock-ins, bonuses and, in their minds, huge sums of money still being paid to bankers while the country is deep in recession."

"The money is bonkers," agreed Mickey. "More than my old man made in a lifetime and then some. But I got a contract says it's mine."

"Doesn't mean you have to take it though," said Weil.

Mickey had thought about it of course. A number of bankers had waived their bonuses, not that it had done them much good. Any other year Mickey might have done the same. Trouble was this year he really needed the money to save his marriage. But he couldn't admit that to Weil.

"It's the principle," he said finally. "Them lock-ins have already been awarded to us. It's just a technicality that they haven't yet landed in our bank accounts. We worked hard for 'em. Almost cost me my marriage. I'm not giving up a penny of mine just because Sir Stanley can't handle the PR. Besides, the public will still hate us all, even if we did give up the lock-ins. So what's the point?"

"The point is the Government own sixty percent of our shares, and they're not happy."

"It's not my job to make politicians happy."

Weil drum-rolled his fingers on the leather table top. "Your intransigence on this won't portray you as much of a team player Mickey."

"I'm no mug. That's all." Mickey suddenly realised what Weil was getting at. "Are you saying it will count against me in the promos?"

Weil folded his arms and sat back in his chair. "You're still my preferred candidate, Mickey. You know that. But ultimately it's Sir Stanley's call and there are others that he is obliged to consider."

"Like who?"

Mickey immediately thought of Daniel. Obviously the only promotion he needed to worry about now was getting through the Pearly Gates.

"There's Ben."

"He's a heart attack waiting to happen."

"Benaifa."

"Not got the experience."

"Vanni's got a lot of experience."

But not a lot of brain, thought Mickey. However he liked the Italian gent and wasn't going to bad mouth him. "I'm the obvious choice, Zac. You know that."

"But will you still be here in five weeks' time, Mickey?"

Mickey's heart skipped a beat. He laughed. "Of course I'll still be here. Why are you asking?"

"Sir Stanley has heard differently."

"Like what has he heard?" asked Mickey.

"Like you have to retire early to save your marriage."

"Cobblers. Who did he hear that from?"

"He didn't say."

"Well whoever said that is just stirring up trouble. My marriage is fine thanks."

Weil frowned. "You just said working for Royal Shire almost cost you your marriage. And I understood you and your wife were separated."

"Helen's just helping out her old man on his farm while he finds his feet after her Mum died. Just temporary like. So you tell Sir Stanley to make sure he pays me my lock-in and gives me the promotion. There's no need for him to worry about me and the missus."

5

Frank explained to Mrs Goldcup for a second time that the postmortem had found no suggestion of foul play. But she was adamant her husband would not have taken his own life.

"Why was there no suicide note?" she asked. "Don't people usually leave one?"

"Not always," said Frank. "But are you sure your husband didn't leave a note somewhere in the house?"

"I'm sure. And Daniel wouldn't have just gone without …" she choked, "… without saying goodbye."

Frank gave her a moment to recover. He started to imagine Julia's reaction to news that he had killed himself, but then stopped. He didn't ever want to go there. "How would you describe your husband's behaviour recently?"

"Normal."

"Not under any stress?" asked Frank.

"He was always stressed."

"But had he been under any extra strain?"

"Why are you asking? Do you know something?"

Frank shook his head. "I was really just thinking about the general climate of banker bashing. They have been getting a pretty bad press."

"Of course Daniel was sensitive to it," she said, wiping her eyes with a neat, white hankie. "Despite what some might think, bankers are human. Many of his colleagues have suffered verbal abuse, some have even had windows smashed and cars scratched."

"Had your property been vandalised at all?" asked Frank, searching for a lead.

"Not that I am aware of."

"Any other changes you noticed to your husband's behaviour recently?" he asked.

"How do you mean?"

"You said he was sensitive to the banker bashing. Would you say this had got to him so that he was actually depressed?"

"No." She shook her head firmly. "He had his ups and downs like everyone else, but nothing serious."

"Was he on any medication?"

"He takes," she sighed, "He took an aspirin a day to thin his blood, but he wouldn't dream of taking anything stronger."

"Any particular problems at work or in his personal life that you were aware of?"

"No."

"Financial difficulties?" Frank would run a financial profile later, but the wife might know something which wouldn't show up.

"Certainly not. Daniel was very careful with his money. We lived off his salary and he invested the bonuses."

"In what?"

"I don't really know. Daniel dealt with that side of things. Mostly property I think. We have a chalet in Meribel. And a farm in Derbyshire. Just a small one."

Frank wondered how many acres 'just a small one' might be, but didn't pursue it. "Might your husband have overstretched?"

She reached for the glass of water. "Look, there's something you should know."

Frank's mind raced. Was she about to reveal a gambling problem or a drug addiction?

"It's confidential," she said eventually. "Can you promise to keep it within this room?"

"If it is of interest to the coroner I will have to tell him," said Frank. "And if he judges it to be of significance then he will have to include it in his verdict. But I am sure he would be discreet."

"It's nothing sinister," she said. "The thing is … Daniel was due to receive a large sum of money in just five weeks, so there really were no financial difficulties."

"How large is large?" asked Frank.

She hesitated. "Millions."

"Millions? As in more than one?" Frank straightened his tie. "Just how many millions are we talking about Mrs Goldcup?"

"Ten, maybe eleven."

Frank tried not to look shocked. 'Ten, maybe eleven', he repeated in his mind. What's a million here or there? He wondered how she could talk so casually about such wealth and not be embarrassed.

"I thought the days of big bonuses were over," he finally said.

"It was a lock-in," she said.

"A lock-in?" asked Eddie, who had been taking notes.

"Not the thing you have in your local on a Sunday night," said Frank. "Golden handcuffs is the other word for it. Am I right, Mrs Goldcup? Money to stop your husband leaving the firm and going to a competitor."

"That's correct," she said. "They were awarded to the senior staff at Royal Shire when the American bank State Financial took a stake in it a few years ago. But clearly, given the climate now, Sir Stanley is anxious that these payments do not leak out to the press."

"Sir Stanley?"

"The Chairman of the bank," she explained.

"This is the man who's mates with our Chief Constable," Frank said to Eddie.

"I wouldn't know about that," said Mrs Goldcup, sitting forward in her chair. "But you see, there were no financial difficulties. In fact Daniel planned to retire after the lock-in was paid."

Frank checked the date of birth in his notes. Two years older than him. "He was only forty six. Bit young to retire isn't it?"

"It wasn't entirely his idea." Her cheeks flushed. "It was more Sir Stanley's."

"You mean he was getting the sack."

She looked down at the carpet. "I prefer to say that he'd agreed to retire."

Have it your way, thought Frank. "How did your husband feel about the prospect of retiring then?"

"He wasn't entirely sure what he would do with his time. He didn't really have much of a life outside work."

Her eyes welled up again and Frank gave her a moment to pull herself back together.

"What do you know about events on the Friday night?" he asked, refilling her glass of water.

17

She drew a deep breath. "Daniel had just won some big deal. I never really did understand what he did. But the team went out to celebrate. He rang me about nine o'clock to say he was coming home. He was agitated, upset."

"Why was that?"

"Well, the thing is …" She paused. "He'd had an argument."

Frank and Eddie exchanged glances. "Who with?"

"A colleague. Mickey Summer."

Frank checked that Eddie had noted the name.

"Do you know what the argument was about?"

"Daniel didn't say. But it had clearly upset Daniel. He'd worked with Mickey for years and never had any trouble. It's odd because Mickey's normally good company. A joker. Maybe you've met him?"

"Not yet," said Frank. "But we will."

6

Mickey had a lunch booked in the Managing Director's dining room, but the news about Daniel left him needing fresh air and space to himself. So he picked up a sushi pack from the canteen, grabbed a first edition of The Evening Standard and walked to a bench beside the wharf. The low sun just did enough to keep him warm without a coat.

To take his mind off Daniel he read a review of the Hammer's game at the weekend and agreed they deserved to lose and were probably going down. He flicked through the other match reports then turned over to the front page.

His eyes popped at the headline.

Payment for Failure Scandal at Royal Shire Bank.

He speed read the article.

Twelve bankers … a hundred and fifty million …

Shit. It was out. The press had found out about the lock-in payments. How the hell? He read on.

Outrageous … theft … bonuses to be cancelled …

He rolled the paper into a truncheon and whacked the seat.

That couldn't be allowed to happen. Without the lock-in his plan to get Helen back would be up the Khyber.

He looked up at the Royal Shire tower and wondered who had leaked it. It could be anyone. So many knew. He needed to think ahead. First check out the facts. Martin in legal. He'd know.

He dialled Martin's mobile.

He answered with a groan.

"Martin? It's Mickey. You seen the front page of the Standard?"

"I'm in LA, Mickey. And it's five in the morning."

"Sorry mate. But listen to this headline: Payment for Failure Scandal at Royal Shire Bank. Twelve bankers at failed bank RSB are set to share a staggering hundred and fifty million pound bonus pot as UK unemployment passes etc. etc. Then get a load of this bit: Wallace Arnold MP described the outrageous payments as theft and called for the bonuses to be cancelled, saying that the taxpayer cannot continue to reward bankers for failure."

"I wouldn't worry about it, Mickey," Martin said, sounding a bit miffed at being woken up.

"You might not worry, mate. But I do. You said the contract was rock solid."

"It is. Relax, Mickey, you'll get your money."

"You sure?"

"Sure I'm sure. Trust me, I'm a lawyer."

"That's not funny, Martin. Look, they can't blame me for the credit crunch."

"I know."

"Blame the egg-heads in derivatives for inventing financial bombs and passing them off as safe investments. Blame the Fed for inflating asset bubbles or the regulators for falling asleep on the watch. Blame every punter who had a credit card and a mortgage. But don't blame me."

"I'm not, Mickey."

"Well this Wally Arnold geezer is. And if he seriously expects me to give up a penny of my lock-in then he's three stops down from Plaistow – we're talking stations on the underground – Barking mad."

"Relax, Mickey. Arnold is just playing politics. There's nothing anyone can do."

"I still want you to check it out when you get into the office."

"I will. Now if you don't mind, Mickey I need a bit of shut-eye."

7

As he manoeuvred the Targa into the slack water behind St Katherine's pier, the pilot pointed to a mound of river rubbish lodged against the wooden struts that supported the overhead walkway. There was the usual driftwood, plastic bottles, a traffic cone, a dustbin lid; but unusually it was all circled by police tape.

"We found him in among all that lot."

The engine slowed and Frank imagined the body, sticking out like a Guy from a bonfire. He'd pulled out seven stiffs during his own stint with the river police. After a time it became routine. Pull on the rubber gloves, reach over and secure an arm and a leg, then haul it on board, taking care not to cause any bruising that might complicate the autopsy.

"Some rich banker wasn't he?" asked the pilot. "He had a Rolex, gold, the works. He must have been loaded. What's he doing chucking himself in the river?"

"Who says he did?"

The pilot turned to face Frank. "You treating it as suspicious then?"

"I'm keeping an open mind."

"Mind you," said the pilot. "It's not as if you'd struggle to find people who'd want to kill a banker. They're still at it according to the Standard. Paying themselves million pound bonuses."

"Don't see why everyone is so surprised," said Eddie. "They're just following the Golden Rule of the City."

"What Golden Rule?" asked Frank.

"I was told it by a uni pal who went into the City," explained Eddie. "The trick is to make a killing, as quickly as possible, then cash in and get out before the stress kills you. So of course they're still paying themselves bonuses. That's the name of the game."

"Makes my blood boil," said the pilot. "Driving Bentleys, living in mansions, holidaying in five-star hotels."

"Jealous are you?" asked Frank.

"Course I am. Aren't you?"

Frank smiled. "Wouldn't want that much money if you gave it to me."

The pilot grunted something, then gunned the engines on full rudder and edged the launch closer to the pier. Frank jumped ashore and held her steady as Eddie tentatively climbed out.

They walked up the steps onto Tower Bridge, taking in the view of the steel-clad HMS Belfast up river.

"Did you mean that?" asked Eddie. "About not being jealous of the money bankers earn."

"Of course," said Frank. "I feel sorry for them. Their sole aim seems to be building up treasure on this earth. And you know what the good book says – it's harder for a rich man to enter the Kingdom of Heaven than for a camel to pass through the eye of the needle."

"Still, I'd take the money now and worry about the after-life later."

"So why didn't you follow this university friend of yours and go into the City then?"

"I tried." Eddie blushed. "He was a straight-A student. I couldn't even get an interview."

They walked on, halting again where the pavement circled round the first blue-and-white tower.

"The briefcase was found on the floor here," said Eddie, checking the notes from the first responder.

Frank leant over the wall and looked down at the grey water below. Turning back he realised he was unable to see the pavement or road around the Tower's buttress.

"It's a blind spot," he said. "Explains why there were no witnesses."

Eddie measured the height of the wall up to his chest. "That's quite a tough climb. He meant what he was doing. He didn't just wobble off."

"He could have been chucked over," said Frank.

"He weighed fourteen stone. You'd need a crane to lift him over here."

"D'you reckon?" Frank suddenly grabbed Eddie around the thighs and lifted him up onto the wall.

"All right!" shouted Eddie, kicking his legs to break free. "I get your point."

Frank helped him back down.

Eddie brushed his trousers. "I've got pigeon crap on me now."

"They needed a clean in any case," said Frank.

"You're keen on this being a homicide all of a sudden. Mrs Goldcup got to you did she?"

"I'm just considering every option."

"But what do you really think happened then?" Eddie continued, brushing his trousers.

"It probably was suicide," said Frank. "Goldcup was about to be made redundant and he didn't have a life outside work. He was depressed at the prospect. Then he has an argument with this Mickey Summer bloke and gets upset. He's had a few beers, he's walking over the bridge and he snaps. Spur of the moment thing. That's why there's no note."

Eddie looked over the edge and shook his head. "All that money about to come his way and he blew it all."

"He didn't follow your friend's Golden Rule," said Frank.

"How do you mean?"

"He made a killing. But he didn't get out in time."

8

"This could bring down the Government!" Cookson's flashbulb eyes glanced next door, as if Number Ten might really collapse at any moment.

"I rather doubt it," said Stanley. "The media outrage is all too predictable and it will blow over."

"The Prime Minister doesn't share your confidence. He promised the electorate there would be no more big bonuses paid out at state-owned banks. And now this!" Cookson slapped the Evening

Standard down on the table.

"As I've told you before, they are not bonuses." Stanley tried to keep the irritation out of his voice. Even by the standards of junior ministers, Cookson was remarkably naïve about finance. "They are lock-ins."

"That's just semantics."

"Not at all. It might help you to understand the difference."

"Try me."

Stanley smiled as he wondered where to begin. Really, Cookson needed to learn something of the history of merchant banking before Big Bang. Or at least try to understand why Royal Shire Bank proudly retained its independence for so long and resisted the temptation to be taken over by a foreign bank.

But he could tell Cookson did not have the patience for a financial history lesson. "Before State Financial took its stake, we ran a very happy ship at Royal Shire Bank. The staff felt proud to be working for what had become the last bastion of pure British independent investment banking."

"Flying the flag?" asked Cookson sarcastically.

"Precisely," Stanley continued, increasingly annoyed by Cookson's tone. "We'd watched over the years as the other great names such as Warburgs, Kleinworts, Schroders and Morgan Grenfell had been taken over and run into the ground by their new owners. And we were determined that should not happen to Royal Shire."

"I'm still waiting to understand the difference between a bonus and a lock-in," Cookson said, pouring himself more water.

"So, there was great resistance to the proposal that State Financial take a major stake in the bank," explained Stanley. "The lock-in money was put on the table to remove that resistance. To ensure the top people, those who could ensure on-going stability and success, stayed on board."

"Bribery."

"If you like. It was also a reward for years of hard work and dedication."

"And so you took the money and lowered the flag," said Cookson.

"Even with the incentive of the lock-ins it was still a very close

23

vote amongst the partners, to accept the takeover."

"And how did you vote?" asked Cookson.

"I voted against."

Cookson looked surprised. "But you managed to overcome your conscience and let State Financial take a stake anyway."

It hadn't actually been the money that had swayed Stanley. It had been the realisation that it was the end of an era. The independent British investment banks would not survive. State Financial would take its forty-percent stake and then inevitably, one day, it would buy out the rest and Royal Shire would disappear completely. Just like the others. Felled, all felled, like Manley-Hopkins' poplars. Ultimately there was no alternative but to join a giant universal bank. State Financial was as good or as bad as the rest.

"The point is that the payments are not bonuses from current profits."

Cookson laughed. "I'm afraid the distinction doesn't help. Certainly not as far as the man on the street is concerned. Whatever you say, they are what they are. Multi-million pound payments to bankers, who quite frankly would be on the dole if the Government had not stepped in and saved the financial system."

Stanley shook his head. Like many, he wished the government had let a few banks fail. Bit the bullet there and then. Better than this lingering death they were having to endure instead. "Whatever the merits of your argument, the point is that the payments are all legal and above board."

"Above board?" Cookson's eyes narrowed. "You don't get it do you. The economy is on its knees, millions unemployed and you can't see anything wrong with twelve bankers sharing a hundred and fifty million pounds."

Stanley wondered whether to tell Cookson that it would now only be eleven bankers. But he said nothing.

"So what do you plan to do about it?" Cookson pressed.

"What do you suggest?"

"Cancel the payments."

"As simple as that?" asked Stanley, almost laughing.

"As simple as that," repeated Cookson.

Stanley gritted his teeth. "I keep telling you, these are not discretionary payments. They are guarantees tied to legally binding contracts. You can't break them. They'll sue."

"Let them."

"And they'll win. And then you'll lose twice."

"Then I suggest you force them to give back the money voluntarily."

Stanley ignored the tautology. "I am working on something along those lines. I hope to persuade them to accept shares instead of cash and to take part-deferrals."

"Defer the money!?" shouted Cookson. "Is that all? You're not trying for any cuts whatsoever."

"No, I can't."

Cookson smiled as if he'd just spotted a move to check. "I wonder if you might be troubled by a conflict of interest here. I wonder what your plan would be if you weren't in the lock-in group yourself."

"It makes no difference."

Cookson puffed his chest. "I'll cut to the chase, Stanley ..."

"Sir Stanley, please." He wasn't one to stand on ceremony. Most of his old colleagues still called him plain Stanley, but this boy had not earned the right. And right now he was, frankly, being plain irritating.

"The omission was intentional." The minister smiled. "I wanted you to think about how you might miss the title."

So, that was his game. Stanley had almost walked out on the chancellor when he'd made the same threat. It wasn't that he was precious about the title. He could quite easily have done without it. But now that he had it, he couldn't face the ignominy of having it stripped away.

"Are you threatening to revoke my title?" asked Stanley. "Surely you wouldn't put me in the same boat as criminals like Blunt and Mugabe?"

The minister looked directly at Stanley. "We've already had a preliminary meeting with the forfeiture committee. Be in no doubt that, if you don't find a way to stop these payments, we'll be after your title."

9

The boys were already down in All Bar One, but Mickey had to stay behind to see Weil, so he spent some time pulling up share price charts and studying bond yields and economic data.

Then he surfed through various football sites and finally decided to see if any new farms had come up for sale since his last look. There was one new instruction. Lower Saddle Farm near Cuffley, Hertfordshire. He glanced at a map. It was commuting distance for Mickey, probably an hour by car either side of the rush hour. Going for two million pounds, so in the price range. The period farmhouse looked homely enough and it was a proper working farm; a hundred acres of arable land and fifty of grazing. It also had its own two-acre wood. Ticked all of Helen's boxes from what he could see, so he saved the page as another alternative if the Whitwell Farm purchase fell through.

For the hundredth time he pulled up the page with details of Whitwell. The range of outbuildings and stores and the hundred-and-twenty arable acres would be Helen's bag. Mickey might whiz around on a tractor or quad bike at the weekends, but that's as close to farming as he wanted to get. The Secluded Grade II Georgian Farmhouse didn't really do much for Mickey either, but Helen had fallen in love with it the moment she'd stumbled upon it on one of those wet, wintry walks she used to drag him out on. He missed those walks.

Out of the corner of his eye, he noticed Manita push back her chair and stand up. She'd never said anything, but Mickey knew Manita didn't approve of his plan to get Helen back. Thought he was chasing a lost cause. But she was wrong.

He switched to his emails just as she walked in the room.

"Looking at your dream farm again are you?"

Mickey turned the screen round to face Manita. "I'm checking my emails actually."

"I believe you!"

"Have you got a spy camera trained on me?"

"I don't need one. I can read your mind."

"Well if you must know I was just looking for a fall-back in case something goes wrong with the dream farm."

"Do you think it might?"

Mickey shook his head. "Just to be on the safe side."

"And you've still not told Helen about it."

"I want it to be a surprise don't I?"

"I wish Ollie would buy me surprises like that."

"He don't need to does he?" said Mickey. He was about to add the explanation that she loved her husband regardless, but he stopped himself just in time.

"While you're in the spending mood," said Manita, "have you chosen your charities yet?"

"All sorted." He passed her a plastic folder with details of various charities that Manita had put together.

She skimmed the pile. "You don't seem to have narrowed it down very much."

"I have narrowed it down. You can forget all that lot. I want to give it all to this one charity here." He held up the leaflet for Manita's Nepalese charity.

She looked at him, testing to see if this was one of his jokes. "Are you sure," she said. "Everything to Nepal?"

"Everything."

Her eyes glistened. "And have you decided how much yet?"

Mickey hadn't. How could he decide when he didn't know the future? If Helen went with the farm idea and was happy with Mickey commuting in to the City then he could give most of the rest of his lock-in to Manita's charity. But if Helen insisted on Plan B and he had to give up the City as well, then he'd need to keep something in reserve.

"It's going to be a million squid for starters," he said eventually.

"A million pounds! Are you sure?"

"Sure I'm sure. Of course this all assumes the Government is still going to give me the lock-in. Otherwise we'll be having a whip round for the Save Mickey Summer Fund."

"I'm sure you'll survive without having to resort to charity, Mickey." She smiled. "Anyway, I came to tell you that Weil is ready to see you now."

"He still won't say what it's about?"

She shook her head.

Mickey stood up and grabbed his jacket. "Whatever it is, it better not take long. The boys have been down the cruiser for half an hour already."

He hurried over to Weil's office.

The door was open so he walked straight in. "All right?"

Weil cleared his throat. "Take a seat, Mickey."

Mickey sat down. "Is this going to take long?"

"No." Weil paused. "Sir Stanley has received a letter of complaint."

"About what?"

"About you."

"What the …? Who from?"

"It was anonymous."

"What's the complaint about?"

"About what you got up to in Amsterdam."

"Got up to? What do you mean?"

"Apparently you took clients to strip clubs."

Mickey loosened his tie. "It was their idea."

"And cannabis cafes."

"Come on, Zac, we do what the clients ask. It's our job. Besides it's legal in Holland. I think."

"Well drugs have never been legal at Royal Shire Bank."

"Don't get at me. I only ever have beer. I leave the Bob Hope to the Dutch. You know we got two-hundred million euros of orders the day after our last trip."

"That's not the point."

"So what is the point then?"

"Sir Stanley wants me to discipline you to set an example."

"Set an example? What is this? Play school? You going to smack my bum?"

Weil shook his head. "It's enough that we've had this conversation. I'll make a note on your personnel file and send a copy to Sir Stanley. I think he'll be happy with that."

"Bloody great." Mickey clenched a fist. "Someone's stitching me up, Zac."

"Stitching you up?"

"Trying to stop my promotion," explained Mickey. "First this rumour about me leaving. Now getting me in trouble with HR."

"I don't think it's a stitch up."

Mickey was sure it was. It had to be a promotion rival. Vanni was too much of a gent to play dirty. Benaifa was too new and would be unsure if it would backfire. It had to be the fat man. "It was Ben, weren't it?"

"The complaint was anonymous."

"I'm going to ask Ben."

"What does it matter if it was him? You haven't denied the allegation."

"This is all bullshit." Mickey stood up and walked to the door. "Just so we're crystal clear on this, Zac. You promote who you want but if I don't get it I'll have to consider my options."

"I understand."

"And be in no doubt, that if I do leave, this place will unravel faster than a mullah's turban."

10

Frank spotted MacIntyre checking his watch as he passed his office and was not surprised to hear him call out.

"Is that you finished for the day then, Frank?"

"Yes it is, Superintendent." Frank actually had some paperwork in his briefcase that he planned to tackle once the kids were in bed, but that wasn't the point. Frank popped his head round the door. "Why do you ask?"

MacIntyre leant back in his chair, twiddling a pen. "I like my senior men to set a good example to the junior officers."

"Thanks for noticing, Superintendent. I do try my best."

MacIntyre frowned. "Your new man, Eddie. He could go far, Frank."

"I'm not stopping him, Sir."

"Policing isn't a nine-to-five job."

Frank realised where the conversation was heading. "Nor is it about hanging about for long hours just to impress the boss. I work flat out during my shifts so that I can spend time with the family. And I do my overtime like anyone else."

"Except on Sundays …"

"I do Sundays if I really have to. But it seemed unnecessary."

"The request came down from the Chief Constable. That not high enough for you, Frank?"

"The request not to work Sundays comes from even higher up, Sir."

MacIntyre shook his head and muttered something under his breath. He pointed to a headline in a newspaper. "Where have you got to with this Daniel Goldcup enquiry anyway?"

"Looking like a suicide so far. I can't really see why the wife or anyone else would think it was murder. I don't think anyone is really that worked up about bankers are they?"

MacIntyre sat forward on the edge of his chair. "Well I'm mad as hell about cuts to this police force because of a global recession caused by bankers like Daniel Goldcup."

"I'm no fan of bankers either," said Frank. "But it wasn't only the bankers to blame for the recession. They're just convenient scapegoats."

"Well whatever you or I think, Frank, there is genuine anger among the public," said MacIntyre. "And that's going to keep simmering so long as the bankers keep paying themselves multi-million pound bonuses when everyone else is taking pay cuts."

"Maybe." Frank shrugged. "But I still don't believe anyone would get angry enough to kill over it."

"Let's hope you're right, Frank."

11

From the thirtieth floor of Royal Shire Bank, Frank counted ten towers just as tall as the one he was in. He understood that inside these totems to the god of money, thousands and thousands of people were busy. But doing what exactly?

From what he could gather, they were simply shuffling around the rest of the population's money. They were alchemists turning it from one form to another. And for this service they took a fee that amounted to billions of pounds every year. Yet the man in the street, who ultimately paid for this through charges on his pensions or savings, didn't have a clue whether any of it was really necessary. The bankers had constructed a financial world so impenetrable that only they could navigate it. The whole thing looked to be a multi-billion pound scam.

Frank's thoughts were interrupted by a knock on the door. A stocky man with thinning brown hair and a boxer's nose walked in with an outstretched hand.

"Mickey Summer," he announced, in a surprisingly loud voice.

Frank shook his hand. "I'm DI Frank Brighouse. I'm making enquiries for the coroner's inquest into Daniel Goldcup's death."

"I was told," said Mickey as he took a seat. "How can I help?"

"You were drinking with Daniel Goldcup in the Dickens Inn on Friday night, weren't you?"

"Not just me and Daniel. A whole bunch of us went out to celebrate."

"What was the occasion?" asked Frank.

"We'd won over a Footsie client on the corporate-broking side."

"Footsie?" Eddie looked up from his notes.

Frank beat Mickey to it. "The Financial Times Stock Exchange Index of the largest hundred companies."

"You're not just a pretty face are you?" said Mickey.

"And how did Daniel appear to you that night?" continued Frank.

"Happy enough. He'd had a few sherbets, of course, like everyone else."

"So Daniel was happy. Not upset about anything?"

"I don't know about everything. There are some big issues in the world that upset everyone – the state of the pitch at Wembley, vote rigging in the Eurovision Song Contest …"

"But you didn't see Daniel upset at any stage in the evening?" Frank interrupted.

Mickey looked away, as if checking his memory. "Nah."

"He rang his wife around nine, to say he was coming home."

"Green card expired had it?" asked Mickey.

"He was leaving early because he'd been upset by you," Frank paused for effect. "You'd given him a dressing down – embarrassed him in front of everyone apparently. Is that right?"

Mickey folded his arms and sat back in his chair. "Daniel had been getting a bit too big for his boots. Claiming the deal we'd won was all down to him. So I brought him down a peg or two and reminded him it's a team game."

Frank checked his notes. "You had another argument with Daniel on the phone that morning. What was that about?"

"Nothing much," said Mickey. "Daniel was planning to have the celebrations on the trading floor at lunchtime but I told him to wait until the evening when I was back from New York."

"Daniel's secretary described it as a 'heated argument'."

"It weren't."

"She says you threatened him."

"That's cobblers."

"She got the impression you swore at Daniel."

"I probably did. I'm a sodding broker. I'll wash my mouth out later."

Frank looked through his file again. "Daniel was a promotion rival wasn't he?"

"I suppose."

Frank could see Mickey's breathing getting faster. "I'm wondering if there was some tension between the two of you because you were both running for the same job and Daniel had just won this deal."

"I had no problems with Daniel."

"Were you aware that Daniel planned to retire in five weeks?"

"He hadn't told me, but I'm not surprised. He was getting on a bit. Broking is a young man's game."

Frank guessed Mickey was mid-thirties, though he looked older. He doubted Mickey could run for a bus. But he was still probably strong enough to throw a drunken man over a wall.

"What time did you leave the pub?"

"Same time as Daniel. I offered him a lift to the train station, as a peace-offering like. But he said no."

"Were you in a fit state to drive?"

"I had a driver for the night."

"What's his name?" asked Frank. "I'll need to talk to him."

"Karim Buchri."

Mickey pointed to a phone book.

Eddie flicked through, found the name and made a note of the number.

"So why did Daniel refuse your offer of a lift?" continued Frank.

"He said he wanted to walk. At the time I thought he still had the hump with me. Now I'm not so sure. Maybe he'd already decided to jump."

"Who says he jumped?"

"Well ain't that what happened?"

"We don't know," said Frank. "That's what we're trying to establish. So tell me, were you angry that Daniel snubbed your offer of a lift – this 'peace offering' as you call it?"

"Look mate, I don't know where you're going with this. It bothered me that maybe I came down too hard on Daniel that night and upset him. I didn't know he was depressed. It might be that I tipped him over the edge but …" Mickey paused. He scratched the side of his face. "I don't mean literally of course."

Frank was pretty sure it was just a slip of the tongue, but Mickey was so cock-sure of himself that it might do him good to be pulled up.

"I must caution you, Mr Summer, that you do not have to say anything to me but it may harm your defence if you do not mention when questioned something which you later rely on in court. Anything you do say may be given in evidence."

"What's this? You arresting me?"

"No. But I think there are reasonable grounds to suspect you had some involvement in the death of Daniel Goldcup, and so I want to caution you to be very careful what you say."

Mickey rubbed the back of his hand across his mouth. "In that case I ain't saying another Dicky till I get a lawyer."

12

Mickey arrived at the Oxo Tower to find his brother already waiting at the table.

"Sorry I'm late. Been busier than Santa on Christmas eve this morning."

"Why so?" asked Marcus, in the public school voice that always caught Mickey by surprise, even though it was decades since his brother had lost his East End accent.

"Weil asked me to keep an eye on the corporate broking desk. You must have heard about Daniel?"

"Yes of course. Poor Daniel. What the hell happened?"

"Took a dive off Tower Bridge, didn't he?" Mickey turned to the window and watched a choppy Thames flowing below. Daniel's face flashed across his mind. He shook his head and looked up to the skyline: the pale dome of St Paul's, the breeze-block Barbican, the gigantic cut-glass shard and the dark Gherkin which he always thought looked more like a giant turd.

"Did he fall?" asked Marcus. "Or did he jump?"

"I've no idea. Though try telling the Old Bill that."

"What do you mean?" Marcus set his wine down on the table.

"I had a bit of a barney with Daniel on Friday night. The police think that might have upset him and made him jump. Worse than that, they're trying to suggest I followed him onto the bridge and pushed him over."

"Shit!"

"It's crazy I know, but they was in this morning asking all sorts of difficult questions. Ended up cautioning me. I shut up shop then."

"I suggest you get hold of a good lawyer."

"Manita's put a call in to Martin. You remember him?"

"Not an in-house, pretend lawyer like Martin," said Marcus. "You need a proper, keep-you-out-of-jail-even-if-you're-guilty-as-sin, criminal lawyer."

"Bloody hell, Marcus I had nothing to do with it. I'm innocent!"

"I know. But so was Dad, remember? Better safe than sorry."

Mickey knew Marcus was right. Dad had found out the hard way that courts deal in law not justice. Come to think of it, if the police connected Mickey to his dad, and who knows, they might already have done so, then they'd really be on Mickey's case.

"You're right," he said. "I'll sort it. Anyhow, I'm starving."

He waved over a waitress who took their order. Then Mickey watched her walk away until she had disappeared into the kitchen.

"Are you back in the market then?" asked Marcus.

"Course not. I'm a married man, remember?"

"I'm glad you didn't pretend to be a happily-married man."

"I am a happily-married man." Mickey twisted his wedding ring. He remembered that Helen had not been wearing hers the last time he'd seen her. "Just a pity that the missus doesn't seem to feel the same way."

The sommelier arrived and passed Marcus a wine menu.

"I'm looking for something that will go well with duck," said Marcus.

"Water?" suggested Mickey.

"I'll have the nineteen-forty-five Mouton Rothschild," said Marcus eventually.

"A beautiful wine," said the sommelier. "The silk tannins give it a very velvety taste."

"Let's have a look." Mickey reached for the wine list. He had to count the zeros to double check. "Bloody hell. It's eight thousand pounds!"

"Carpe diem!" said Marcus. "Don't worry, I'll pay."

The sommelier smiled as he turned away. Mickey guessed he was on some sort of commission.

"That's silly money for a bottle of plonk, Marcus."

"You can't take it with you, Mickey. Anyway, once you come on board you'll be so seriously rich you won't worry about eight thousand pounds."

Mickey sighed. "Don't start on all that again. I've told you before. I couldn't have you as my boss. It wouldn't feel right."

"I won't be your boss, Mickey. I want you to join as my partner. Run it with me. That's why I want to change the name to Summer Securities. It's got a better ring to it don't you think?"

"Like the bell on The Titanic," said Mickey. "There's no money in equity research anymore."

"You're wrong there, Mickey. The business is really taking off. We turn cash flow positive in the second quarter next year. It's all in the plan." He slid an A4 envelope over the table. "For your eyes only. Take it home."

Mickey folded it and slipped it into his jacket pocket. He knew that if it hadn't been for Marcus he'd never have got into the City. So the least he could do would be to give his brother's business plan some serious thought. "If the numbers stack up, I'll help you out and make an investment."

"You'll be helping yourself out, Mickey. I'm giving you a chance to make serious money. Get yourself on the Rich List."

* * *

"Money wasn't an issue," Eddie declared, having completed the financial profile of Daniel Goldcup. "It's just like his wife said. He was loaded."

Frank sat back from his desk. "How loaded is loaded?"

"Worth about six million at the peak. Nearer five now. Seems his investment manager screwed up on some sub-prime investments."

"My heart bleeds."

"Plus, of course he was about to land a ten-million-pound lock-in. So if he was worried about retiring it wasn't from a financial perspective. Lucky sod."

"He's dead," said Frank. "That's not so lucky in my book."

Eddie blushed. "Anyway, the point is we can't use money problems as a reason for him to jump."

"You've got this the wrong way round, Eddie. We don't have to prove it was suicide. We just have to rule out anything else, which we have."

"So do we mention money at all to the coroner? The fact that he was about to land a shed load."

Frank thought about it a moment. "We'll mention it and let the coroner decide if it has relevance."

"So what do you think happened then, Sir?"

"He was a sad, rich banker facing a future with too much time on his hands. He was drunk and he jumped."

Eddie nodded. "So what do we do with Mickey Summer?"

"Nothing."

"But he's waiting for us to fix up an interview."

"Let him wait," said Frank. "Patience is a virtue."

* * *

The sommelier returned with the wine and removed the foil from the bottle. Marcus nodded appreciatively. "I think this is the right manner in which to celebrate our new venture."

"Steady on," said Mickey. "Even if I do decide to invest I'm not coming on board myself. I'm not leaving Royal Shire now I'm about to get Weil's job."

Marcus laughed. "You're not going any higher at Royal Shire, Mickey."

"What would you know about it?"

"You don't have the credentials for senior management."

"Cobblers. What ain't I got?"

"An education, stupid. The Americans are not going to let someone without a GCSE run a billion-pound business."

"It's not up to them. It's Sir Stanley's call."

Marcus shook his head and smiled. "Every senior appointment at Royal Shire Bank needs to be approved by State Financial now."

"Well I've got no problems with the Septics."

"But the Yanks have got a problem with you, Mickey. Not personally of course, but with the idea of a barrow boy running their European Equity businesses. They pretend to be all about meritocracy and opportunity but they're not. Trust me."

Mickey tried to think of an example of someone in senior management that had come up the back route like him. But he couldn't think of one. He let it drop and turned to watch the sommelier tease out the cork then pour the wine into a glass flask. He then decanted this over a flame to remove decades of sediment. Finally, silently, he poured Marcus an inch.

Marcus circled the crystal glass on the table top then lifted it to his nose and sniffed. He sipped and washed the wine around in his mouth. Finally he looked up to the ceiling and swallowed.

"How's the mouth wash?" asked Mickey, who thought the whole thing was barmy.

"It's excellent," said Marcus, nodding his approval at the sommelier, who smiled with relief, poured them both a glass and departed.

Marcus closed his eyes and took another sip of wine. "Right then, let's leave aside the exact timing of you physically coming on board. How much are you able to invest?"

"Only what I could afford to lose."

"So how much is that?"

Mickey was beginning to feel uncomfortable with his brother's hard sell and was relieved when the waitress arrived with the food.

He tried to change the subject as he cut into his steak. "This is perfect. The chips are a bit skinny posh though."

Marcus was undeterred. "How much have you got, Mickey?"

"You show me yours first."

"Read the plan," said Marcus. "You'll see the business will be worth a hundred million when I sell it. Quite possibly considerably more. Now don't be shy. Tell big brother how much you're worth. Or more accurately how much you will be worth."

"I presume you're referring to my lock-in."

"That also, but you've obviously got something squirreled away already."

"Not much," said Mickey. "About a million."

"Is that all?" asked Marcus. "What have you spent it all on then?"

"Well, I dropped a few hundred big ones subsidising Helen's dad's farm over the years. And I paid for all that work on Mum's house. The rest of it I've blown on cars, holidays and all the rest."

Marcus set his cutlery back on the plate and dabbed the sides of his mouth with his serviette. "So you have a million plus your lock-in. That's worth ten million, five after tax. That still gives us a fair amount to play with."

"There are three big problems with that calculation," said Mickey.

Marcus loosed the top button on his shirt. "Pray tell."

"You've seen all this old Tom in the Standard about the Government trying to stop our lock-ins getting paid."

"I can't read the Standard," said Marcus. "It hurts my brain thinking down to that level. But I wouldn't worry. They can't stop the lock-ins. You've got a contract. It's legally binding."

"Maybe, but there's still a risk."

"Relax. They'll pay it. Now, what are the other two problems with my calculation then?"

"I'm buying a farm."

Marcus almost choked on his wine. "A farm? Why would you buy a farm?"

Mickey wished he hadn't started. Marcus was not going to approve. He rolled the pepper pot around on its edge. "Farming could be a good investment."

"Nonsense. This is Helen's idea isn't it?"

"She don't know about it."

Marcus laughed. "I get it now. You think that buying Helen a farm will win her back, don't you. You're mad. But whatever. How much does a farm cost then?"

"Two million."

"Bloody hell!"

"It's pricey because it's near London," explained Mickey. "So I can commute to Canary Wharf."

"I see. And what's the third problem?"

"I want to give a chunk of the lock-in to Manita's charity in Nepal."

"You're kidding? How much?" asked Marcus, a bit too loud. The woman at the next table glanced over.

"I was thinking maybe a couple of million."

"Don't be ridiculous." Marcus' eyes widened. "What would that achieve?"

"An education for the kids, homes for orphans, medical treatment for the elderly. You know, Marcus, I've never really been in this game for the money. I just like the buzz. Plus I always felt uncomfortable about the lock-in. How did you describe it? Forty pieces of silver?"

"You've earned that money, Mickey. Worked your way up from the bottom. Worked all the hours that God sent. You deserve it."

"But you didn't do it," said Mickey. "You didn't take the bribe."

"How could I? Me work for the Americans after everything I'd said."

"I guess it would have been a bit of a climb down," said Mickey. It had never been clear how much of Marcus' anger at America was put on for show. He hated everything and anything American. But he reserved a special anger for the American banks and how they had come to dominate global finance. He'd made a great play of Royal Shire Bank being Britain's last chance to take on the Americans.

"You know, State Financial ain't as in-your-face as you might think," said Mickey. "It's actually giving us a pretty long leash."

"Only because it's flat on its back from the credit crunch. Once it recovers it will move in and wrap you in a bureaucratic straight jacket, just like every other American bank."

"They say they're going to leave us with our own identity."

Marcus laughed. "You're so naïve Mickey. That's what they said to BZW, Cazenoves, Schroders and all the other great names that the Americans discarded. Hundreds of years of tradition poured down the drain. And Royal Shire Bank will be next."

"So that's why you didn't sell out."

Marcus nodded. "I also realised the market still needed independent investment advice. The point is that I had good reasons not to take the thirty pieces of silver. You, on the other hand, have good reasons to take it. You've no need to feel guilty about taking your lock-in."

"Maybe you're right," said Mickey. "I could give half what I was going to give to charity and the rest I can stick your way."

"Invest it all with me." Marcus placed a hand on Mickey's shoulder. "Forget about the charity donations. Do that in your will. Right now your money is needed in Summer Securities."

13

Manita checked her watch as Mickey approached the desk. "The lawyer has been waiting twenty minutes."

"How did you get hold of one so quick?"

"You said it was urgent. I've booked you room sixteen."

"Why can't I see him in my office?"

"I thought you'd appreciate meeting *her* somewhere more private."

"What are you talking about?" asked Mickey.

"The lawyer's name is Veronica Edwards."

"So she's a woman."

"Miss Veronica Edwards."

"And she's single. Good for her."

"And maybe for you. She's very good looking." Manita winked.

Mickey hurried off the trading floor and over to the lifts. He couldn't help be a little annoyed at Manita's attempt at matchmaking. He was still married to Helen, happily as far as he was concerned, but Manita, like Marcus, didn't seem to believe it anymore. The real question was whether Helen believed it.

On the top floor in room sixteen, Miss Edwards was taking in the view over to the Greenwich observatory. She wore a cashmere cardigan and a tight-fitting red pencil-skirt. Quite racy for a lawyer, Mickey thought.

He didn't want to sneak up on her so he coughed and she turned. Her dark hair was harshly scraped back off her face but there was no denying she was attractive. Mickey tried not to stare.

"Hi. I'm Mickey Summer. Pleased to meet you. I see you were enjoying the view."

She turned back to the window and threw off a whiff of something fruity. "I was actually thinking of how exposed this building is to a nine-eleven style attack."

"Why?" asked Mickey. "Are you planning one?"

"No." She laughed and turned back into the room. "So how can I help you?"

"A colleague of mine drowned on Friday night. He jumped off

Tower Bridge. You might have read about it in the paper."

"I didn't, but I'm sorry to hear that. That must have been a shock for you."

"Yeah, really shocking."

Mickey walked back to the table and poured tea.

"So why do you need a lawyer?" she asked.

"The Old Bill seems to think I had something to do with it."

"Then you'd better sit down and tell me why."

Mickey described his meeting with the police. Veronica took the occasional note but said nothing until Mickey had finished.

"It sounds like routine enquiries ahead of an inquest. I don't believe you have anything to worry about."

"But what about me having a go at Daniel?" asked Mickey.

"You said you didn't physically assault him."

"My tongue-lashings can be worse than a real whipping."

She set her cup back on the table and looked at the biscuits without taking one. "An argument will be of legitimate interest to the coroner, but you can't be held in any way accountable for his death just because you shouted at him."

"What if the Old Bill tries to fit me up?"

"Fit you up?"

"Say that I followed Daniel on to the bridge and pushed him off."

"Why on earth would they say that?"

"To get me in court. And then it's a lottery. Depends on what mood the jury is in. If they're lucky they get a conviction."

Veronica folded her arms. "Hang on. I think you're putting two and two together and getting rather too much."

"But you read about miscarriages of justice all the time."

"You've been watching too many cop shows. The police are just going about their duties. You'll probably hear no more from them."

"The copper gave me his card and told me he'd be in touch. I don't think it was for a social."

"Well, I'd be surprised if this went any further, but if the police do ask you to go in for further questioning then call me straight away."

She handed over her own card.

Mickey slipped it into his jacket pocket. "So if it did go further you'd be happy to represent me?"

"Of course."

"But you haven't even asked me if I did it?"

"I don't need to know whether you did it or not."

"So you'd represent me even if you thought I was guilty?"

"That's how the system works."

"I couldn't do that," said Mickey.

"So all your clients are whiter than white then?"

"So far as I know. The City works on trust. You know the motto: my word is my bond."

Veronica raised an eyebrow. "Given the collapse in the financial system, do you think that still holds?" She glanced at her watch. "Now I'm afraid I have another appointment."

Mickey stood up.

She smiled. "I'm happy to see myself out."

"No can do. All guests have to be accompanied back to reception. Besides, after your comments on suicide bombers I need to keep my eye on you."

She laughed and Mickey gestured towards the door.

"Well thanks for the advice," he said as they arrived at reception. "I feel much more relaxed."

"Good. Hopefully you won't have to see me again."

"Hopefully," said Mickey. But he realised he didn't really mean that.

14

Stanley slammed the paper onto the table. The damn Telegraph was at it now. He wasn't overly bothered about the tabloids. But The Telegraph should be defending him, not joining in the braying for his knighthood to be revoked.

It seemed that nobody outside of the City understood that he could do nothing about the lock-ins. That he hadn't even wanted them. That he'd voted against the Americans. That none of this was his fault.

He turned to look up the Thames at the jigsaw of spires and towers of the old City. It was a reminder of a better place in a gentler time. Some blamed the demise of the old City on the Americans, with their braces and cash-register mentality that had little regard for risk or reputation. But in reality Big Bang had already done the damage by mixing retail banking with investment banking. It was always going to end in tears.

His secretary called through on the intercom. "I have William Morris on the phone."

Stanley had put a call in to his PR manager as soon as he'd read the headlines. He turned back from the window and snatched up his phone.

"Well? What have you got to say for yourself?"

"I knew nothing about it, Sir Stanley."

"Why do I pay you hundreds of thousands of pounds a year to manage my PR when you don't even know that a national newspaper is about to write about me?"

"They never called," he said. "We got no warning at all. It was a Treasury hit job. I know the journalist. They've used him before."

"Do you think Cookson set it up?"

"Undoubtedly."

"And have you found anything on him yet?"

"Not yet. He appears to be squeaky clean."

"Then make something up."

Stanley slammed down the phone, screwed up the cutting and threw it at the bin. And missed. Typical of his luck at present.

His secretary called through again. "I have the Chief Constable."

He took up the phone again. "Anthony. Thank you for calling back. Look I'm sorry to trouble you. It's perhaps a trivial matter..."

"Don't worry. What is it?"

"It's about Daniel Goldcup."

"What about him?"

"You told me you'd concluded it was suicide. Is that still the case?"

"That will be for the coroner to decide. But it's looking that way. Why?"

"This detective you sent round led one of my staff to believe he was under suspicion for murder."

"He must have misunderstood. It's not a murder enquiry."

"Well Mickey Summer, one of my best chaps, was told to get himself a lawyer ready for an interview."

"Very odd. I'll look into it straight away."

15

Despite the recession, the late-night Christmas shopping was full on. Mickey had washed around the West End for hours but found nothing suitable for Helen. The farm was the real Christmas present of course, but he wanted to get her something to open on the day as well.

He took shelter from the rain in an arcade off Regent Street and decided to call her and see if she had any ideas. Besides, he hadn't spoken to her in over a week and he missed her voice.

She picked up on the second ring.

"Helen Cooper."

She'd kept the maiden name. Bit of a leading indicator. "It's Mickey."

"Mickey. Are you all right?"

"Fine."

"You sound a bit flat."

"Never could reach the high notes."

"I read about Daniel. It's been all over the papers."

"Yes he made quite a splash."

"You shouldn't joke about it."

"Sorry. I still can't quite believe it."

"Me neither. Why did he do it?"

"Nobody seems to know."

"Stress of work I suspect," said Helen. "Bankeritis."

"Actually work was going well for Daniel. We were out that night celebrating a big deal he had brought in." Ironic, thought Mickey.

Now that Daniel was dead he didn't mind giving him the credit for winning the business.

"How are things with you, anyway?" she asked.

"Been better. You've seen all this fuss about our lock-ins I suppose."

"It's understandable though isn't it?"

"It's understandable how people who don't understand anything about the City can misunderstand lock-ins for bonuses."

"You don't need to be a City insider to know that the banks shouldn't be paying out bonuses after they caused the credit crunch."

"Even if that was true, our lock-ins ain't bonuses."

"It's the same thing isn't it?"

Mickey sighed. "No. It's payment for work done years ago. Nothing to do with the credit crunch."

"Still …"

"Still nothing."

There was an awkward silence. Mickey broke it first. "Forget about all that anyway. I'm Christmas shopping. Wondered if you had any ideas for yourself?"

"Oh, don't go spending money on me."

"Do you want me to nick your present then?"

"I'm happy with just a card. Or, if you want to get me a present, then you know the sort of thing I like: something simple, anything natural or better still handmade."

That's all she ever wanted; shells from the beach, rocks from the hills, a hand-drawn picture, a made-up song or poem, anything 'from the heart', as she put it. Mickey was desperate to tell her about the farm. That was from the heart, even if it did cost a couple of million quid. But he was worried she might stop him buying it if she knew. Safer to tell her once it was a done deal.

The conversation moved on to life on her dad's farm. The sick cows, the fox and chicken wars, the lost cat, the hole in the barn roof and the leaking radiators. It was the sort of remote conversation Mickey imagined a soldier on tour of duty might have with his wife back home.

"You still coming home for Christmas?" he asked eventually.

There was a long pause before she answered.

"I've been thinking about that, Mickey. I'd like to spend Christmas up here."

Mickey felt sick. He probably shouldn't have been surprised, but he'd been banking on her coming back for Christmas. "So when do you think you're coming back to London?"

"Well actually I'm coming next week. I was hoping we could meet up and talk."

"Talk about what?"

Another long pause.

"About us," she said.

"Sounds ominous."

"Are you free Thursday night?" she asked, ducking his comment.

"I can be."

"Shall we say seven o'clock in the Punch and Judy?"

That had been their favourite boozer when they'd first been married. "All right."

"I'll see you then."

She rang off. He'd had more intimate business calls. He wanted to slam the phone into its receiver. But it doesn't work with a mobile. So he shoved it into his pocket instead.

16

Another week down. A little over a month to go. Ben Stein smiled as he poured out the last of the Chateau Faugeres. Sociologists claimed people only smiled in social situations. Yet here he was, with no-one around, practically laughing his head off because in just over a month he could cash in his lock-in and never work again. Cheers State Financial. Here's to you.

Did he feel any guilt at earning so much when the plebs wouldn't get any bonus this year and when millions were on the dole? A pang of course. But did he think he should give some back like the press was saying? Would they do the same if the roles were reversed? Of course not.

He'd earned it, just like a footballer or a pop star or anyone else who was at the top of their game. And he'd paid his dues; two marriages, a dodgy ticker and burnt out at forty-four. He probably couldn't work again even if he wanted to. This last pay cheque was his retirement fund.

Distracted by movement outside, he wandered over to the window. Fir trees swayed behind the tennis court at the back of the garden. Beyond, the flag on the fourteenth green fluttered in the moonlight.

He shook his head as he recalled the wild slice into the lake that had cost him the match that afternoon. Still, he had been playing a client and so would have had to throw the match at some stage.

Resolution to self: once retired, take lessons, get handicap down, replay all clients and thrash them. Except those who managed the family trust fund.

That reminded him. He had yet to call his daughter on her birthday. She answered immediately.

"Happy Birthday my little jewel."

"Daddy!"

"Sorry I couldn't get to the phone earlier. It's been a mad day."

"I understand. Thank you for the lovely flowers. You remembered orchids."

"Of course." Note to self: congratulate secretary for remembering daughter's favourite flowers. "Have you had a good day?"

"I've been in lectures, but Sam is taking me out to dinner any minute."

"That's good." Ben tried not to sound disappointed that the gentile was still on the scene.

Rachel reeled off a list of presents she'd received and Ben's attention wandered. He thought he heard a rattle on the fencing at the bottom of the garden. He moved over to the window, but saw nothing out of place. Possibly a fox.

"Daddy? Are you still planning to keep all of your bonus?"

"Of course I am. Anyway it's not a bonus sweetie."

"It's just that everyone seems to think it's wrong. They say the money belongs to the taxpayer."

"It doesn't. And you shouldn't be talking about it. There are people who might harm you if they knew about me."

"I haven't told anyone that you are one of them." She giggled nervously. "I wouldn't dare."

"Well don't go worrying about it. Concentrate on your studies." He looked at the three-quarter moon reflected in the pond. On the far side he imagined something move. A shadow. It was probably the neighbour's irritating children garden hopping again. Last time they'd trampled a flower bed.

"Rachel my dear, I've got to go now. Just wanted to wish you happy birthday. Enjoy your dinner."

"Love you Daddy."

"Love you."

Ben hit the red button and moved out onto the balcony to get a better look at the garden.

A shadow again, crossing in front of the pagoda. A big shadow. Not that of a child. A man. He ran over the grass and up the wooden steps.

Ben jumped back inside the house and pulled the balcony door shut. The man raced up to the door.

Ben fumbled with the lock but the man yanked the door open. Ben strained to pull the door closed again but the man was stronger. Ben's feet slipped on the carpet as the door opened wider. One foot, two feet, three feet and then, with a final jerk the door was fully open.

The man jumped inside. His 'Guy Fawkes' mask grinning manically.

"Get out, or I'll call the police," shouted Ben.

The man pulled out a long knife. Sharp. Not for show.

Ben backed away. "You'll get no trouble from me."

The man drew the curtains closed behind. Then he walked slowly toward Ben, leaving muddy footprints on the white carpet as he went.

"Take what you want," said Ben. "The Star of David. On the fireplace. It's solid gold. Go on. Take it. Take it."

Suddenly Ben felt a stab of pain in his chest. It couldn't be the knife. No. He remembered this pain, the squeezing sensation in the centre of his chest. He dropped to his knees.

"Heart attack. Help me. Please."

But the man just stood there with the knife held out, like an actor who'd forgotten his lines.

Ben pointed to the phone. "Call an ambulance."

The intruder picked it up, held it for a moment and then dropped it on the floor.

"Please, my pills," said Ben. "In the first aid box on that shelf."

He was struggling to get any breath in his lungs and he was surprised at how loud the wheeze which came from his throat sounded. He pointed at the first aid box, but still the intruder didn't move. Just stood there. Watching from behind the mask.

The mangle squeezed tighter. Ben forced himself back up onto his feet. He struggled across the room and reached up for the first aid box, took out the tablets. He was turning the lid when the intruder snatched the container from him.

Ben dropped to the floor, his hands tugging at the buttons on his shirt as he tried to get air to his chest. "For God's sake," he rasped. "I'm dying."

"That is the idea."

17

Vanni started the morning meeting with a minute's silence. Mickey wasn't in the mood to give his usual market view. The few analysts that managed to speak struggled to make contact with eyes that were mostly staring into space.

The meeting finished early and people put in some half-hearted calls, then gathered in huddles to discuss Ben's death. He'd been a control freak to his traders and a bully to the rest of the floor. If they'd been asked what they thought of Ben the day before, ninety-nine per cent would have said they disliked him. But nobody would have wished him dead and it was difficult to think he'd never be seen again.

But there was no surprise he'd died of a heart attack. It was common knowledge that Ben had had a dodgy ticker and he smoked and ate and boozed like a troll.

"Ben wasn't the only one who drank too much," said Ole. "It's the British culture. You drink more than anyone else in Europe."

"Since when have you Vikings been teetotal then?" asked Mickey.

"Ole is right though," said Glen. "We all drink too much and our diet is all wrong. I'm going to book myself in for a well-man medical."

"Don't you need to be a man for that?" asked Mickey. "Seriously though, that's not a bad idea. Daniel's depression was also probably stress related. A medical should pick up problems like that as well. I'll get HR to organise medicals for everyone."

Mickey struggled through his second round of calls until it was time to go and check in with Manita.

He realised from the smudges on her cheek that she had been crying. "Are you all right?"

She shook her head and tried to wipe away some of the smudges.

"So you're half left as well?"

"I'm not in the mood for jokes, Mickey."

He remembered that Manita had worked for Ben, way back sometime.

"Do you want to go home?" asked Mickey, putting his arm around her.

She dabbed her eyes with a tissue. "I'll be all right in a minute."

"You sure? I can pretend that I can do this job without you. I can bluff through for a day."

She laughed. "Really, I'm fine. It's probably better for me to keep busy."

Mickey noticed a bunch of red roses on Manita's desk. "Are those for Ben's wife?"

Manita shook her head. "Vanni has sorted that already. These are the flowers you asked me to get for your mother. I've also wrapped up that gold bracelet you asked me to buy." Manita removed a packet from her top drawer and handed it to him. "She's expecting you later this morning."

"This morning? There's too much going on. With Ben …" Mickey couldn't finish the sentence. "Weil asked me to keep an eye on the traders. I'll have to go see Mum after work."

"It has to be this morning," said Manita. "You're blocked out with appraisals and meetings from twelve o'clock right through to a seven o'clock dinner with a client."

"Can't you cut a couple of the appraisals?"

"You're too far behind as it is."

"How about if we courier the present over today and I'll go see her tomorrow."

"I think you should see her on her birthday, Mickey."

He knew she was right. Ben and Daniel's death were reminders of how fragile life was. He couldn't be sure how many more birthdays his Mum would be having. He looked at his watch. "I'm on my way then."

"You'll also need these." She held up some keys.

"What's that about?"

"Marcus has bought her a car and he asked if you could drive it round. It's down in the basement."

"A car? What the hell is he playing at? I didn't know Mum wanted a car."

"I don't think she knows about it. It's a surprise."

"Well Marcus can bloody well drive it round himself. I'm not his delivery boy."

"Stop competing with him all the time. It's about making your mother happy on her birthday, not about who bought the biggest present."

She held the keys out again.

* * *

Frank found MacIntyre sitting behind his desk, arms folded, lips pursed.

"Problem, Sir?"

"I had a call earlier from the Chief Constable," he said. "Do you want to tell me what it was about?"

"Might be easier if you tell me, Sir."

"Guess."

"I've really no idea, Sir, and I'm actually a bit too busy for games. At a wild stab I'd guess it has something to do with Daniel Goldcup."

"You guessed right. Apparently you told someone at Royal Shire Bank that he was under suspicion of murdering Daniel Goldcup."

Frank had been half expecting this. "It wasn't like that, Sir."

"What was it like then?"

"I cautioned him."

"You told him to get hold of a lawyer before the next interview."

"That was his idea. He said he wouldn't talk until he'd seen a lawyer. I didn't actually tell him I'd be back to interview him."

"But you didn't disabuse him of the opinion?"

"I suppose I didn't."

"And why did you caution him?"

"He said something about pushing Goldcup over the edge. He probably didn't mean it literally but there was a double meaning and as they'd had a big argument that night I thought it only right to caution him."

Frank left aside the fact that Mickey's fat-cat banker attitude had irritated him.

"So are you genuinely concerned that Mickey Summer was involved in Daniel Goldcup's death?"

"It's a possibility," said Frank.

"Are you going to question him then?"

Frank shook his head. "Not as things stand."

"Well you'd better set the record straight," said MacIntyre. "Call Mickey Summer and tell him that you don't need to see him for an interview and you're sorry for any unnecessary aggravation you may have caused."

"Why the kid glove treatment, Sir?"

"Because Mickey Summer's boss is friends with the Chief Constable."

"Good for him. If it's all the same with you, Sir, I'd rather just leave things as they are."

"It's not all the same to me. Make the call."

53

18

Mickey was annoyed to find no parking space outside his Mum's red-brick terrace. He'd wanted to buy her a bigger house with its own drive but she wouldn't have any of it. Wouldn't move from the street where she'd lived nearly all her life.

So he parked further up, still miffed to be running his brother's errand. He hurried back to the house and rang the bell.

His Mum took a long time to answer. She wasn't so quick on her feet anymore.

"My little Mickey!"

He whipped the flowers out from behind his back. "Happy birthday."

"I don't need flowers at my age."

"Yes you do." Mickey pushed them into her hands and kissed her on both cheeks.

"I'll put these in some water," she said as she moved off to the kitchen.

Mickey followed. It was like being stuck behind a learner on a country lane. "Now I can't stop long, Mum. I'm meant to be at work."

"You and your work, Mickey. You've always been such a hard worker. You'll have time for a cuppa though?"

In the kitchen she filled a yellow vase with water, dropped in the flowers and set it down on the window sill. "That brightens the place up."

Mickey sat on a stool. "So, is it twenty-one again, Mum?"

"Twenty-one and a matter of months."

She lit the gas under the kettle.

"Well you look twenty-one to me." He produced the wrapped present from his pocket. "Happy birthday."

"More presents? Honestly Mickey, you shouldn't keep spending your money on me." She unwrapped it slowly. Mickey knew she'd re-use the paper. Her eyes widened as she opened the box.

"Do you like it then?"

"Looks expensive, Mickey."

"Don't worry about the price, Mum. Do you like it?"

"She held it over her wrist. It's lovely. But when am I going to wear something like that?"

"When you go out."

"I only go down the bingo."

"Wear it then."

She put it back in its box. "I'll wear it Christmas Day. Thanks."

Mickey knew she wasn't one to make a big deal about a present, but he hoped she did genuinely like it. The kettle whistled and she turned off the gas, made the drinks and carried them through to the living room. Mickey followed with a packet of biscuits he found in the cupboard.

They sat beside each other on the old sofa.

"Have you seen our Marcus recently?"

"We went for lunch the other day."

"How was he looking?"

"Through both eyes," said Mickey, though he knew she wouldn't get the humour. "Same as usual."

"He looked terrible thin when I last saw him. I'm worried for him. All that stress he's under."

"No more than the rest of us."

"But you don't have to run your own business like he does."

"His job's no bigger than mine." Mickey felt himself getting defensive.

"I suppose," she said quietly.

But the bias was obvious. The eldest son always had to be doing bigger and better. "Work's going well thanks."

She smiled. "That's good."

"I'm in line for a promotion."

"Well done."

But his Mum didn't appear interested in the detail and busied herself with pouring more tea.

"Is Marcus coming round to see you then?" It was a cheap shot but Mickey couldn't stop himself.

"He said he'd try but he couldn't promise. He's very busy."

"So am I."

"Thank you." She smiled. "You've always been a good boy."

She sipped her tea and then asked from nowhere: "You seen Helen recently?"

"As a matter of fact I'm seeing her next week."

"She coming back then?"

"Well she's coming back for a day in any case."

"You planning to take her out somewhere nice? Make a fuss of her."

"We're going to her favourite pub."

"Take her a little surprise," she said. "A little present. Always helps."

"Well I could tell her about the farm," said Mickey, thinking aloud.

"What farm?" Mum frowned. "You're not wasting your hard-earned money on Helen's dad again."

"No. This is a farm for me and Helen to live in. For her to manage but close enough to London so I can commute in to Canary Wharf."

"So she's agreed to come back and live on this farm then?"

Mickey dunked a biscuit in his coffee. "I haven't told her about it yet. Don't want to promise what I can't deliver. But I'm exchanging in January, just as soon as I get my lock-in."

Mum sighed. "Well I hope it works out for you, Mickey. I really hope it does. I can't say I agree with everything Helen's done. Leaving you like she did. But she is your wife and I think she's good for you."

She was right about that. That was his biggest fear about losing Helen. That he'd go back to being the idiot he'd been before he met her. He checked his watch. "Look, I've got to get back to work, Mum."

"You only just arrived."

"Sorry it's such a short visit. But we can keep talking while you drive me back to Canary Wharf if you like."

"Drive you back?"

Mickey winked.

They walked out into the street and along to the black Golf.

"You didn't buy that for me?"

Mickey handed over the keys. "It's from Marcus."

56

19

Frank went into an empty office to make the call to Mickey Summer. He was kept on hold for a couple of minutes. He couldn't help wondering if Summer was doing that on purpose.

There was no apology for keeping him waiting when he did finally pick up the phone. "What can I do you for Inspector Brighouse? Price and size in which stock?"

"I don't gamble," said Frank.

"It's called investing."

"Same difference. Anyway I am actually ringing to let you know that we've finished our enquiries and we won't need to interview you again. The coroner will give his verdict next week and I expect him to declare Daniel Goldcup's death as a suicide."

There was a long pause and then Mickey said: "Is that it?"

"That's it," said Frank anticipating what was coming next.

"No apology then."

"Apology for what?"

"For accusing me of murder?"

"I didn't accuse you of anything, Mr Summer. I cautioned you, that's all. It's quite common during interviews. I think you over reacted."

"Were you ordered to ring me?"

Frank resisted the temptation to lie. "It was suggested I call you to clear up the misunderstanding and I agreed that would be a good idea."

"Look mate. You had a problem with me for some reason and you put the frighteners on me. Right?"

"I wouldn't describe it like that."

"Well I can put the frighteners on you too. You know that Sir Stanley is big pals with your Chief Constable don't you?"

"I understand there's a connection," said Frank.

"A good connection. So I reckon you should go do something useful with your time like arrest a traffic warden. And leave me to get on with helping the economic recovery."

Frank lost it. "D'you know what's funny? Is how a little bloke like you doing a pretty meaningless job can have such an overblown view of his own importance."

"Pot, kettle, black," said Mickey.

"I know my place in the world. I know I'm irrelevant in the scheme of things. But I get on with my little life, look after my family and friends, try and be good and treat people as well as I can. I do my job to the best of my ability to help the community and I take the pay I'm given without complaint. Can you say the same?"

"Look mate, if it wasn't for City tax revenues the Government wouldn't have the money to pay for the police, the doctors, teachers and all the other stuff."

"You pay yourselves a fortune out of other people's money. It's a scam."

"We get paid well because we work bloody hard," said Mickey. "Why do you think Daniel Goldcup got depressed? And another guy at our place died this week. Heart attack."

Another banker who'd made a killing but not got out in time, thought Frank.

"If you're looking for sympathy," he said, "you're talking to the wrong bloke."

20

The orange gas lanterns flickered over the entrance to the Claremont Club but there was no name plate or information plaque, nothing to show that this was where high-rollers from Lord Lucan to Jimmy Goldsmith had won and lost fortunes over the years.

When he'd been a member himself, Mickey had mostly lost. Then Helen discovered he'd been down every night one week and she'd made him ring Gamblers Anonymous. One of the many good things she'd done for him.

Mickey found his brother in the Pembrokeshire Room. The leather-backed door closed silently and Mickey nodded at Marcus and the other men around the green table.

They turned back to their game.

He recognised Alistair Beers, who slid some chips into the middle of the table. "I'll see your thousand Marcus and raise you another thousand."

The two players on Alistair's left folded fast and all eyes turned to Marcus, who counted his chips then turned to look over his shoulder at Mickey. "For reasons too tiresome to go into, I have a short term cash-flow problem. Could you help me out, Mickey?"

"Do I look like a cash point machine?" asked Mickey. "Is that why you got me over here? To bankroll your card game?"

"Of course not. I need to see you about something else, just as soon as I've finished this hand. But as you are here, can you help out?"

Mickey shuffled in his chair. He'd promised Helen he'd quit. He'd promised himself. But this wasn't gambling, it was just lending money. And anyway, Helen wasn't around to care.

"How much do you need?"

"Two thousand," replied Marcus. "Would you like to come in on the hand? I've put in four thousand already, but I'll split the winnings fifty-fifty."

Mickey's mouth turned dry and he looked around for a glass of water. "Just leave it as a straight loan."

"Come in for old time's sake, Mickey." Marcus turned to Alistair. "Is it all right with you if Mickey comes in on my hand?"

"I've no objection," said Alistair.

"Well I have," said Mickey. "I don't play anymore."

"I'm the one playing the cards," said Marcus. "You're just banking the hand. Have you got your cheque book on you?"

Mickey shook his head. He hadn't carried a cheque book in years. "Do you take plastic, Alistair?"

"I'll take a promissory note if that helps," said Alistair.

"Thank you," said Marcus. "Write one out for two thousand pounds then would you, Mickey?"

Mickey grabbed a pen and did as Marcus asked.

Marcus snatched the paper and placed it in the centre of the table. He sat back in his chair and fixed Alistair with a stare.

"So," he said eventually, sliding his last chips into the pile. "I've seen you and now I raise you another …"

"Hold on!" shouted Mickey. "I lent you the money to see him."

"Hush," said Marcus. "So I raise you another one thousand five hundred, Alistair."

Alistair nodded and looked at his cards as if he'd quite forgotten what a good hand he held. Then he slid forward a stack of red chips. "That's to see you and raise you a further five thousand pounds."

Marcus smiled. "Can you lend me another five then, Mickey, so that we can see Alistair? Remember we'll split the winnings."

Reluctantly Mickey wrote out another note. "This is to see Alistair. This is the end of the game, right."

"Of course," said Marcus.

Alistair studied his hand. Then with a magician's flourish he unveiled three kings and two jacks.

Marcus's smile vanished. "Beats me."

"What did you have?" asked Mickey.

"We don't have to show."

"I want to know."

Marcus laid down his cards. Three queens, a nine and a six.

"Bloody Hell, Marcus. Three sodding queens." Mickey shook his head. "That's a worse hand than Captain Hook's."

Alistair gathered up his winnings. "Given the financing situation I rather think that's the end of the game isn't it?"

"I'm on for more," said Marcus. "How about you, Mickey?"

"On for handing more money over to Alistair. No thanks." Mickey picked up Marcus by the elbow and led him away to the lounge.

"Sorry about that," said Marcus. "Win some, lose some."

Mickey squeezed Marcus' arm hard. "You must be off your trolley. You're just throwing away money."

Marcus shrugged. "Must be losing my touch. I was sure Al was bluffing."

"What do you want to see me about anyway?" asked Mickey. "It's eleven o'clock. Why did you drag me over here at this time?"

"I need to know what you thought of the business plan."

"I haven't read it all yet."

"But did you like what you saw?"

Mickey stood up to leave. "I can't believe you made me come round here to discuss this. You gave me the impression it was something urgent."

"It is. I told you I have a short-term cash flow problem. If I know you are buying in then I can use that to arrange other financing around it."

Mickey sat back down. "I can't commit just like that. Anyway, if you're short of cash what are you doing blowing money here? And why did you buy a car for Mum's birthday if you're so hard pushed? Not to mention that bottle of expensive plonk at lunch."

"They're all small change, Mickey. That's what you don't realise. I'm talking about serious money when we sell the business." He grabbed Mickey's arm and pulled him closer. "It's a no-brainer."

"Maybe that's my problem. I have got a brain. And it's telling me it needs more time to make a decision on something this risky."

"Come on, Mickey. Join me. We'll have a riot together. And if it doesn't work out after a few years you're still a big name and you'll walk back into another job."

Marcus' grip on Mickey's arm was uncomfortably tight. Mickey released it.

"It's not like the old days. Moving firms is much riskier now."

"There's far more risk staying where you are, Mickey. Royal Shire Bank is on death row. The Government won't let management pay market rate, you know that. So people will drift off to those banks that can still pay proper bonuses. And the winners will be the Americans, of course, but also new entrants like Summer Securities: independent, financially unconstrained, entrepreneurial. It'll be just like the old times. Can't you see that?"

"You could be right," said Mickey. "I just need more time to think."

"You've had days already."

"I've had a lot on my mind."

"Well hurry up. If you aren't coming on board then I'll need to let the private equity boys come in instead. I just need this last bit of capital and then its take-off in the New Year. Don't miss out."

"When I've made a decision Marcus, you'll be the first to know."

21

Mickey and Ole sat opposite each other in Mickey's office. Ole carefully watching Mickey write. Mickey read out loud as he filled in the summary box.

"A much improved year. Ole is now a genuine franchise player."

Ole nodded but said nothing.

Mickey placed his hands flat on the table as a signal that the appraisal was over and Ole was free to leave.

Ole sat firm. "You haven't said anything about my bonus."

"Correct."

Mickey had been trying to duck money conversations since discovering that the bonus pool was shrinking faster than the arctic ice cap. "It's all very political, Ole. What with the UK Government owning part of us and with State Financial owning the rest and both sides being in a mess themselves. I've really got no idea how big the bonus pool is going to be. It's safe to say it will be well down on last year."

"My friend at Finsburg says their pool is up thirty percent."

"I heard twenty," said Mickey. "But in any case we ain't Finsburg."

"But Ben and Daniel are out of the pool now aren't they," said Ole. "And they would both have been in for a big bonus. So if you spread what you save from them around the department then it's going to help."

Mickey was shocked at Ole's mercenary thinking.

"It don't work like that, Ole. Their bonuses won't come back into the general pool."

"What happens to them then?"

"I suppose they'll go to the next of kin."

Ole shook his head slowly. "Check your own lock-in contract, Mickey. There's no death benefit in it."

"How do you know that?"

Ole tapped the side of his nose. "I take an interest in these things. The money doesn't get paid out to the relatives. So the question is: where does it go?"

Mickey hadn't bothered with the small print in his contract. "I'll have to look into that. But in any case, Ole, I can't give you a steer this year. I just have no idea."

Ole folded his arms. "And I don't suppose you're going to fight very hard for us either. You're only bothered about whether the Government blocks your lock-ins."

"Don't you get yourself bothered about what does or doesn't bother me, Ole. I'm looking out for my team like always. I told Weil we still need to pay market to keep everyone."

"Too right you do. I'm getting plenty of calls from head hunters."

"Mind your head then," said Mickey. "Now we're drifting into Friday night drinking time. So I need to get on."

Mickey kept his smile on until Ole had left the room. Then he unlocked a drawer and pulled out the bonus sheet. After the final cut with Weil, Ole had been put in for a big fat zero. The toys would definitely be out the pram. Mickey shaved ten grand off three others to allow him to give thirty to Ole. He also made a note in the margin: 'Claims he's getting calls.'

Mickey put the sheet back in the drawer and locked it. He checked his watch. Almost six o'clock. He packed up a bag of weekend reading, then left.

Manita was on the phone as he passed. He waved goodbye and she held a hand up for him to stop.

"It's your Mum."

"Is she all right?"

"Her car has been stolen."

Mickey took the phone. "You all right, Mum?"

"It's the car. Someone's thieved it."

She sounded close to tears.

"When did it happen?" asked Mickey.

"I went out just now and it's not there. I think I might have left the keys in."

That'll impress the insurers, thought Mickey. "Don't worry about it, Mum."

"I'm scared to tell Marcus."

"It's not your fault. Anyway, it might turn up yet. Could just be joyriders."

"Do you think so?"

"The main thing is whether you are all right?"

"Just cross with myself."

"Do you want me to come round?"

"I'm all right. Marge is here."

"Good. Now leave everything to us. We'll call the Old Bill and the insurers and Marcus. You just relax."

"You're a good lad, Mickey."

He handed the phone back to Manita.

"When you say 'leave everything to us', you really mean me, don't you."

"I'd stay and help you," said Mickey, "but I've got all them chores to get done."

Manita checked the diary. "What chores?"

He kissed her on the cheek. "A pint of lager thanks. But I'll get it myself."

22

Vanni's GPS showed he'd been running at sub eight-minute mile pace. Not bad, in the dark and the rain and considering his knee was hurting. If he could keep it up over the last two miles he'd get home in under the hour.

On that thought he found a little extra spring in his stride. Then, as so often recently, his thoughts wandered to retirement. Provided the Government didn't stop the lock-in payments he could leave in just three weeks. Sell the house in Hadley Wood and move permanently to the summer house on Lake Como. It was the only place Camilla was truly happy. They'd been too long in England. It was time to go home.

Up ahead on the country lane a car switched on its headlights. Vanni put his hand up to shield his eyes. Suddenly the car pulled out, wheels screeching. It accelerated down the narrow lane. Boy racers from Southgate or Barnet probably. Vanni stepped to the side of the road and glared disapprovingly, hands on his hips, shaking his head.

It seemed though, that despite Vanni's high visibility clothing, the driver had not yet noticed him. Certainly he was making no attempt to slow down or move over.

The car was closing quickly.

Vanni tried to squeeze into the hedge on the side of the road but it was thick with spikes. He pushed harder in to the hedge but there was just no way through. The car was almost on him.

How could the driver not see him? If he was going to swerve to avoid hitting him he needed to do it now.

The last few metres ran in freeze-frame and Vanni's thoughts flashed back to a school physics lesson on the kinetic energy of a body being proportional to the velocity squared, with the implication being that the most important determinant in the impact was the speed of the car rather than its mass …

Vanni's legs broke as they were taken away from him. His stunned body rolled up the bonnet and crashed against the windscreen before being dumped on the side of the road.

The driver braked hard and jumped out of the car. He ran back up the road searching frantically by torchlight for the man he'd hit. He found him face up in some brambles. He looked for signs of life. The eyes were open but vacant. The chest was still. He felt for a pulse but found none.

Satisfied, he removed his mask and walked back to the car.

23

Eddie parked up beside the blue-and-white crime scene tape. He and Frank climbed out of the car and ambled over to a fresh-faced uniform talking into his shoulder piece.

Frank showed his badge.

"I was told to expect you," said the sergeant. "Come on through."

They ducked under the tapes and walked down the narrow lane.

"Clearly not a very sensible place to go running," said the sergeant. "Especially at night."

"Depends what he was wearing," said Frank, who felt naturally defensive of a fellow runner. He often ran down such lanes. If he ran facing the oncoming traffic he got plenty of warning that a car was coming and it was a simple matter of stopping for a moment and stepping off the road until the car had passed.

"He had a high-visibility bib on. But still. He was asking to be run over."

"Any witnesses?" asked Frank.

"None have come forward."

Frank walked over to a woman in a white coat, who knelt beside a hedge that had clearly been run into by a car. The black tweezers in her gloved hand were picking at the broken branches.

"Got anything?" asked the sergeant.

"A few flecks of paint," she said without looking up. "Should be enough to establish the make of car."

She pointed to a tyre mark on the mud bank at the side of the road. "And we should be able to match those."

Frank turned to look at the white outline in the road. "Killed instantly, is that right?"

"Apparently," said the sergeant.

"The car must have been motoring some then."

"That's how people drive down these lanes. The speed limit is sixty miles an hour. He was asking to be killed running round here."

"Will you stop saying that," said Frank. "He wasn't asking to be killed. He was out running to keep fit. He was asking to live."

* * *

The shock at the death of the popular, easy-going Italian spread rapidly across the trading floor.

Mickey thought immediately of Vanni's wife, Camilla. She'd be devastated. He also thought of their three kids. He remembered back to the news of his own dad's death. The numbness. The aching pain in the gut. All complicated by Dad being locked away in prison for something he hadn't done. A lot of bad memories he wished he could let go.

The initial shock wave was followed by a rising sense of panic as people wondered at three deaths among their colleagues in as many weeks.

"This is getting to be a dangerous place to work," said Ole. "It can't just be coincidence can it?"

"What are you getting at?" asked Glen. "Of course it's just co-incidence. Isn't it?"

"Think about it," interrupted Mickey. "Daniel drowns, Ben has a heart attack and now Vanni gets killed in a hit and run. All work in the same bank and all die within a few weeks of each other."

Glen swivelled round fully in his chair. "You think they might have been killed?"

"You've got it, Sherlock."

"Don't talk like that," Glen laughed nervously. "You'll get people frightened."

"Maybe they need to be." Mickey looked up the phone number for one of the egg-heads in derivatives and called him on the intercom. "That you, Paolo?"

"What do you want, Mickey?"

"You've heard about Vanni?"

"Yes. What's going on Mickey? Three deaths now. And all senior staff Mickey. It's scary."

"Scarier for me than you," said Mickey. "All three of them were in the lock-in group."

"Were they?" asked Paolo. "Are you sure you should be telling me that. I thought us ordinary mortals weren't supposed to know the identity of the lock-in group – even though we all do."

"Well keep that bit to yourself and the other ten-thousand who know," said Mickey. "But tell me, knowing that they were all three members of a group of twelve, what are the odds of these three deaths just happening by chance?"

"How would I know?"

"Come on. You can work out the odds for anything. Just ball park."

Paulo sighed. Mickey could hear him muttering numbers as he tapped on his keyboard. "It's got to be something near to a million to one shot."

"Thanks mate."

"And you take care, Mickey."

Mickey turned back to the others on the desk, who had been listening in. "Paulo puts the chances of these three deaths being a coincidence at a million to one."

"That doesn't mean they were murdered," said Ole. The word murdered seemed to linger overhead.

"Not for certain," said Ed. "But it's still bloody scary. I mean, who's next?"

"Could be anyone," said Glen.

"We need to alert security then," said Ole.

"Maybe we should stop coming in to work," said Glen. "At least until this all blows over."

"You can't do that," said Mickey. "Besides which, none of them died at work."

"It makes you think," said Glen. "Whatever the explanation for the deaths, is the job worth the trouble? Why not just cash in your chips and go live on a desert island? I bet there'll be a few resignations coming in now."

"After bonuses of course," said Ed.

"That's if there are any bonuses this year," said Ole.

"Will you two shut up about bonuses," shouted Mickey. "Vanni and the others aren't going to be getting bonuses now are they?"

They stopped talking and turned their attention to the far side of the room, where Manita was running across the trading floor, waving a newspaper over her head.

"We're under attack," she shouted.

"Who's under attack?" asked Ole.

"Royal Shire Bank!"

"What are you talking about?" asked Mickey.

"It's true. We're under attack from the anti-capitalists. That's who killed Vanni, Ben and Daniel."

A crush formed around Manita and her paper. Mickey stepped away, pulled up the online version and quickly found the article. It mentioned the three deaths and said police were investigating the possibility that the anti-capitalists had upped the ante.

The story whistled around the room. Mickey tried to calm nerves by touring the floor but he quickly realised he was in no position to counter the story. It was precisely what he'd been thinking. He left them to it and went to his office to call Martin in legal.

"Martin, have you seen the Standard?"

"We're just drafting a response now."

"What are you going to say?"

"That the article is without foundation."

"How do you know that?"

"We've talked to the police. They haven't connected the deaths at all."

Mickey sighed with relief. "Are you sure?"

"It's just some journalist making up a story. The police say the deaths are a coincidence. Daniel was a suicide and Ben died of a heart attack. Vanni was just a hit and run. We're drafting an announcement now. Got to go."

Martin cut him off.

Manita burst into the room and closed the door behind. "Can I have a word?"

"What's up now?"

"Everyone's nervous," she said. "Three people have been murdered, Mickey."

"I've just talked to legal. They say it's a load of cobblers. The police haven't connected the deaths. They don't think we're under attack. It's just the boys in the press making headlines."

Manita looked sceptical. "Three deaths in as many weeks."

"Look, I admit that's odd. I was worried about it myself. But the police say it's just coincidence."

"What if it's not? What if the anti-capitalists are really that mad? They might kill again. And they might kill everyone who works for Royal Shire Bank."

"They'll need to nuke the Tower to do that." Mickey smiled, though it was definitely forced.

"I mean they might target anyone who works for the bank. We're all at risk."

"Well I don't think you should worry about it."

Manita coughed and looked down at her toes.

"What is it?" asked Mickey. "Shoes need a polish? Come on,

spit it out."

"It's just …" she looked up. "I've been asked to put a suggestion to you. Something that people out on the floor have been thinking."

"Go on then."

"They think this has been brought on by those headlines about the lock-in group."

"Do they now?"

"They think if you all give the money back, or at least some of it, then whoever is behind this will leave us all alone."

"I see." Mickey turned to look out on the floor. Eyes that had been watching now flicked away.

"At the end of the day, it's only money," said Manita. "You can make it all up again in the future. Once all the fuss has died down."

"No I can't. I'll never get a chance to earn money like that again. Besides, I need it to buy the farm for Helen."

"You don't need all of it though."

"Manita, you know the rest is going to your Nepalese charity and to help out my brother. Besides, if someone really has killed Vanni, Ben and Daniel over the lock-ins it would be betrayal to give in to blackmail."

"Will you think about it?"

Mickey sighed. "Look, it won't be my decision but I'll pass on the suggestion to Sir Stanley. See what he thinks. In the meantime I don't think you have anything to worry about. The police think it's just coincidence. But even if the scaremongers are right, remember it's the lock-in group who appear to have been targeted, not secretaries, not even brilliant secretaries like you. So relax."

"What about your safety then?"

"I'm working on that."

24

Julia had chosen an especially dull history programme for the kids to watch, as it was late and she didn't want them getting over-excited. Frank's attention wandered. He wondered what sort of summer holiday they'd be able to afford with a pay freeze, a cap on overtime and rising mortgage payments. They'd manage to get away somewhere, even if it was only camping. That would actually suit him fine. Open air. Plenty of quality time with the kids. He snuggled in between Billy and Grace and stared back at the screen.

His mobile rang in the hallway and reluctantly he got up and went out to answer it.

"Sorry to trouble you so late, Inspector Brighouse, this is Mickey Summer."

"We do long hours in the police as well, Mr Summer. What do you want?"

"I just wondered if you read the Evening Standard?"

Frank knew why he was ringing but didn't feel like helping him out. "I glanced at it, why?"

"It says the police are investigating the possibility that the three deaths at Royal Shire are connected. Done by the anti-capitalists."

"Don't believe what you read in the papers," said Frank. "The Met have looked into it and as of now the view is that the deaths are unrelated. A suicide, a hit and run and a heart attack."

"But three deaths."

"There are thousands of deaths every week across London."

"But three deaths out of such a small group of bankers. Don't you think that's odd?"

"I did wonder about it," said Frank. "Which is why I looked into it personal like. But, realistically, there are thousands of bankers at Royal Shire Bank."

"There were only twelve in the lock-in group," said Mickey, who suddenly realised that the police would not know. "And now there are only nine."

Frank remembered the conversation about lock-ins with Mrs Goldcup. He rolled his eyes, cross with himself for missing the connection. He suddenly had a hunch why Mickey was ringing.

"And where do you fit in then?" he asked.

"How do you mean?"

"Are you in or out of the lock-in group?"

"I'm in. That's why I'm ringing. I'm scared."

Frank appreciated Mickey's honesty. He probably had good reason to be scared. "How does the rest of the bank feel about the lock-in group?"

"How do you mean?"

"What sort of bonuses are the rest going to get?"

"Down. Big time. A lot of fat zeros as well."

"So, there must be a bit of friction between them and the lock-in group," Frank said.

"No more than on your average tectonic plate."

"Last time we spoke, you told me to back off and stay away from you. Or words to that effect."

"Yeah, well I'm really sorry about that, Inspector. I was bang out of order. I've got a big mouth and sometimes I don't know when to shut it. The thing is, Inspector, I think there is something weird going on. I'd really appreciate it if you can look into it."

"Why don't you use your very good connections with the Chief Constable and Sir Stanley?"

"Sir Stanley is happy with what he's been told, that the deaths aren't related. He doesn't want to cause a panic. But maybe you could have a little sniff around and see what you find out?"

Summer sounded genuinely scared. Despite the apology, Frank still didn't much like him. But he was asking for help and Frank couldn't refuse.

"Leave it with me."

25

Frank couldn't even guess a value for the mock-Tudor mansion, but he was certain the coach house alone was worth millions. The housekeeper answered the door and took his coat.

He followed her through to a room with white carpets and walls. A portrait hung in an elaborate frame over the white stone fireplace. It was a young and handsome face.

A few moments later its owner opened the door, strode confidently into the centre of the room and held out a hand high enough to kiss.

Frank shook it awkwardly around shoulder level and introduced himself.

"Kate," she said. "I've been expecting someone. After I read in the paper that the police were investigating whether the deaths were linked."

"The official line is there is no link."

"You say that as if you don't believe the official line."

"I don't have a view at the moment," said Frank. "That's why I'm here, to check out a few things. If that's all right with you?"

"Of course." She looked a little rattled. "You won't mind if I get a drink? It's past noon after all."

"Go ahead." It's your liver, he thought.

"Can I get you something?"

"Water please."

"Ice?"

"That'd be champion."

Kate walked over to a black, art-deco drink cabinet and fixed herself first; a large gin with a dash of tonic. "You're from the north are you then?"

"Yorkshire," said Frank.

"I like a northern accent," she said, moving in a little too close as she handed Frank his glass.

"This must be a difficult time for you," said Frank.

"Life goes on." She retreated to a chaise longue and pulled her knees up as a table for the glass. "I'm sorry Ben's dead of course. But our marriage died a long time ago. We've been nothing more than housemates for the last five years."

"I see." Frank perched on the edge of a dark-blue leather settee. "I understand this was Ben's second heart attack."

"Third," she corrected him. "So he'd had his warnings. He was on medication but he refused to look after himself other than that. He ate rubbish, he smoked and he was a heavy drinker." She raised her glass and smiled. "Good health!"

Frank raised his glass awkwardly in return. "Could you tell me what you know about the night Ben died?"

She spoke with her eyes half closed. "I'd been out at a fashion show. Ben had dinner at the golf club then came home and rang our daughter to wish her happy birthday. That was around eight-thirty. Sometime after that he had the heart attack." She pointed to a space in front of the fireplace. "I found him there when I came home."

"And what time was that?"

"Ten-thirty. At first I thought he'd just passed out drunk. It wouldn't have been the first time. But when I shook him he wouldn't open his eyes. I tried to massage his heart. I took a first-aid course once. If only I'd come home earlier."

"Ifs and buts," said Frank. "You can't worry about them. Besides, it might have made no difference even if you were here."

"You're probably right." She took a long sip of her drink.

"What else do you remember?" Frank continued.

"Such as?"

"Anything that struck you as strange."

"My husband was dead. That was pretty strange."

"Sure. But anything else? However minor."

She frowned. "Well. Not that it matters, but he'd made a mess of the carpet with his dirty shoes. And he was normally very fussy about that, so I presume he was very drunk."

"Do you mind showing me?"

"Why?"

"Please."

Kate stood up and moved over to the patio windows. "The housekeeper cleaned it all up but his footprints were all over here. He must have wandered in the garden, had a smoke and then just traipsed back in."

Frank looked down at the carpet and tried to wish the footprints back into existence. He looked at the patio doors. "Were they open or closed?"

"I can't recall."

"Would you mind if I had a look outside?"

Kate took another sip then set her glass down on a side table and opened the doors.

Frank went out onto the wooden patio. He walked down some steps to a path made of wood chippings and then he stopped beside a flower bed, run through with heavy footprints.

"Have you got a pair of Ben's shoes?" he asked.

"I've started to pack his things away. I'll be back in a minute."

She left him for a while then returned with a pair of golf shoes. Frank held a shoe over one of the footprints.

"It's at least two sizes too big," he said. "Whoever made these footprints wears size nine shoes I reckon. Do you have a gardener?"

"Only in the summer."

"Have you had any work done in the back? Or is there any other reason why someone might have walked through your flower bed?"

"Not that I know of."

Frank followed the path down through a garden that looked like it had been transplanted from Kew. At the bottom was a high metal-framed mesh fence with a golf course beyond.

The fence was a good twelve feet high but a relatively easy climb for a fit man. In the damp grass at the foot of the fence he found two more footprints that looked to have been made by someone landing from a jump. He measured them up against the golf shoes. Same size as the other footprints.

He walked back up to the house and picked up two dustbin lids which he arranged carefully over the prints in the flower bed. "Don't let anyone disturb these."

"What's going on then?" asked Kate. "What's so special about the footprints?"

"I don't think your husband left those footprints on your carpet."

"Who did then?"

"I don't know yet." Frank checked the patio doors again, but there was no sign of forced entry. "Are you sure you can't remember whether these doors were open or closed."

She thought about it again. "They were closed but not locked. I had to lock them myself that night. I'll have to lock them myself every night now I suppose."

"That would be a good idea. Has anything been stolen? Anything missing?"

"Not that I'm aware of. Why?"

Frank didn't want to alarm her unduly. He didn't think she was likely to be in any danger. But he couldn't lie. "I think there was an intruder that night."

"But what are you saying? Do you think Ben was murdered?"

"Not as such. The doctor issued a death certificate for a heart attack and I suppose that was right."

"So what are you thinking?"

"I'm just interested in identifying the person who made those footprints."

Kate looked down the garden. "Now you've got me scared."

26

Mickey didn't know why he'd woken up but he sensed something was wrong. He checked the time. Ten past one.

Something clattered outside his bedroom window. He sat up in bed and tried to picture what had made the sound. Perhaps a dustbin, knocked over by a river rat; he'd seen one the size of a cat the other night. That was probably it. He raised his head off the pillow and listened carefully but could only make out the tap of rigging from the boats in the dock.

Nothing more than rats. He was worrying himself silly over rats. He puffed up his pillow and lay back down.

Then he heard a long, metallic scraping sound. No rat that. He jumped out of bed and ran over to the window. The dockside was empty. But a shadow moved down below. He pressed his face against the window to get a better angle. A man was pulling a bin over the ground. What the hell was he up to?

The man climbed on to the dustbin and reached up to an open window. Mickey's downstairs toilet window.

Oh God. They'd come for him.

He snatched his mobile from the bedside table, pulled some trousers on over his pyjama leggings and grabbed the baseball bat he'd bought that day. He was about to dial 999 when the doorbell sounded.

He hesitated. Should he still call the police? And say what? That someone had rung his doorbell.

He crept along the landing, switching on the lights as he passed. The doorbell rang again. Who the hell was it at this time of night? And what was he doing on his bins? Mickey edged down the stairs, baseball bat in his right hand, mobile in the other, thumb over the number nine.

In the hallway he stopped by the shoe rack. His Churchills would be useful if he needed to kick. But his trainers were better if he had to run. He slipped on the Churchills and then, with the bat raised, he crept the last few steps to the door.

"Who is it?"

* * *

"Me," called a voice from the other side of the door.

"Who the bloody hell is 'me'?" asked Mickey.

"Marcus."

Mickey opened the door an inch on the chain. His brother looked like a street drunk; specs skewed over a black eye, one sleeve hanging off his jacket like a tailor's workings.

Mickey lowered the bat. "For God's sake, Marcus. You scared the shit out of me. And it's the wrong night for the fancy dress party."

"Are you going to let me in?"

Mickey slid the chain and opened the door. "What the hell happened?"

"I was attacked."

"Who by?"

"They didn't leave a business card. Big boys though. England could do with them in the front row."

"That's not funny, Marcus." Mickey checked the dockside for rugby types before closing the door and replacing the chain. "What were you doing dragging that bin along the ground? I thought you were trying to break in?"

"Didn't want to wake you up. I saw the window was open but it was too small to climb through."

"That's the idea."

Mickey stood aside as Marcus walked into the living room and helped himself to a large glass of whisky. He offered the bottle to Mickey.

"No ta. Where did it happen?"

"At home. In the driveway. They took the car."

"You've had *your* car nicked as well?" asked Mickey.

"Yes. And it had the house keys in. That's why I came round."

"Haven't you got a spare?"

"At the cottage."

"Bloody hell," said Mickey. "What is happening to the world?"

He picked up the house phone.

"What are you doing?"

"Calling the Old Bill."

"Don't. It's only a car. I'll buy another one."

"But you can't let them get away with it," said Mickey. "Besides with Mum's car getting nicked as well, there might be some connection."

"If you tell the police then the press will find out. I don't want the publicity. The press will write it up as another revenge attack on bankers and then my picture will be out there for everyone to see."

"I don't know, Marcus. Three colleagues are dead, two cars nicked, you've been beaten up. I've got to admit I'm bloody scared."

"Nothing has happened to you, Mickey."

"Not yet."

"Relax. And put the phone down."

Mickey did as he was told. "It's your call."

"Thanks." Marcus smiled. "I presume I'm not disturbing anything. I can stay the night?"

"You can have the guest room."

"Much appreciated." Marcus finished his glass and poured another. "Now have you come to your senses about joining me?"

"What? How can you think about that now? You've just been beaten up?"

"Tis but a scratch." Marcus winked. "So come on. Have you made up your mind?"

"I haven't been able to give it any thought. Can't stop thinking about Daniel, Ben and Vanni. And that I might be next."

"Dying is getting to be a bit of a bad habit round at your place," said Marcus.

"It's no joke."

"Sorry. What do the police think about it all then?"

"Official line is the three deaths are just coincidence and Sir Stanley doesn't want anyone to think otherwise because he doesn't want to spread panic. But I've asked that copper who came to see me to take an extra look at it."

"Well, you take care all the same."

"And you," said Mickey. "You're the one who's been attacked, Marcus. It might be the same people. You used to work for Royal Shire Bank. And you were in the first draft of the lock-in group. They might not know you didn't take up your lock in. You could be next on the list. You should definitely take care."

"Don't worry about me, Mickey. I'll be fine. Now back to the subject in hand. You are going to come on board, aren't you?"

"I can't decide until I know whether I'm going to get Weil's job."

"Still think you're in with a chance?"

"Hell, yes. My sales-trading desk has been voted the best in Europe."

Marcus raised an eyebrow. "I didn't know the results were out."

"I've been given a heads-up."

"Good. That will be a useful marketing tool when you come on board."

"It'll be a useful tool to win promotion more like."

Marcus shook his head. "You just don't get it do you. You've hit the glass ceiling at Royal Shire Bank. The Americans won't be impressed by your poxy prize. They'd be more impressed if you got an MBA."

Mickey smiled. "You're just jealous that little brother is going to go higher than you."

"Hah! Is that what you think? I'm just telling you how the world works. Think about it Mickey. Gants at Wharton Bank is Harrow and Oxford, then an MBA at Harvard. Finsburg is run by Antoine

Collette. He came out of …"

"I run the best sales-trading desk in Europe," interrupted Mickey. "That's what will win me promotion."

"Well you'll find out soon enough."

"How do you know?"

"A little bird told me. The whole management reshuffle gets announced tomorrow."

27

It was obvious from the comings and goings in Weil's office that something was in the air. Mickey was sick of waiting. He couldn't concentrate on work and was pleased to be distracted by Manita calling through.

"Helen's on the line," she said.

"I'll take it in my office."

He ran off, not wanting to keep her waiting, and picked up the line. "Hi. You all right?"

"Fine. How are you?"

"A bit on edge. I'm about to find out whether I got that promotion."

"I see," she said. "Well I hope you get what you want."

"Fingers crossed."

There was a moment's silence. "I read in the newspaper about Ben and Vanni's death."

"Yeah. Bad news just keeps coming thick and fast."

"Why didn't you tell me?"

It hadn't occurred to him, which said a lot for the state of their relationship. "Sorry."

"The paper said that their deaths might not have been accidents."

"It's possible. But the police aren't concerned."

"I'm worried about you."

"Really?" Mickey was pleased. Last time they'd spoken she'd been so cool. "I'll be all right. Anyone attacks me and I'll talk them to death."

"Seriously, Mickey."

He noticed Manita waving to get his attention. She pointed at her watch and then to Weil's office. "Look I have to go see Weil now."

"Be careful then, Mickey."

"And you."

There was a pause then he heard her hang up. She had definitely been genuinely concerned. Of course she was concerned. He was her husband.

A husband who was about to win a promotion. He put on his jacket, straightened his tie, then walked as slowly as he could to the corner office.

Weil was sitting behind his desk, pulling at an ear lobe. "Shut the door behind you."

"How's it going?"

"Fine. Fine."

"So … you want to see me about something?"

Weil scratched his cheek then folded his hands on the desk in front of him. "I want to give you advance notice of a number of announcements that will be made later on today."

So it was happening today. Marcus had been right.

"Management reshuffle?"

Weil nodded. "The headline is that Carrick is moving from Royal Shire to be CEO of all State Financial's ex-US businesses."

"Smart move," said Mickey. "Getting on board the mother ship early. So that means we need a new CEO for Royal Shire Bank. Who's got that?"

"Bernard Madden."

That made sense. He was a long-serving retail banker. Having seen the bank, like so many others, almost collapse after being run by investment bankers it was no surprise that the Government wanted change at the top. "So, who's taking over from Madden."

"Frank Muller."

"So we can assume that you will be the new Head of Capital Markets?"

"I am," said Weil, but without the display of emotion Mickey would have expected. Perhaps it had all been in the price.

"Congratulations."

"Thanks." Weil opened then closed his mouth without anything coming out, as if his disk was stuck.

"So come on then. Who's taking over from you?"

"It's been a difficult decision …"

"Difficult?" Mickey laughed, waiting for the pat on the back from Weil. But when he took in the serious look on Weil's face he started to worry.

"I'm afraid you haven't got it Mickey."

Haven't got it. Mickey pursed his lips. Had he heard correctly? Was it a wind up? He looked into Weil's eyes. No twinkle. No joke.

Mickey felt like someone had kicked him in the nuts. "So who has got it?"

"Benaifa."

"Benaifa," repeated Mickey.

"That's right."

Benaifa? Mickey didn't even have her down as a serious contender.

"I'm sorry, Mickey. I knew you'd be disappointed. That's why I wanted to see you in advance of the announcement. To let you down gently."

Mickey fought the urge to scream. "Why Benaifa over me?"

"As I said, it was a close call."

"Is it this business over Amsterdam? Has that cost me?"

"That didn't help," said Weil.

"And this rumour about me leaving."

"Sir Stanley was worried about that as well."

"But I told you someone started that rumour deliberately to mess up my chances. The same person who grassed me up on Amsterdam. It was probably Benaifa wasn't it?"

"I don't know," said Weil. "But in any case we made a positive choice for Benaifa, rather than a negative choice against you."

"You still haven't explained why."

"On balance, we thought Benaifa had a better skill set to bring to the party."

"Skill set? What's that all about?"

"She's got both banking and equities experience."

"Give me a break. She ain't ready for the job."

"Benaifa learns fast. She's a very smart lady. She graduated top of her year from INSEAD."

"So it's suddenly all about qualifications. Surely it's what you do in the office that counts?"

"And you're doing a great job, Mickey. That isn't in doubt."

Mickey looked away. Marcus had been right about the glass ceiling. He'd been found out. He was a barrow boy; a fruit-and-veg trader; and he'd gone as far as he could in the City.

28

"Take the next left," said Frank, looking up from his A-Z. "No, sorry, it's the one after this. Camelot Road."

Eddie dropped down a gear and sped back up. "Sure you don't want me to switch on the sat nav?"

"Never used one. Never will."

"They're dead easy."

"I'm sure you're right," said Frank. "But I don't want to be driven around by a robot."

"I'm doing the driving," said Eddie.

"Well concentrate on it. This is the turning now."

They drove past huge houses hidden behind high walls and protected by cameras, until they came to the Gamberoni residence.

"You wait here," said Frank. "She'll talk more if I'm on my own."

Eddie turned on the radio.

Frank walked up to the gate and pressed 'Reception' on the entry box.

After a short time a voice crackled on the intercom: "Who is it?"

"DI Frank Brighouse." He held his warrant card up to the camera. "I'd like to talk to Mrs Gamberoni."

The gate clanked then swung open and he walked up to the front door. It opened on a frozen face. No makeup. No jewels. Lots of strain.

"Mrs Gamberoni?"

"Yes," she whispered in a tired voice.

"I'm DI Brighouse."

"I've already spoken to two policemen."

"I appreciate that." He realised he was not going to be invited in so he pressed on. "I've just got a couple of questions, if you don't mind."

She shrugged.

"Did you or your husband notice anything strange or out of the ordinary at any time over the last few weeks?"

"Like what sort of things?" she asked, her voice quivering.

"I'm wondering whether either of you had a feeling of being followed perhaps? Or maybe you noticed a car parked near the house that you didn't recognise? Anything unusual."

She thought for a few moments then shook her head. "I didn't, and Vanni didn't mention anything."

"Did your husband go out running often?"

"Three or four times a week."

"Do you know if he always ran the same route?"

"I don't know. What does it matter?"

"A lot of runners run the same route so that they can check whether their times are improving, to see if they're making progress. I do a bit of running myself. Do you have any idea whether your husband would check how quickly he covered his route?"

Again she thought for a moment. "He did say he was trying to get round in under the hour. It seemed to be a target."

"That would suggest he did run the same route then."

"Is this about what the papers are saying?" she asked. "You think it was deliberate. Is that what you're suggesting?"

"I'm not suggesting anything. Just thinking aloud."

"But you do think it's possible."

"Anything is possible," said Frank.

Mrs Gamberoni turned to study a minor commotion in the hallway, as her three children pulled on boots and gloves. She kissed each child as they were shepherded outside by a lady who, from the similarity in face, Frank guessed was her younger sister.

The eldest boy studied Frank carefully. "Are you a policeman?"

"Yes, son."

"Have you found the person who killed my dad?"

"Not yet," said Frank.

"But you will do won't you?"

Frank nodded. "I'll do my best." He watched the kids shuffle down the drive and imagined how his own children would cope with the situation.

"I couldn't send them to school today," said Mrs Gamberoni, as if some justification were needed.

"Of course," Frank agreed. "There'll be plenty of time for school later. Right now they'll need a bit of space I suppose."

"It's not that," she said. "It's because some of the other children were teasing them. They said their dad deserved to be killed."

"Deserved it?" asked Frank, thinking back to the sergeant who kept saying the same thing.

"Because he was a greedy banker," explained Mrs Gamberoni. "Can you believe anyone would think like that? It was just a job. When he started in the City it was a job that held a lot of respect. Now people think bankers deserve to die."

29

The email announcing the promotion news was out by the time Mickey got back on the trading floor. People stood around in groups, reading the screens and discussing the implications. At least it gave everyone a break from murder conspiracy theories.

"So, how do you feel?" asked Glen.

"With my fingers," said Mickey. "How do you do it?"

"I'm talking about the promotions." Glen patted Mickey on the shoulders. Mickey realised the rest of the sales traders were all listening in, so he turned to address them all.

"Its good news for Equities that Weil has been made Head of Capital Markets, because he won't treat brokers as second-class citizens to bankers."

"But what about Benaifa?" asked Ole.

Ears now tuned in from elsewhere on the floor, especially the sales desks.

So Mickey raised his voice. "You all know Benaifa. She's done a great job on sales. There's every reason to expect her to do a great job as Head of Equities."

"But why didn't they give it to you?" asked Ole.

"Weil thought Benaifa was the best person for the job."

"Well, I don't get it," said Glen. "You're the obvious choice."

The rest of the sales traders grumbled in agreement.

"What are you going to do about it?" asked Ole. "Are you going to accept it?"

"I can't do anything else but accept it," said Mickey. "And so should you."

He left them all moaning and gossiping as he walked slowly over to his office.

Manita was sitting inside, her face flushed red. "Benaifa is the new Head of Equities."

"Tell me about it."

"Is that what Weil wanted to see you about?"

"He did mention it in passing, I think."

"You don't seem all that bothered."

"Appearances can be deceptive." Mickey realised Manita was also gutted. She would have been expecting to move up herself as personal assistant to Head of Equities. "Don't let it bother you. We've got more important things to think about."

"Like what?"

"Like three of our colleagues being murdered."

"You said you didn't believe in that."

"I'm having a rethink. The way I feel right now I could kill both Weil and Benaifa. And there are sixty million people out there who feel the same way about all of us."

* * *

"The Met are certain whoever left those footprints at the Stein's house was a burglar," said Eddie. "Not a murderer."

"How can they be so sure?" asked Frank.

"There's no evidence a murder was committed. No sign of any

struggle. Whereas there is evidence for a burglary."

"Such as?"

"The stolen ornament."

"What stolen ornament?" asked Frank, who was beginning to regret letting Eddie look into it instead of doing the job himself. "Mrs Stein told me she didn't think anything was missing."

Eddie checked his notes. "She's since realised a statue of the Star of David was missing from the mantelpiece. Gold-plated. Not very valuable, but probably looked it to an amateur."

"Any leads on this burglar then?"

"The Met have been round the local pawn shops and fences. Nothing showing. They've checked out all the persistents within five miles of the house and ruled them out. So they reckon it was probably opportunistic, someone coming home from the pub on the public footpath through the golf course. He sees the patio doors open, thinks that no-one is in, so he jumps over the fence. Ben Stein was probably already dead when he got there."

"They've checked CCTV, done door-to-door?"

"All the usual," said Eddie. "Obviously they've got the footprints. They're trying to match them to the shoe make. But that's not really going to help is it?"

"Was anything else missing?" asked Frank.

"Not that Mrs Stein noticed."

"So why did this burglar take only the one ornament?"

"Easy to carry," said Eddie. "Remember he had to climb back out over the fence."

"Does sound amateur and opportunistic," agreed Frank. "A professional would have known it was only gold plated and that it would be easy to trace. But what if it was really a killer who wanted to make it look like a robbery?"

"Why bother? Ben Stein was dead of a heart attack. Job done. Walk away. Why risk being discovered by taking a cheap ornament."

"It doesn't make sense, I agree."

"By the same token, a killer would have walked round on the path and not left footprints in the flower beds and on the white carpet."

"Unless he was off his head on something."

Eddie shook his head. "You're clutching at straws, Frank. Whoever was there was an opportunistic bungler."

"But three deaths."

"The three deaths at one bank is just down to bad luck," said Eddie. "Why can't you accept that?"

"Because God doesn't play dice."

* * *

Mickey forced a smile as he walked into the meeting room that Benaifa had commandeered as her new office, while she waited for Weil to move out of his.

Mickey held out his hand. "Congratulations."

Benaifa shook the hand cautiously, as if he might be holding a toy shocker. "Thank you. Are you not still angry?"

"I was," said Mickey. "But I've got over it."

"So soon?"

"It's the trading mentality," said Mickey. "Don't let a bad position eat into you. Accept it and move on."

Benaifa nodded silently. She sat back with her elbows on the armrest and her finger tips touching each other in front of her lips. "I think it's best if I set out my stall very clearly from the outset."

"Suits me," said Mickey. "You selling fruit or veg?"

She ignored the joke. "I'm going to run things differently from Zac. There's been a lot of confusion on the floor about what your role was exactly. People got the idea that you were de facto head on the floor and Zac concentrated on managing upwards."

"It was a bit like that," said Mickey.

"Well it won't be, going forward. People like clear reporting lines. You'll run sales trading and nothing else."

"I'm all for an easy life."

"And I want you to stop," she paused while she looked for the right words, "Strutting around the floor."

"That might be more difficult. I'll need an operation to change the way I walk."

"You know what I mean. I don't want you acting as if you run the floor."

"Fine."

"There's something else."

"More good news?"

Benaifa grasped the ends of the armrests. "I'm giving your office to Tim Skellon. It's ridiculous that the Head of Corporate Broking sits out on the floor."

"So where's my office going to be?"

"The Head of Sales Trading doesn't need an office. You may have noticed that I didn't have one as Head of Sales. You need to be out on the floor, on the phone or managing your team."

It was probably true that he didn't need an office. But he knew that if he lost the one he already had he would also lose a lot of face. "I have confidential material to look at. Bonus sheets and budgets and stuff."

"You won't have so much in future. And what you do have you can take off to a meeting room."

"So what's going on here? Is this your way of telling me to push off? Is that it?"

"There is no hidden message. That's not my style. I'm happy for you to stay as Head of Sales Trading. But it's a free market. If you don't like the greater clarification of your existing role, then I can't stop you going." Her eyes narrowed and she sat forward in her chair. "But if you do decide to stay then I won't tolerate any bad attitude."

"I don't do bad attitude."

"I must also let you know that I won't be as tolerant as Weil was on sexist behaviour."

"About time someone took a grip. The way some of the women out there treat the boys on my desk is a disgrace."

"So for example, what happened in Amsterdam. One more repeat of that and you'll be out."

"So it was you that grassed me up," said Mickey.

She shook her head. "I did not. I only heard about it today. But I would have told personnel if I had known."

"Did you start the rumour that I was leaving after my bonus?"

"No. But as you raise the subject I would be interested to know if you are planning to leave?"

"I bet you would. Well it's not long to go now before you find out."

30

Two inches of snow had fallen overnight and settled. It was the sort of real snow Frank remembered as a child up north. Not the will-o-the-wisp southern snow that has melted by the time you get your boots on. Although he knew it could land him in trouble, he decided to go into work late and take the kids sledging. He would catch up in his lunchtime.

He called Eddie and told him not to advertise where he was, but to tell the truth if anyone asked. Then he dug the sledges out of the back of the garage and packed them and the family in the car. It should have been a ten-minute drive to the golf course, where the hill on the ninth hole made the best sledge run for miles around. But it took almost half an hour struggling through the poorly-gritted roads. Billy and Grace were out of the car before Frank had pulled up the handbrake.

Julia unstrapped Lucy while Frank got the sledges out of the boot. Then they crunched up the hill and took their turn in the queue at the top of the run.

Frank sat Lucy inbetween Billy's legs on the sledge.

"Are you ready?" he asked.

"No!" shouted Lucy at the last moment. She kicked her legs and wriggled free of Billy's arms.

Frank picked her up off the snow. "It's all right. You don't have to go if you don't want to."

"Lucy go with Daddy," she said.

"All right little monkey. You go with me. In a minute."

He shoved Billy and Grace off and they screamed as their sledges gathered speed.

"Isn't this snow wonderful?" said Julia. "It makes me think we should try skiing some year. Everyone who's ever been says it's a fantastic holiday."

"Bit flash," said Frank. "And I don't see how we can afford it this year. Unless we sell the kids."

"Spoil sport."

"We've got a pay freeze," said Frank, "but our spending keeps going up. Food, heating bills, the mortgage. They're all rising. If I could make Chief Inspector ... but that doesn't look to be on the cards, with MacIntyre calling the shots."

Billy and Grace came panting back up the hill.

"Push me faster this time," said Billy.

"Hold tight." Frank ran with the sledge a couple of paces and then pushed as hard as he could. Billy squealed away down the hill. Then he gave Grace a gentler push.

Lucy scowled. "Lucy go Daddy."

"Sorry little sausage. I forgot. Next time."

They watched the others race downhill again.

Frank's mind wandered back to work and he thought again about the enormous sums of money that were washing around in The City. "I bet none of them bankers will be worrying about their fuel bills. Even now, after partly causing this recession, some of them will get million-pound bonuses."

"You're not jealous are you?" Julia took Frank's arm.

"Of course not." Frank squeezed her hand. "I wouldn't know what to do with that sort of money. But it don't seem right that they earn so much more than everyone else. I understand it when it comes to top sportsmen and pop stars. It's obvious they have special talents."

"Maybe you just can't see the special talents bankers have."

"Maybe," said Frank. He thought of Mickey Summer. The only special talent he seemed to have was for verbal diarrhoea. Billy came back up the hill with his sledge. Frank picked up Lucy. "Do you want to go now with Daddy?"

"Yes."

"Give me your sledge then Billy." Frank held out his hand to take the rope from his son. But his phone rang, and as he pulled it from his pocket Billy jumped back on the sledge and escaped downhill. Frank saw it was a number withheld and pictured MacIntyre on the other end of the line. He hesitated, then duty got the better of him. "DI Frank Brighouse."

"It's Mickey Summer."

Frank turned his back on the hill. "Morning Mr Summer. What can I do for you?"

"Just wondering if you followed up that lead I gave you."

"I wouldn't exactly call it a lead."

"Whatever. You said you'd make some enquiries."

"I did," said Frank. "I've talked to the DI investigating the hit-and-run and he suspects a drunk on the way home from Christmas drinks. It's that time of year. I've told him to keep an open mind though and I've asked him to keep me in touch."

"And what about Ben Stein?"

"The DI there is certain the intruder was a burglar."

"What burglar. What intruder?"

Frank realised Mickey wouldn't have known and was cross for letting it slip. "It looks as if there was an intruder at the house the night Ben had his heart attack."

"How can he be so sure it was a burglar? Maybe it was someone out to kill him?"

"An ornament was stolen. A murderer wouldn't bother."

"He might have wanted to make it look like a burglary instead of a murder."

"But Ben died of a heart attack," said Frank. "A murderer could have just walked clean away. No-one would be any the wiser. Taking the ornament only drew attention to the fact someone was there."

"That is strange," agreed Mickey reluctantly.

"By the same token," continued Frank. "The intruder walked through flower beds and traipsed his muddy shoes over the carpet. That sounds like an amateur burglar. A bungler."

"So what happens now?" asked Mickey.

"In what sense?"

"Well ain't you going to do something? Launch an investigation? A murder enquiry or whatever?"

If it were down to Frank he probably would. But everyone appeared happy with the coincidence theory and he wasn't going to break rank for Mickey Summer. "A murder enquiry would be a job for the Met homicide squad," he said. "But we don't have a homicide. We have two accidents and a heart attack."

"What if they ain't accidents? What about the rest of us?"

"What about the rest of who?" asked Frank.

"Us at Royal Shire Bank. Especially the nine of us left in the lock-in group. What are we supposed to do? Just sit here and hope no-one else has an 'accident'. Aren't you going to protect us?"

"To be safe, I think you probably should get yourself a bodyguard."

"So do I have to protect myself?" asked Mickey. "You're not going to do it? What the hell do I pay my taxes for?"

"My job is to solve crime," said Frank. "And as to why you pay your taxes, I imagine you might like to give a little bit of your good fortune back into society, but I don't really give tax advice."

"Well I've got some free advice for you mate. Your customer care approach is piss poor."

"Don't use bad language when you're talking to me, Mr Summer."

"I won't bother using any language. Waste of time talking to you by the look of it."

Mickey cut the call.

Frank took a deep breath and put away the phone. He realised someone was tugging at his trouser leg.

"Lucy go Daddy now!"

He picked her up. "Yes, Lucy go with Daddy now."

31

European markets were rallying on upwardly revised economic growth forecasts. But it was on thin trading volume and first indications from the economists were that the revisions resulted from technicalities rather than genuine underlying growth. Mickey didn't expect the rally to last and spent an hour ringing round the client base to tell them not to get sucked in.

When he finally put down his phone, Manita appeared beside him. She looked unusually anxious as she took an empty seat. She spoke in a whisper. "Benaifa has stopped you going to the awards lunch."

"What?"

"Benaifa has cancelled your place at the Financial Excellence Awards."

"She can't do that. Me and Glen are looking forward to that."

"She's cancelled Glen's place as well."

Mickey looked over at Benaifa doing paperwork in her temporary office. "We've gone to the awards lunch every year for fifteen years. We're not missing it this year of all years, when we might be picking up a trophy." Mickey pushed his chair back.

"Don't get angry," Manita called after Mickey as he marched away.

He swung back round and tensed his muscles like the Hulk. "Don't you like me when I'm angry?"

"Seriously, stay calm."

Manita was right. Benaifa was deliberately trying to rile him, to get him in trouble, and he wasn't going to fall for it.

He walked straight into her office. "Can I have a word?"

"Yes. But next time maybe you'd knock." Benaifa placed the expense form she was holding back on the pile. "I wanted to see you in any case, Mickey. Do you actually look at these expense forms before you sign them off?"

"I skim through to see if anything stands out."

"How about a drinks bill of three hundred and twenty pounds? Does that stand out?"

"Clearly not."

"Well, it should. Especially as Glen made no mention of any client being present."

"It was probably a team-building exercise."

Benaifa shook her head. "They can buy drinks with their own money. I've sent it back. What did you want to see me about?"

"The Financial Excellence Awards lunch on Friday. Me and Glen go every year. It's a good way to find out what the oppo are up to. A bit of networking over a few sherbets."

"I can imagine. But we can't be seen going to back-slapping award ceremonies in the current climate."

"I'm not a banker."

"We're all bankers as far as the public is concerned."

"But I have to go this year. I've been given the nod that we've won the Sales Trading Award." He might have added that he had never won any award before in his life.

"I'll collect it for you."

"You're going?"

"I won't be drinking and there isn't any harm in one member of management going as a representative. I'll take some clients as well."

"No thanks. I'll collect it myself."

"I've already given your seat to a client."

"I'll get a seat at another table."

"You are not going!" Benaifa stood up and set her hands on her hips. "I want you at your desk, working that day. If you ignore my instruction you'll face a disciplinary hearing."

"Better book the meeting room then," said Mickey. "Because I'm going."

He turned and left the room. As he walked back to his office he realised the whole floor had been watching.

Manita followed him into his office and shut the door. "Are you all right?"

"Sure."

"What did she say?"

"Mickey shall not go to the ball."

"What are you going to do?"

"I'm going to get help from my Fairy Godmother, ain't I?"

"Who's that, as if I didn't know?"

Mickey thought about it a moment. He couldn't risk another disciplinary hearing. If he got too many yellow cards he'd end up with a red. And if he was dismissed for misconduct he'd lose his lock in. At the same time, this was the only award he'd ever won. He'd give it to Mum to put on the mantelpiece and show Marge. "Book me in for a holiday that day and see if you can find me a seat at another table."

Manita made a note. "Why has Benaifa got it in for you?"

"She wants to show she's top dog."

Glen had obviously seen Mickey in Benaifa's office and came over to have a chat. "She's lucky she's behind glass doors. I tell you Mickey, there are some very angry people out there on the floor."

Mickey knew. The mood had been growing darker as the bonus day drew nearer.

"Here's a thought," he said, lowering his voice. "What if it isn't some nutter outside that resents bankers getting bonuses? What if it's an inside job?"

"What job?" Glen asked.

"Daniel, Ben and Vanni."

"You said they were accidents."

Mickey shrugged. "What if they weren't? Maybe the papers are right that someone is out for revenge. Only it's someone out there."

"Where?"

Mickey nodded towards the trading floor. "What if someone thought the best way to protect the bonus pool was to take some of us lock-in boys out of the equation?"

Glen looked at Mickey as if he had just landed from Mars. "No-one would even think like that."

"Ole did. In his appraisal he pointed out that with Ben and Daniel dead their money was up for grabs. He also knew that there was no death benefit so the money didn't go to the next of kin."

They both turned to look out on the floor. Ole was on the phone, standing at his desk on the end of a row. He liked to walk as he talked, out into the corridor and back again, with the result that his cord wrapped with every turn and at the end of each day he would get the desk assistant to dangle the phone upside down for a minute to unravel the cord.

"Are you actually saying you think Ole killed Ben and Daniel and Vanni?" asked Glen.

"I don't know what I'm saying," said Mickey. "But there are three hundred people out there who would do almost anything for a bonus. What if one of them was angry enough to kill?"

32

MacIntyre said he had only five minutes before he had to go out, so Frank cut to the chase.

"I want to apply for a RIPA on Mickey Summer."

"Why?"

"Suspicion of involvement in murder."

"What murder?"

"The three bankers."

"Hang on a minute. Last you told me Daniel Goldcup was going down as a suicide and the Met think the other two are accidents."

Frank hated it when he had to admit he was wrong. "I'm no longer so sure."

"Explain. But quickly."

As Frank finished talking, MacIntyre looked unconvinced.

"Why do you suspect Summer if it was him that put you on to this murder idea in the first place?"

"It was the press that first came up with the idea, not Summer."

"Right. But you said he rang you to put you on the case. Why would he do that if he was involved?"

"Smokescreen," said Frank. "Appearing helpful. Classic criminal behaviour."

"Hmmm. Do you have a motive?"

"Summer and the others were promotion rivals."

"I thought Goldcup was retiring?"

"Summer might not have known that."

"Nah." MacIntyre shook his head. "There's easier ways to win promotion. Give me a proper motive."

"I haven't got a better one than that yet," admitted Frank. "Surveillance might come up with one."

"Do you have means then?"

"Summer had the means to do all three, and of course he's got enough money to have paid someone to do them."

"I still don't see why you suspect Summer."

"Gut instinct."

"You're a policeman, Frank. Not a gastroenterologist."

"Funny. Not. Look it's one thing after another. The suspicious comments he made in interview. Then the inconsistency in his behaviour. He clams up after I cautioned him. After that he's in my face. Then he tells me to back off. Next thing he rings me about the other deaths and tells me to investigate them. He's behaving oddly."

MacIntyre checked his watch, then pushed his chair back from the desk and rose to his feet. "What level RIPA are you after?"

"Not intrusive," said Frank. "I'd just like to follow him around a bit. See what he gets up to out of the office."

MacIntyre grabbed his coat from the door peg. "I'll see what I can do. But make sure you're not seen, Frank. I don't want the Chief Constable on my case saying you're harassing Summer again."

33

TO: European Investment Banking Managing Directors
Many of you are concerned that the deaths of Daniel, Ben and Vanni are somehow connected. The police think otherwise and are not treating the deaths as suspicious. But consider the following:
1. Vanni was killed by a driver who did not stop.
2. There was an intruder in Ben's house the night he died of a heart attack.
3. Daniel was in high spirits at the Dickens Inn, did not leave a suicide note and was not being treated for depression.
Having previously dismissed the conspiracy theories I am now concerned that all three of our colleagues may have been murdered. Hopefully I am wrong, but it would be wise for all staff, particularly senior staff to take extra precautions for their personal security.
Best.
Mickey.

Mickey stopped reading aloud and looked at Manita. "What do you think?"

"As I've said before, I think you should show it to Benaifa first."

"She'll block it," said Mickey. "She's towing the party line. And she won't want me to send this because she'll think I'm doing it to big myself up."

"And are you?" asked Manita with an eyebrow raised.

"Nah. Tell you the truth I think it makes me sound a bit stupid."

"Show it to Ruth then."

"She'll also block it. Just send it, please."

Manita tilted her head to one side and put on her half smile. This was her signal that she was washing her hands of the decision. "And you'd like me to send it to all Managing Directors, not just the lock-in group?"

"To be safe."

Manita returned to her desk to send the email while Mickey decided to tackle his 364 unread emails. As usual he deleted everything that he was only copied in on without even looking and then glanced at the headlines of everything else as he pressed delete. He was down to two hundred and picking up speed, when his cull was stopped short by Manita calling through on the intercom.

"I've got a Dave Casey for you."

Casey was an old school pal that Mickey hadn't seen since a stag do many years back. When Mickey learnt he'd done time for dealing drugs he figured it was a friendship he didn't need.

"What does he want?"

"He won't say. Shall I put him through?"

Mickey nodded.

There was a pause, a couple of clicks and then:

"Is that Mickey Summer?"

"It is. And is that Dave Casey?"

"Yeh."

"All right mate? Long time no see."

"Stuff you, Mickey. You know why I'm calling."

Mickey double checked his memory files. "You're going to have to give me a clue, Dave."

"I'll give you a hammer in your face, that's what I'll give you. And I still haven't forgotten you nicked my girl neither. I still owe you for that 'n all."

"I honestly don't know what you're talking about, Dave."

"I'm talking about the money you and your posh brother owe me."

34

The Fine Line was heaving. Mickey fought his way through the crowd and was pleased to discover that Marcus had already got the beers in. Mind, it was the least he could do. As if Mickey didn't have enough on his plate without having his brother land him in trouble with a nutter like Casey.

"I'm all ears for this good explanation of yours."

Marcus nodded. "First of all, I really am sorry to have got you involved. It's just as I told you, I need short-term working capital to see the business through to the New Year."

"So you borrowed money from Dave Casey?"

Marcus nodded. "But you've seen the business plan. I'll have enough money to pay him back in January. I thought Casey would give me more time, but he's called the loan in early."

"But why did you use my name?"

"He knows you. Casey wouldn't lend to me without your name as collateral."

"How much did you borrow?"

Marcus wriggled in his seat. "Two-hundred thousand. Our cash burn is running at one-hundred thousand a month."

Mickey hadn't realised the numbers were that bad. "But what are you doing borrowing money from Casey? Why don't you go to a bank?"

Marcus rolled his eyes. "Have you tried borrowing from a bank recently?"

Mickey's thoughts were interrupted by a cheer as someone dressed in a Santa suit appeared in the doorway. Santa joined his friends at the bar and Mickey now noticed the red noses, antlers and tinsel. Another works Christmas party. He doubted there would be many takers for the Royal Shire Christmas party this year.

He turned back to Marcus. "I ain't happy about this. Not happy at all. I don't have two-hundred thousand pounds lying around. And this really isn't my problem."

"I know. I'm sorry."

"So how are you going to pay back Casey?"

Marcus shrugged. "I don't know. Every spare penny I have is in the business."

"Sell assets."

"Such as?" asked Marcus.

"Re-mortgage the house in Kent."

"I can't. It's under water." Marcus laughed. "Not literally of course, though it nearly was during the flooding. But it's in negative equity."

"What about your main house then?"

"Same situation."

Mickey shook his head. "And people wonder how the credit crunch happened."

"I wasn't the only one who over-borrowed."

"That's right. There were millions of other idiots doing the same thing. How about your Ferrari then? Have the police found it yet?"

"Casey has it. It was his boys that took the car the other night. Part payment. I get it back when I pay off the loan."

Mickey hit replay. "So that's what happened? It was no random robbery. That's why you didn't go to the police. You total idiot."

"It's simply a short-term cash-flow problem. The sort that many growth companies experience. If it wasn't for the credit crunch, banks would be falling over themselves to lend to me."

"Can't you ask Casey to give you another month? You can pay him a premium interest rate to allow for the time factor."

Marcus raised an eyebrow. "I don't think Casey understands discounted cash flow. He wants his money tomorrow. Plus interest."

"Which is?"

"Five percent per month."

"How much?"

"Extortionate isn't it."

Mickey sighed. "If I sort this out, when can you pay me back?"

101

"We could consider the two hundred thousand as payment for a stake in Summer Securities. You're going to have to come and join me now that Benaifa is in charge."

"That's a separate issue. I want this loan paying back in cash. And pronto."

"Of course. Then I can pay you back in January. February at the latest. With interest, of course. I don't want you to lose out in any way."

Mickey slugged his beer and collected his thoughts. Although he was using him, Marcus was only asking for a loan. It was his brother. He owed him a lot. And, after all, it was the season of goodwill.

"I'm still not happy," he said eventually. "But I'll pay it."

"Thanks, Mickey. Really."

Marcus offered his hand and Mickey shook it.

"But you'll have to put it in writing. I want it all legal."

"Of course."

"And you better not do anything like this again."

"I promise. Thank you. When can you pay him?"

"I'll have to get the bank to advance me a loan on my lock-in. I'll try and fix it up tomorrow afternoon."

"Do it first thing Mickey. Casey isn't a man to leave waiting."

Mickey pictured Dave Casey sitting below a clock, polishing his hammer. "I'll get out as soon as the bank opens."

"Thanks. Another pint?"

"No. I've got to get home and write up a bunch of appraisals."

"It'll flow better after another pint."

"I want to stay sober. I've got things on my mind."

"Like what?"

"Like making sure I'm not number four on the Royal Shire hit list."

Marcus frowned. "Are you genuinely concerned about that?"

"Too right I am."

"I promise you, Mickey, you'll be fine. The world isn't that angry with the City."

"I'm not so sure it's an outsider anymore," said Mickey.

"What? You think it's someone in the bank?"

"Who else knows all the members of the lock-in pool?"

"Better watch your back then."

"I am. Turns out Karim, one of the drivers, also did a spell in police protection. He's going to shadow me."

"A bodyguard?" Marcus looked around the pub. "But where is he?"

"He can't start until the morning."

"I still think you're over-reacting but I guess it'll come in handy having a bodyguard when you go see Dave Casey."

"When I go? You're coming as well ain't you?"

"Sorry. I'm in Milan. Signing a two-million euro distribution deal with an Italian broker. I can't miss that."

"Never mind. I'm probably safer in the company of a nutter like Casey than I am in the office." Mickey finished his beer. The crowd at the bar started singing Slade's Merry Christmas. They ran into trouble with the second verse and collapsed into giggles and drinks.

Marcus set a hand on Mickey's shoulder. "Thanks again for helping me out."

"As if I had any real choice. If you can't count on your family, then who can you count on? Now I've got to shoot. See you later."

Mickey stood up and squeezed his way outside. He stopped in the doorway to reflect on the irony of the smokers puffing under the monument to the Great Fire of London. As he buttoned his coat he thought he saw someone watching him from the doorway of a pub on the other side of the road.

Mickey pulled up his collar against the cold and headed up to London Bridge to get an Evening Standard. On the far side of the road the rush-hour traffic crawled south. He flagged a cab, which made a tight turn and pulled up alongside.

"Royal Docks mate."

Mickey sat back as the cab settled into the rush-hour queues. The driver treated Mickey to twenty minutes on the changes he would make to London transport policy if he were Mayor.

They made slow progress, despite the driver's knowledge of the back roads, but Mickey tipped him heavily anyway. As Mickey walked towards home he realised he'd left his copy of the Standard on the seat. He ran back, but the cab had already pulled away. It passed a parked car on the other side of the road and Mickey watched a man freeze as he climbed out the passenger door. It was the man from the pub doorway. He looked away from Mickey's stare and climbed back into the car. It did a quick three point turn and was gone.

Mickey hurried back home. He double-locked the front door and jammed a table up against it. He securely locked the windows, upstairs and down, and placed ornaments against them, so they would crash if the windows were forced open. Then he sat downstairs beside the phone, with a large whiskey in one hand and a baseball bat in the other.

35

Frank stood at a screened counter, doodling numbers on a paying-in slip while keeping an eye on proceedings in the glass meeting room on the other side of the bank.

The cashier had been counting out twenty-pound notes for ages. When she had finally finished Mickey signed some more forms and loaded the bundles into his briefcase. He then shook hands and walked briskly out of the bank.

Frank waited a few seconds then followed him out, in time to see him getting back into a waiting cab.

He ran back to Eddie's car and jumped in. "He's just taken out a ton of cash."

"How much?"

"We'll go back and find out later, but it was a briefcase full of twenty pound notes."

Eddie checked his wing mirror then pulled out into the road. "How many twenties can you get into a briefcase?"

"Never tried it," said Frank. "Likely never will."

* * *

Mickey was grateful for Karim's presence as he sat beside him in the back of the cab. Partly because he was carrying so much cash, but also because the geezer from the pub doorway had got him rattled. Although he probably wasn't really being followed. It was surely just his imagination doing overtime.

He settled back and watched east London pass by, trying to identify the parts of his old stomping ground which had been transformed into the Olympic Park and Village.

Twenty minutes later the driver pulled into the off-street parking beside a gym that looked more like a Victorian swimming baths, with its red-brick walls and glasshouse roof.

The receptionist set aside her magazine and looked curiously at Mickey's suit and briefcase.

"I've come to see Dave Casey," announced Mickey.

She turned to a hulk shovelling breakfast for three at a nearby table. "Winston."

He pushed aside his plate, looked down at the briefcase and said, "Follow me."

They passed into a mirror-walled gym filled with bench presses and weights. Mickey noticed that unlike the City gyms there wasn't a rowing machine, stair climber or a TV in the place. It was a proper bodybuilder's gym, and the half dozen men in there all had forearms thicker than Mickey's legs.

A big man eye-balled Mickey as he followed Winston to a red door marked 'No Entry'. Winston knocked. The door was opened by a skinhead in an England shirt. Mickey followed him through the door, making sure Karim was still close behind. Casey was sitting behind a desk, tipping a supplement powder into a cup. Mickey recognised him from the neck up; the grey-blue eyes and crooked teeth. Below the neck was a pumped up body that looked ready to burst.

Casey stirred his drink then downed it in one. He dabbed the side of his mouth with a hand towel and looked Mickey up and down without making eye contact. Then he did the same to Karim. He sniffed. "Expecting trouble were you, Mickey?"

"The bag was heavy."

"You should build up your muscles. Join a gym."

"We've got one at the office," said Mickey. "But by the time I've done the sauna, Jacuzzi and the Turkish bath I ain't got energy left over for lifting weights."

Casey sniffed again, shuffled out from behind the desk and walked forward until he was just two feet from Mickey. He fixed him a stare and pushed a thick finger into Mickey's chest. "You got here in the nick o' time. I was just coming to look for you."

"I had to go to the bank didn't I? I don't have this sort of money just lying around at home."

"I thought you did, Mickey. Small change for you, from what I hear." Casey took a step back. "Is it all there?"

"Two hundred and ten thousand pounds."

Casey picked up the briefcase and undid the lock. He nodded to the skinhead. "Count it Tony." He looked Mickey up and down again. His chest expanded as he breathed in deeply.

"Forty-four inches, Mickey," he said.

"I do all right with six."

Casey grunted. "So how's high finance? You guys finished destroying the world yet?"

"The worst is behind us I reckon. How's the gym business?"

"The gym is just a hobby."

"Money lending your main thing then?"

Casey laughed. "I'm in the same business as you, Mickey. Supplying money to those who need it and taking a little commission for my services."

"Difference is I take point two percent. You're taking five, and that's not including the car you took from my brother. Oh and yeah, what I do is legal."

"There's some think it shouldn't be."

They stood in silence while Tony counted the rest of the money. Finally he set aside the last bundle. "It's all there."

Casey closed up the empty briefcase and handed it back to Mickey. "It was good doing business with you."

"Is that it then?" asked Mickey. "Don't I get a receipt?"

"You don't breathe a word of this to anyone, Mickey. We never met." Casey's smile disappeared as he looked into the gym and saw Winston pounding down the corridor, as quickly as his oversized body would allow.

He came panting through the door. "There's a fella watching the gym from Almerston Road."

"Filth?"

"Don't know, boss."

Casey swung round to Mickey. "Have you brought someone along?"

"Are you mad? We came alone."

"Looks like you didn't, even if you meant to."

"What does he look like?" Mickey asked Winston.

"White. Big guy. Around thirty."

"Sounds like the same geezer I saw yesterday," said Mickey.

Casey pointed to the cash. "Tony, you disappear that. Winston, you go out front and keep an eye on him."

Mickey started to follow Winston.

But Casey pulled him back. "You follow me."

"I want to know who's been following me."

"No you don't."

Casey led Mickey and Karim down a corridor and through a fire exit into a yard piled high with tyres. They walked through to a garage on the other side.

Mickey watched two mechanics pulling apart an engine. "Is this business yours too?"

"And scrap metal." Casey pointed to the far end of a yard where a dozen bashed up cars were piled one on top of another.

"Spread yourself around a bit don't you?"

"First rule of finance," said Casey. "Diversify your portfolio to spread your business risk. You should know that Mickey."

Out the other side of the garage they passed into a yard full of rusting cars and parts. Casey pointed to a gate on the far side. "Turn left out there, then take the second right back up to the high road. There's a cab rank near the post office."

"What about that guy out front? I want to know who the hell he is."

"If he's filth then I don't want you talking to him. We're just old school mates. Right?"

"The Old Bill will never believe that."

107

"It doesn't matter. They have to prove otherwise. Right?"

"OK."

"Besides, it's more likely to be a private detective sniffing around ahead of your divorce."

"Who says I'm getting a divorce?"

Casey tapped the side of his nose. "Second rule of finance, Mickey. Know your customer."

36

Weil re-read Mickey's email while he waited for Benaifa to cross over to his office. It was a typical Mickey memo, subtle as a baby elephant. But Weil knew Mickey well enough to realise he'd sent it with the best of intentions. He'd have had no problems with it. But as for Mickey's new boss …

He looked up and smiled as she entered the room. "Benaifa. How's it going?"

"Fine," she said. "I feel like I'm really getting to grips with things now."

"That's good."

"You wanted to see me?"

"Ruth tells me you want to discipline Mickey over the email he sent out."

"That's right," said Benaifa.

"Do you think that's a good idea?"

"I wouldn't do it if I thought otherwise."

Weil pursed his lips and nodded a couple of times. "Is there really anything wrong in what he wrote? I mean, he could be right, that we're all being targeted. I'm certainly going to get myself a bodyguard."

"That's not the point. He should have asked me before sending it."

"So it's the breach of protocol that upsets you?"

"I'm not upset."

"What are you then?" asked Weil.

"I'm angry. Mickey sent it to undermine my authority. It was a power play."

"That's not Mickey's style."

"I beg to differ." Benaifa crossed her arms. "I insist on disciplining him."

"To what purpose?"

"I want everyone to know he's been disciplined."

Weil sighed. "It's your call of course. But you realise that if you push Mickey too hard he'll leave. His brother will take him in with open arms."

"Good."

"Together they could be a serious competitor and take a lot of clients with them."

"This is a matter of principle."

"I understand," said Weil. "I'm just checking you've thought through the business impact as well. Mickey is more than just the best sales trader in the business. He'd leave a serious hole behind. He's a big personality on the floor."

"That's the problem. I told him to stop strutting around like a peacock. But he hasn't stopped. This email is just the latest example."

"He says he didn't ask you because he knew you wouldn't allow it."

"In that case he shouldn't have sent it at all. And it follows then that he should be disciplined."

"Well if you do discipline him then I wouldn't advertise the fact."

"That's the point of it. So people know."

"But this is a private matter," said Weil. "It looks unprofessional if everyone knows about it. Moreover, they'll sympathise with Mickey."

"Let them."

"Then when he leaves, which is now looking more and more likely, he'll have more ability to take people with him."

"Let them go," said Benaifa. "We both know we're going to have to cut heads in the New Year."

"That's as maybe, but I'd rather we didn't lose our best people."

"So would I. But it's very simple. Am I in charge of this business now or am I not?"

He sighed. "You are."

37

"Hello Detective Brighouse, this is Martin Newsome. The Head of Legal at Royal Shire Bank."

"Thank you for ringing back," said Frank. "I was wondering if you'd found out the answer to my question about what happens to the lock-in monies of the three dead employees."

"The money stays in the pool."

Frank sat back in his chair while he tried to think through the implications. "Then what?"

"The extra money gets shared equally between the nine surviving members of the lock-in group."

"Surely it's got to go back to the Government or to the other employees," said Frank.

"No. It's a contractual arrangement. There's a clause to say that if anyone leaves the firm before their lock-in is paid their money stays in the pool, to be shared out between the others. It was designed to stop a mass defection. The more people that leave, the greater the incentive for those remaining to stay at their desks."

"You sure dying is the same thing as leaving the firm?"

"Quite sure."

"Interesting," said Frank. "Really interesting." Now there was a clear motive of financial gain for each and every one in the lock-in group. It really could be an inside job. And Mickey Summer was prime suspect. "Have all members of the lock-in group got twenty-four-hour protection?"

"I think so."

"Make sure of it."

"Why are you saying this now? How does this news on the contract change things?"

"It's probably nothing," said Frank, trying to sound calmer than he felt. "Probably the deaths are still a weird co-incidence. But, if it is murder, then it might not actually be out of revenge or anger at the bonuses. It's just possible the lock-in members are being killed by one of their own, for financial gain."

"No way. That's not possible. These are professional men and women we're talking about, Inspector. They're not a gang of cut-throats."

"They're not a gang of cut-throats," agreed Frank. "They're a gang of bankers."

38

Ruth and Benaifa were already in the meeting room when Mickey arrived. They were sitting together on one side of the table, Benaifa reading some papers, Ruth granite-faced as usual.

"Take a seat please," Ruth said. "As has already been explained to you, Mickey, this meeting is to discuss the memo you circulated regarding the recent deaths of colleagues. Having looked into the matter I agree with Benaifa's assessment that the email was entirely the wrong way to communicate something like this."

"I tried carrier pigeon, but the floor got covered in bird crap."

"Please try and be serious for once in your life, Mickey."

"Look, I wrote what I thought was right."

"You sent it without authority from your line manager."

"And would you have let me send it, if I'd asked you?" Mickey asked Benaifa.

"Certainly not. It was alarmist."

Mickey smiled. "That's why I didn't check with you. Anyhow I sent it in a personal capacity. Just giving my personal opinion. I can't see how anyone can have a problem with it."

"Someone did." Benaifa said this in a way that suggested the 'someone' was important.

"Who?"

"I'm not going to go into names."

"Suit yourself. I still can't see what harm's done."

Ruth cleared her throat. "Do you appreciate how sensitive everyone is given the recent deaths?"

"I'm as sensitive as anyone."

"Well your email was a highly emotional jolt for your colleagues. Did you not consider the impact it would have?"

"I wanted them jolted. There's too much complacency. Everyone's gossiping about murder but no one is taking any precautions. And I've since discovered something that makes me even more convinced we are all in danger."

Ruth tilted her head to one side. "What's that then?"

"I'm being followed."

"Followed? Are you sure?"

Mickey nodded. "As sure as I can be."

"Have you told the police?"

"I put in a call to DI Brighouse, but he ain't rung me back yet."

"Well, hopefully you're mistaken. But returning to the email, it's for the police to decide whether there is a security threat to staff. They are the professionals. At the present time they have advised us that we have no cause for concern. There is no connection between the three deaths. Your email has resulted in needless confusion and alarm."

"I pointed out some basic facts," said Mickey. "Let everyone decide for themselves what to believe."

"That's not good enough," said Benaifa.

Mickey checked his watch. "Look, I haven't got time for all this, so can we just skip straight to the punishment? Forty lashes is it?"

"It's enough that we have had this conversation," said Ruth. "I'll make a note on your personnel file that we explained to you that your action was inappropriate. Provided there is no repetition of this or similar behaviour, then that will be the end of the matter."

"And if there is a repetition?"

"We would have to look at that very seriously," said Ruth. "Depending on the circumstances at the time."

Benaifa sat upright. "Further mistakes could result in your dismissal for gross misconduct."

Mickey nodded. "I thought that might be the plan. Wait until I step out of line again and then dismiss me, so I go without my lock-in. Then you can keep it to spread round the department, is that it?"

Benaifa didn't answer.

Ruth closed her folder and set her pen down on top. "You have the right to appeal against this decision in writing."

"I might just do that," said Mickey.

39

The sign in Mitre chambers announced that the crumpled building dated back to the fourteenth century. Mickey watched a wigged lawyer lower his head to pass out the narrow doorway. Veronica came out a moment later.

"I'm really on a very tight schedule today," she said, looking at her watch. "I can only spare about ten minutes."

"I'll talk quickly then."

"I hope you don't mind going outside, but this is my only chance to get some natural sunlight."

"Good idea. If you're lucky it will rain and then you get watered as well."

Veronica suddenly noticed Karim. "Is this man with you?"

"He's my bodyguard."

"Bodyguard?"

"A lot's happened since we last met. I'll explain."

Mickey told her about the deaths of Vanni and Ben and the theory doing the rounds that they had been murdered. He also told her about his fear that he was being followed.

"This is all very worrying," she said, as she opened the black gates into the lawns of Temple Gardens. "So what are the police doing about it?"

"They don't seem interested. When I rang DI Brighouse about the bloke that's been following me he said it was probably my imagination. He thinks I'm just spooked."

"That sounds terribly complacent. It's just as well you've got yourself a bodyguard."

Mickey was pleased. Veronica's concern seemed more than a professional interest. "I guess Brighouse will take it more seriously when I become 'accident' number four."

"I hope that won't happen."

"Snap."

"Of course, it could be the police that are following you. That's why DI Brighouse isn't following up on it."

Mickey hadn't thought of that. "Why would the police be following me?"

"You might be under suspicion."

Mickey stopped walking and held her arm. "I told you that might happen. They're trying to fit me up."

"And I told you they wouldn't do such a thing. If they are following you, it must be for a reason. Hopefully there's a simpler explanation."

"Like I'm about to be simply murdered."

"I meant a more innocent explanation. But if you are really in fear of your life, then why don't you just disappear?"

"I don't do magic."

"I mean jump on a plane and go somewhere out of the way for a few weeks, until the lock-in is paid."

"That's another story." Mickey explained about the disciplinary hearing. "If I go AWOL, then Benaifa has the perfect excuse to give me the tin tack. Then I lose the lock-in." They walked on to a fountain guarded by a ring of leafless trees. "That's really what I wanted to see you about. I was hoping you'd give me advice on how to defend myself against Benaifa. I need to know what legal tricks she might use to catch me out."

Veronica took a seat on a bench and Mickey sat on the other end. "That's not my area," she said. "But I can get someone who specialises in employment law to give you a call. Sam has done a lot of work on unfair dismissal."

"That would be good. But I'd be interested in your ideas as well." Mickey noticed Veronica seemed pleased that he valued her opinion.

"Primarily you need to be very, very careful what you do and say. If you must send any more emails, write out your message long hand. Get your secretary to type it up. Then check it very carefully before you let her send it. Be conscious that emails are public communications. Imagine you've sent it to the whole firm even if you have only sent it to one individual."

"That's good advice." Mickey made a mental note.

"But you really need to speak to Sam."

Mickey took out a pen and a business card. "Sam. What's his surname?"

"Her surname is Smith. Samantha Smith. Sexuality is also an area where you need to tread very carefully."

"I've done my perversity training."

Veronica frowned. "That's the wrong attitude for a start. Joking trivialises the issue."

"But everyone thinks it's a joke."

"Of course they do, on your trading floor. It's a sexist environment."

"No it's not. Some of my best traders have talked to women. Seriously though, we've got women on the team."

"How many?"

"Two," said Mickey. "Well only one at the moment but we had two until the spring."

"And why did the other one leave?"

"We had to let her go."

"Why was that?"

Mickey could feel his cheeks warm. "Well, she wasn't really coping with the job."

"Wasn't coping with the environment more likely." Veronica shook her head. "A trading floor is one of the last bastions of sexism in the workplace. Although that's not really surprising. Neurologists have shown that the same part of a man's brain lights up whether he looks at erotic pictures or takes a financial risk."

That was a new one on Mickey. "So I should be reading Frankie Vaughan instead of the FT in the morning. Is that what you're telling me?"

"I'm just pointing out that a trading floor is a high testosterone environment. So don't be complacent on sexism, just because all the men you work with think it's a joke. It is not, and you need to be very careful to avoid any rude or lewd behaviour. And certainly never be alone at any time with a female member of staff. If they accused you of, say, molestation it would be just your word against theirs."

"This is getting scary. What else?"

"Don't look at women's breasts."

"I don't," said Mickey.

"You just looked at mine."

"I never."

"You did. Men do it subconsciously, particularly if the word breast is mentioned."

Mickey realised he had just done it again. "I'm sorry. But I can't get into trouble just for looking can I?"

"Sexual harassment is defined as unwanted conduct which has the purpose or effect of violating a person's dignity. So if the woman felt violated then in theory you could be charged with sexual harassment just for looking at her breasts."

This time when he heard the word Mickey made sure he held his gaze forward, staring at the white upper deck of HMS President on the other side of the embankment. He reckoned it needed a lick of paint.

"And of course diversity awareness is not just about equal treatment for women," continued Veronica. "It covers disabled, racial, sexual orientation, religious beliefs and a whole bunch of things."

"This ain't going to be easy," said Mickey.

"Nobody said it would be." Veronica looked at her watch. "Now, I really do have to be going."

They walked back along the gravel path and all too soon arrived back at the entrance to Veronica's chambers. Mickey had a sudden panic that he might never see her again. "What are you doing after work?"

"Going home to do more work."

"How about you take a break in between with a quick sherbet in Ye Olde Cock Tavern? It's just round the corner."

"I really don't have the time."

"Tomorrow then?"

Veronica half smiled, half frowned. "What would your wife say to you going out for a drink with another woman?"

"To tell you the truth, I think she'd be chuffed. I'm almost certain she's about to divorce me."

"Oh, I'm sorry," said Veronica. "I didn't realise."

"Neither did I, until the other day. So how about that drink?"

She seemed to give it some thought, or maybe she was just wondering how to say no.

"Some other time," she said eventually.

40

The suits of armour on the walls looked down on several hundred brokers and bankers, packed into the Guildhall for the Financial Excellence Awards. Unlike previous years, it was a buffet rather than a sit-down lunch. A sign of the times, thought Mickey, as he helped himself to the meat selection.

Benaifa hadn't budged on her refusal to let him attend, so he'd booked the day off as holiday. He noticed she'd let her old mucker Turrell come along though. He also noted that the bankers, who were also expecting an award, were out in force: Carrick, Nav, Vincent and Percy.

It occurred to Mickey that seven of the lock-in group were in the same room. If someone really was out to get them, then a well-placed bomb could do the job.

His thoughts were interrupted by a tap on the shoulder. Mickey turned to see his brother beaming, holding a glass of champagne. "Thanks again for sorting out our friend Mr Casey," said Marcus.

"Just make sure you steer clear of him in future," said Mickey. "How'd your trip to pizza land go?"

"Excellent. Signed a deal giving Banca Intermedio exclusive distribution throughout Italy. They'll be our biggest client. Good people. You'll like them."

"What's it got to do with me?"

Marcus winked and tapped the side of his nose.

"Seriously, Marcus. I still haven't made up my mind what to do."

"You can't stay at Royal Shire. It's a busted flush. With Madden as CEO, it'll become a retail bank. They'll have you helping out behind the tills before you know it. The future belongs to the new independents."

Marcus grabbed another glass of bubbly from a passing tray and handed it to Mickey.

"To us," he toasted.

"I don't want to talk about it now," said Mickey.

"I can't wait forever. Make a decision, Mickey."

Mickey was about to respond when Marcus heard someone call his name. He made his excuses and moved away.

Mickey spent a good twenty minutes working the room. One way or another, he probably was going to leave Royal Shire Bank in the New Year and he would need to work hard to transfer his client base. But Mickey had never been scared of hard work. And he was good at this.

He was stopped by the sound of a gong, and a liveryman in tails approached the microphone. "Ladies and Gentlemen, I'm pleased to introduce our guest speaker, the newly appointed Minister for the Environment, Mr Anthony Stuart."

Mr Stuart took his place at the microphone, shuffling a wad of papers. He had apparently been asked to stand in for the Deputy to the Treasury at short notice, and clearly hadn't had time to prepare a speech. He tried to ad-lib something about the role financial markets had to play in creating a green future but people began to drift back to their food and their own conversations. Sensing defeat, he finished quickly, to a ripple of applause.

There was another chance to circulate, and Mickey found himself near Benaifa, who caught his eye then turned away. He walked up and stepped in front of her. "Enjoying the grub?"

"It's passable," she said. "Are you enjoying your holiday?"

"Best I've had in years," said Mickey. "What with the pound so low, you have to holiday in England don't you?"

She forced a smile and picked at a leaf of dodgy looking salad, turning it over to examine it before popping it into her mouth. Mickey had noticed Benaifa arrive at the Guildhall with a giant of a man who had since taken up sentry duty on the entrance. He couldn't resist a dig.

"Starting a zoo are you?"

"A zoo?"

"How else do you explain the gorilla you turned up with?"

"Have you by any chance been drinking, Mickey?"

"Of course. But I'm still sober enough to spot a hypocrite when I see one."

"I have hired a bodyguard because the Head of Legal advised me to do so. Did you not see his email?"

"Manita read it out to me. The police still think the deaths are not suspicious, but they do suggest we all get a bodyguard. Genius. It's basically the same message that you disciplined me for."

"I never said your advice was necessarily wrong. It was the manner in which you delivered it that was the issue. "

"Cheers!" Mickey raised his glass. "I'll take that as a climb down."

"Take it in whatever way you like, Mickey. Now I'd like you to leave me alone. And I suggest you stay off the drink."

"I'll drink as much as I like on my holidays."

She shook her head disapprovingly and moved away.

Percy Hetherington suddenly appeared beside him and whispered in his ear. "Trouble with the new boss?"

"The trouble is the new boss," said Mickey.

* * *

Eddie emerged from the Guildhall, spotted the car and climbed into the passenger seat.

"What's the score then?" asked Frank.

"He's at an award ceremony," explained Eddie. "Hundreds of bankers in there, swilling champagne and scoffing canapés."

"Awards for what?"

Eddie looked at an invite card. "Categories are for best Overall Investment Bank, best Equity Sales team, best Equity Trading …"

"I get the picture. Patting themselves on the back, oblivious to the mess they've caused out there in the real world. It beggars belief."

"Mickey Summer's hoping to pick up a prize himself."

"Is there a category for biggest gob in the City then?" Frank felt irritated that Mickey Summer might win an award. "So what else has our Mickey been up to today?"

"Went round to see a lawyer earlier. Tasty one too."

Frank turned in his seat. "Corporate lawyer?"

"Criminal."

"Interesting. Looks like Mickey Summer is getting rattled."

* * *

A crystal rang from the back of the room and the liveryman called out: "Your attention, please, ladies and gentlemen. The Awards Ceremony is about to begin."

People handed plates back to waiters, topped up glasses and turned to face the stage. After some obligatory publicity for the sponsors, the Environment Minister moved on to the first award for most improved broker.

Mickey looked over to Marcus who was standing nearby. This was the category he hoped Summer Research would win, and he looked anxiously around the room until he caught Mickey's eye and winked. The minister called out the third placed name and paused to allow polite applause. The second place was called and now Marcus looked again at Mickey and held up his crossed fingers.

"And the award for most improved broker goes to …" the Minister fumbled with the envelope, "Taurus Securities."

Marcus and Mickey exchanged disappointed glances. The minister rattled through various other awards until he came to the award for best Equity Sales Trading desk. Now it was Mickey's turn to feel nervous. He tapped his feet on the wooden floor. In third place was Finsburg, fallen from first the year before. In second was Aralia, a big surprise given their tiny market share.

"The first place award for best Equity Sales Trading team …" the Minister paused for effect, "goes to Royal Shire Bank."

Mickey punched the air. He looked over to see Marcus grinning and clapping loudly. Others he knew around the room were giving him the thumbs up. It was a popular win.

"Well done," said Percy, nudging him in the ribs. "Go on up and collect it then."

Mickey started to push his way through the crowd. But he stopped when he saw Benaifa already approaching the platform. "What's she doing?" asked Percy. "You go up, Mickey. It's your award."

Mickey fought the temptation to run up and grab the award before she reached it. Now he did really know how it felt to want to murder someone. Benaifa was soon up on the podium with the award in one hand, smiling for the photographer. She went to the microphone, pulled it down to her level and blew on it to clear the static. Boy she was milking it.

"On behalf of Royal Shire Bank, I'd just like to say thank you to all those clients who voted for us. We are very aware that sales-trading is at the heart of the equity business. Clients have voted for us because we can find liquidity quickly and we give valued-added sales calls. It takes a great sales trading team to be able to do that and … well, we …"

Mickey smiled as he realised Benaifa had run aground. Having used up the sum total of her knowledge on the subject of equity sales trading, she was standing with nothing more to say, her wild eyes staring at the crowd, almost pleading for someone to step in and finish the speech. Fat chance, thought Mickey. Benaifa then touched her tongue a couple of times before resuming her speech.

"And in so far as this is a survey of client opinions and therefore intentions. We look forward to seeing the future rev…"

She stopped and pulled back from the microphone, her face contorted into a huge grin.

"She's gone mad," said Percy.

Benaifa staggered backward, as if pulled by an invisible cord then she rose up in a slow arch and fell back off the podium. Mickey ran forward, pushing his way through the crowd. By the time he got to Benaifa she'd pulled herself back into a sitting position

"I can't see anything," she said. "Everything has gone dark."

"You'll be all right," said Mickey. "You just fell over."

"I can't see you."

"It's Mickey. I'm here. You just fainted, Benaifa. Can someone get her a glass of water?"

She touched her tongue again. "I can't feel anything."

"I'll call an ambulance," said Mickey, pulling his phone out of his pocket. "Shit! I've got no reception. Someone call an ambulance."

Mickey just had time to put his phone down before Benaifa collapsed in his arms. "For God's sake, someone call an ambulance."

41

The emergency room door swung open and a young doctor appeared. He pulled down his mask as he turned to the relatives. "I'm sorry," he said. "We couldn't save her. We did everything we could."

Benaifa's father shook his head and put his arm around his wife, who collapsed, sobbing, into his chest.

"How did … how did she die?" the brother asked the Doctor.

"Her respiration and blood pressure slowed until she eventually asphyxiated. She seems to have poisoned herself."

"Poison? What poison?" asked Mickey.

"The leaves of Aconitum Ferox. The ambulance crew found some in her handbag so we knew immediately what we were dealing with. But unfortunately there is no antidote."

"Why would she eat poisonous leaves?"

"It can be medicinal in certain preparations," said the Doctor. "It could be she ate the leaves for a medicinal purpose."

"She did often use traditional Indian medicines," said the father. "But she knew what she was doing. She wouldn't poison herself."

"It may have been an accident," said the doctor.

Mickey wanted to protest. He was certain Benaifa had been murdered. But he didn't feel he was the right person to say it. Surely now the police would start doing their job.

The family stood in silence as they tried to understand what was happening. "Can I see her?" asked the mother.

"Of course," said the doctor.

He stood to one side and a nurse guided the mother into the emergency room. The brother and father followed behind.

Frank, who had been watching from the nurses' station, walked up and introduced himself to the doctor.

"Is this Aconitum Ferox something you've come across before?" he asked.

"Not personally," he replied. "But it's well known as the queen of poisons. It's been around forever. You'll know of it as Wolfsbane perhaps."

"I've heard mention. You're sure eating a few leaves could kill her like that?"

"The autopsy will tell us for sure, but I'm fairly certain."

The doctor's caller beeped and he excused himself and hurried off down the corridor.

Frank walked over to Benaifa's bodyguard who was sitting with his head in his hands. "You all right in there?" he asked.

The bodyguard looked up. "It was no accident, was it?"

"Well," said Frank. "If it is an accident it's the fourth one in as many weeks at this bank."

"Of course it's not an accident," said Mickey, marching over. "None of them have been accidents."

"Benaifa was also one of the lock-in group wasn't she?" asked Frank.

"Yeah. Eight of us left. Still think we've got nothing to worry about?"

"I think you've got plenty of reason," said Frank. "That's why I told your head of legal to arrange bodyguards for everyone in the lock-in group."

"Didn't do Benaifa any good," said Mickey.

"This is crazy," said the bodyguard. "Surely this is a job for homicide?"

Frank nodded. "It will be now."

* * *

Frank didn't wait to be summoned when he returned to the station. He went straight in to see MacIntyre.

"I was just about to call for you," said the Chief Superintendent.

"Thought I'd save you the trouble," said Frank.

"Save me the trouble! You have no idea just how much trouble

123

you've caused me, DI Brighouse. There are four people dead on your watch."

"My watch?" asked Frank.

"You put Mickey Summer under surveillance. You were suspicious of multiple murders being committed in London. So I'm being asked why we didn't escalate this to Met homicide earlier."

"We didn't have a homicide," said Frank. "You got the RIPA for surveillance of Mickey Summer off the back of my own enquiries into Daniel Goldcup's death. Ben Stein and Vanni Gamberoni were Met investigations anyway and they didn't think either was murder. And that's despite me giving them a heads-up. So how come none of the Met DIs escalated it to homicide? They didn't join the dots either."

MacIntyre took a deep breath and relaxed a little. "Well it's a Met investigation now. DCS Armstrong is running the show out of Snow Hill. You need to get round and brief him ASAP."

"Will do."

"And Armstrong will probably look to second you to his team. If he does then offer him up DC Shore."

"Why Eddie and not me?" asked Frank.

"Because I don't want to lose a DI when I've got a dozen outstanding enquiries," said MacIntyre. "Besides, a major homicide enquiry will be really useful experience for Eddie."

"It'd be useful experience for me 'n all," said Frank.

"I'd like DC Shore to go."

* * *

It had been only three hours since the Met had been assigned the enquiry, yet Frank arrived at Snow Hill to find that one hundred officers were already on the case.

Most were uniforms given the donkey work of fielding calls from the public, house-to-house enquiries, fingertip searches, checks on vehicle registrations, mobile phone records and the rest. There were also a dozen detectives, led by DCS Armstrong. He was tall, fit, mid-thirties, sharp dresser, quick talker in a home-counties accent. A classic fast-tracker.

"So how long have you had Mickey Summer under surveillance?" he asked Frank.

"Three days," said Frank, who could guess where the questioning was going.

"Given that you had suspicions he was involved in multiple murders across London, why didn't you escalate this to the Met earlier?"

"I wish I had," said Frank. "But I had no evidence. I was just working on a hunch. And procedure doesn't allow for hunches."

"You're right there," said Armstrong. "So then, we have four dead people out of a group of twelve. Apparently a suicide, a heart attack, a hit-and-run and an accidental poisoning."

"Apparently," said Frank.

"But we can forget about appearances, this is now a murder enquiry. And I'd like to second you onto our team for the duration."

"DCS MacIntyre is short-staffed at present sir. He asked me to suggest you take DC Shore, who's been working with me. He's very good."

"I'm sure he is. But your hunch proved to be right and so I want you on this enquiry, DI Brighouse. If you're up for it."

"I'm up for it all right," said Frank.

42

A Union Jack tussled with the Ritz's own blue and gold flag in the sharp wind sweeping Arlington Street. Mickey jogged up the steps with a nod to the blue-suited bell boys, then passed through the revolving door into the foyer.

The concierge side-stepped into Mickey's path. "Can I help you, Sir?"

"I'm all right thanks, mate."

"I'm afraid we have a dress code."

Mickey looked at his chinos and fleece in the polished metal wall panel. "This ain't the right number then?"

"We request a jacket, collar and tie in the restaurant and a jacket and collar elsewhere."

"What's your name, mate?"

He cleared his throat. "Anthony."

"You're not the geezer what went out with Cleopatra are you?"

"No."

"Have you got a favourite charity, Anthony?"

"I give what I can to Great Ormond Street Children's Hospital."

"Good on you mate. Do me a favour and give them this from me."

Mickey counted out ten notes.

"I can't do that, Sir. It's the hotel policy."

"Well you tell Mr Ritz you decided on a charity dress-down day." Mickey pushed the money into the concierge's hands. "Think of the kids."

As the concierge hesitated Mickey slapped him on the back and walked into the hotel and up the sweeping staircase to the first floor.

He followed signs to the Grosvenor suite, along the heavy carpet to a door with two security staff, one of whom checked his ID before letting him pass.

He took a seat at the oval table while Karim joined the other bodyguards standing against the oak-panelled walls. Sir Stanley was the last to arrive. He sat at the top of the table and ran his fingers back through his thinning grey hair.

"You called this meeting, Mickey. So please, take the chair."

Mickey nodded. "Thanks everyone for coming. I'm sorry to drag you all over here but as I got into trouble for that email I put round last week, I wanted to make it clear I was calling this meeting in a personal capacity."

"Don't worry about that," said Sir Stanley. "Carry on."

"You've all heard what happened to Benaifa. I think it's time to accept that someone is killing members of the lock-in group."

"That's a given," said Carrick.

"I'm not so sure," replied Richard Turrell. "I heard she died of poisoning and she was carrying the poison in her handbag. It could be she took an overdose, and given how she was always messing around with alternative medicines I'm frankly not surprised. It's still possible this is just a series of freak accidents."

"It's possible Elvis Presley is living at ET's house," said Mickey. "But it's not very likely is it?"

"They were all murdered," said Stanley. "That's why the homicide squad have been called in. They'll solve this quickly."

"It shouldn't be too difficult," said Mickey. "They only have to check out eight people."

"What do you mean?" asked Carrick.

"I think someone in this room is responsible for the deaths."

43

As soon as Frank received a copy of the autopsy report he went straight round to Forensics. He felt a little lost and out of place amongst the white lab coats but quickly found the technician who had analysed the aconite found in the handbag.

"Have you seen the autopsy report?" asked Frank.

"Just read it," said the technician. "It confirms that it was aconite, the active compound in Aconitum Ferox, that killed her."

"And you're certain that the leaves found in her handbag are Aconitum Ferox?"

"Absolutely."

"So what's it used for?" asked Frank. "I mean medicinally, not for poison."

"Any number of things," he said. "But mostly as a cure for a fever or cold."

"And did she have a cold?"

"Yes," he said.

"So you don't think it's anything out of the ordinary."

"I didn't say that," said the technician. "If she was taking aconite to treat her cold this was a hell of a strange way to treat it. She didn't take the aconite as part of a medicinal preparation. She seems to have simply eaten the raw leaves."

"And are a few leaves enough to kill?" asked Frank.

"Certainly. You can purify the plant to get the pure alkaloid. But the toxicity of the leaves is virtually identical and that's what she had eaten."

"How long between eating and death?" asked Frank.

"Within the hour."

"So she ate it at the Guildhall." Frank checked the notes he'd made at the hospital. "And she told the ambulance crew she didn't recall buying the leaves."

"What are you thinking?"

"I'm thinking someone mixed these leaves into her salad at the Guildhall."

"Did they serve salad?"

"Sure as eggs is eggs," said Frank. "But I'll check. So the killer slips some on her plate and then plants some more leaves in her bag to throw us off."

"Why are you so sure she didn't just eat some on her own?"

"This was an intelligent woman who used traditional medicine all the time. She'd surely heard of Aconitum Ferox, the queen of poisons. She'd know better than to go munching leaves of it for her cold."

"We all make mistakes."

"Yeah, but usually they don't kill us," said Frank.

"The thing is she'd been ill with aconite poisoning before."

"I didn't know that."

"She'd complained to her GP of dizziness and cramps and diarrhoea. These are symptoms of the poison. So that would suggest she'd eaten the leaves before. And that in turn suggests she didn't realise that the aconite was poisonous."

"How do you work that out?" asked Frank.

"Because she didn't mention aconite to the doctor. He didn't know what the problem was and neither did she."

Frank thought about it a moment and realised there was a better explanation. "Maybe someone had tried to poison her before."

44

"What are you talking about?" asked Turrell. "Why would any of us kill our own colleagues?"

"To concentrate the lock-in pool," said Mickey. "Each one of us who dies makes those who are left richer. Much richer."

Sir Stanley nodded slowly. He read aloud from a copy of the lock-in contract. "If an individual leaves the firm, for whatsoever reason, his or her lock-in immediately passes into the moat pool to be shared amongst those individuals remaining in the lock-in group."

"Surely not if he dies though?" asked Turrell.

"We never thought of death when we drew up the contracts," Sir Stanley admitted. "But technically it is a reason for leaving the firm."

Mickey watched the horror on their faces and then the suppressed smiles as they worked through the financial implications of the last few weeks for their personal balance sheet.

"My God!" Vincent scratched his head. "Does anyone really believe that someone in this room is capable of murder? Perhaps you have a particular person in mind, Mickey."

Mickey didn't answer and the room fell silent.

"What do you think, Stanley?" Vincent shuffled in his chair. "You've known us all for years. Can you imagine any of us being involved in murder?"

"Who could have imagined any of this?" Sir Stanley said.

"Then we are all under suspicion," said Turrell.

"Well it is not me," said Vincent, scratching his neck now.

"Nor me," said Weil.

Hurried denials flew across the table.

"I can't believe you're all saying this," said Carrick. "I still think it's just a terrible series of accidents. But if not, if we really have been targeted, then it's much more likely to be someone acting out of jealousy rather than one of us."

"Someone outside the bank?" asked Turrell.

"Possibly someone inside," said Carrick. "They would appear to know a lot about us."

Sir Stanley held up his hand. "I don't think we should speculate on who it might be. That is a matter for the police. We must all be on our guard, but most importantly when we get back to work tomorrow I want everyone to concentrate on their jobs. Business as usual."

"How can you say that?" Vincent was trembling now. "It can't be business as usual."

"I don't want to even go into work tomorrow," said Turrell. "Maybe none of us should. Maybe we should all go into hiding until the lock-ins are paid. What do you think?"

"I think you need to pull yourself together and show some steel," said Carrick. "The franchise of the firm is in this room. If we don't show up to work, the bank will collapse."

"There is something that might help." Sir Stanley waited until all eyes had turned to him. "I could redraft the contracts so that there is no longer a financial incentive for murder."

There was silence while they thought and then Carrick spoke. "Redraft how exactly?"

"The easiest thing to do would be to cancel the moat pool arrangement."

"And what about the money that is already in the moat pool?" asked Turrell.

"It goes to the Government," said Sir Stanley.

"Why?" Turrell looked to the others for support. "It's our money now."

"Given the economic climate, I think it would be right and proper to give this unearned windfall back to the State." Sir Stanley raised his chin. "Besides, it's unethical to keep the money of dead colleagues."

"They don't need it now," said Vincent. "And there is no good reason for us to give it to the Government, especially after the way they are treating us."

"Imagine the headlines if the press find out," said Sir Stanley. "We'd be crucified."

"Who cares about the press?" asked Percy. "The public hate us anyway. I don't think we should let PR dictate the issue."

"Maybe it should be given to the next of kin," suggested Mickey. "It was simply a mistake that there was no death benefit in the contract because it was drafted in a hurry."

"It belongs to us," said Turrell.

"But as Stanley said, it is blood money," said Mickey. "Do you really want it?"

"We don't know that for sure," said Vincent. "Until the police find evidence of foul play we can take the money in good conscience."

"Agreed," said Turrell. "It's an accidental windfall. I am happy to keep my share."

"You're all mercenaries," said Mickey, pouring a glass of water that he wished was something stronger.

"Right now, the money belongs to the people round the table," said Turrell. "Let each individual decide what to do with it. Keep it, give it to the Government or to charity. You give yours to the next of kin if you like Mickey. But let it be a personal choice."

"I'm keeping mine," said Vincent. "Call it danger money."

"All right," said Sir Stanley. "We leave the existing pool as it is. I'll draw up new contracts that say if anyone dies from now on then their lock-in money goes to their next of kin. That will remove the danger if one of us is behind the killings."

"Of course this does nothing to protect us if we are being targeted by anti-capitalists," said Turrell.

"Unfortunately not," said Sir Stanley. "I take it everyone now has a bodyguard and is following the safety guidelines I circulated from the police."

Sir Stanley checked around the table.

"Good. And if you haven't done so already, I recommend everyone gets hold of a good lawyer. We may all be potential victims but we are also suspects."

45

The Great Hall of the Royal Courts of Justice had been invaded by Japanese tourists. They looked up in awe at the stained-glass windows and Frank's gaze was taken up with them. As a boy he'd always loved the huge windows in Leeds Cathedral.

He cupped both ears to catch the guide's explanation of the building's ecclesiastical design.

Eddie appeared at the entrance. He checked through security then ran across the marble floor.

"Sorry I'm late."

"It's only a fifteen-minute recess," said Frank. "And I need the little boys' room as well. So we've got ten."

They sat down on the stone bench. It was cold and Frank stuck his hands in his pockets. "So, are we any further forward on Mickey Summer?"

"That's what kept me late. We definitely are."

"Really? What have you got?"

"Dynamite."

Frank sat up. "Dynamite?"

"Of the high-explosive type."

"Come on, stop teasing me."

"Mickey Summer's dad was Tommy Summer."

The name didn't mean anything to Frank. "Go on."

"Tommy Summer was a convicted murderer. Killed a teacher at Woodhouse School thirty-odd years ago."

Frank clenched his fist. "I knew it. Like father like son. You said 'was'. Is the old man out?"

"Died in prison."

Frank watched the Japanese shuffle over to view the memorial to his left. "You're right. This is dynamite."

"Will the CPS accept it though?"

"Of course not," said Frank. "We need to build the case without it. But it tells us we've got the right man."

"Do you think we have a strong enough case yet?" asked Eddie.

"Let's try it out," said Frank. "You play devil's advocate. So, first there is his odd behaviour, the way he's always cheerful and joking despite everything that's going on around him."

"I'd have a permanent grin on my face if I got a fraction of what Summer gets paid."

"Don't start me on that." Frank undid his collar button and loosened his tie. "Then there's the way he's always ahead of the curve. He was the one who rang me with the murder theory linking the first three deaths."

"A lucky guess."

A door shut down the hall and Frank waited for the echo to die. "He also handed over a pile of cash to Dave Casey."

"Casey says Summer was paying back a private loan," argued

Eddie. "All above board."

"Come on. Mickey Summer is a banker. Why does he need to borrow money from a loan shark like Casey? Next, we know Summer had an argument with Daniel Goldcup and was the last person to see him alive. Summer was at the awards ceremony where Benaifa Bendiri was poisoned and helped her into the ambulance. And his alibis for the other two nights are shaky."

"And the motive?"

"Money. What else?" Frank uncrossed his legs, stretched his arms and checked his watch. "He's a gambler and he's split from his wife. Could be a divorce on the way. Plus he and two of the dead men were in a power struggle. So he kills two birds with one stone."

"It sounds good to me," said Eddie.

"The problem is, all our evidence can be dismissed as circumstantial. We need at least one bit of hard evidence to tip it over I reckon."

"Can't we search the house? We're bound to turn up something."

"I can't get a search warrant with what we've got so far. I haven't got reasonable cause."

"Let's pull him in then. Rattle his cage."

"DCS Armstrong won't let us bring him in until we've got evidence." Frank reached for his phone. "There is something else we could try though. A bit of old-style police work."

46

The door opened as far as the chain would allow and two brown eyes peered out. "Who is it?"

"DI Brighouse." Frank held up his card. "I'm here to see Mickey Summer."

The bodyguard unhooked the chain as Mickey arrived in the hallway, dressed in tracksuit bottoms and a sweatshirt.

"Bit Terry Waite for a social," he said. "So I assume you're here on business."

"I'm off duty," said Frank. "But I happened to be passing so I thought I'd call round, to see how things are."

"See how what things are?"

"From a security perspective," said Frank. "I have a duty to protect you remember? I'm glad your bodyguard opened the door. That's a sign you're taking the threat seriously."

"Of course I am," said Mickey. "Four of my colleagues are dead, in case you've forgotten."

"Can I come in?"

Mickey stepped aside. "I've got nothing to hide. I got rid of the uranium enrichment plant yesterday."

Frank ignored the joke and walked into the reception hall. The bodyguard disappeared into the kitchen.

Mickey turned to Frank. "At last we are alone!"

Frank smiled then looked round the room. "Nice pad. Bigger than they look from the outside these old warehouses."

"Built by the Time Lords," said Mickey. "Fancy a drink? I'm on the wine myself but I can do you something soft if you like."

"I'll have a glass of wine too, thanks."

Mickey went through to the kitchen and Frank studied the lightly-furnished room. His attention was drawn to a large, heart-shaped crystal on a sideboard.

"Rose quartz," said Mickey, returning from the kitchen. "Otherwise known as the Love Stone. Don't look at me too close while you handle it."

Frank read the label on the stand. "It claims to have healing powers. Do you believe in all that?"

"The missus does. That reminds me, she wants it back to cure her bad circulation."

"Superstitious nonsense if you ask me," said Frank.

"I agree it's a load of ol' cobblers, but the wife is into all of this new-age religion stuff."

"Black magic is old age," said Frank. "She'd be better off walking to church to cure her circulation."

"Better still a doctor," said Mickey, handing over the wine.

Frank raised it a couple of inches and took a sip. "Your wife doesn't live with you, does she?"

"Not at the moment."

"Why did she leave?"

"She ain't left. She just needed a break."

"Why did she need a break then?"

"She's not the city type," said Mickey. "Likes the countryside. Like I say, it's all part of the new-age stuff."

"Living in the countryside is also very old age," said Frank. He moved to the window. The lights of Canary Wharf brimmed nearby. "It's certainly not very countrified round here. Handy for work though."

"Door to desk in ten minutes."

Frank's eyes drifted to the moonlit harbour below, where boats rocked in the breeze. "You've come a long way from Leyton, haven't you, Mickey?"

"About six miles as the canaries fly."

"I bet your Mum's very pleased for you. Given the tough start you had in life."

"Things weren't so bad as all that."

"Got into a bit of trouble though, didn't you?"

"No more than any other kid," said Mickey. "Even you messed around I bet."

"Nothing to tell about. I certainly didn't go round hitting anyone with a baseball bat."

"Not surprising you ended up as a copper then is it. Must be in your genes."

"Could be," said Frank. "I reckon a lot of who we are is hardwired. I can't stop myself behaving just like my old man. Saying the same lines. Holding the same views. Do you find that?"

"Not really."

Frank forced a laugh. "I still won't cross the road until the green man comes on, no matter if the road is completely clear. Why is that?"

"I wouldn't worry about it."

"What about yourself? Do you reckon your fighting instincts come from the same gene as your dad?"

Mickey smiled. "I take it you know about my dad going to prison then?"

Frank nodded. "Interesting case. What did he have against the school? It took your brother on a free scholarship. It was giving him a chance he wouldn't have had otherwise."

"I don't know," said Mickey. "Dad never would talk about it. I don't know why he flipped that day, but he should never have got murder."

"Twelve jurors good and proper thought different."

Mickey shook his head. "They were wrong."

"It must have been tough for you; first your dad going to prison and then for him to die there."

Mickey said nothing.

"Left you a bit angry with the world did it?"

"Just determined to make the most of it. Now can we change the subject?"

"If you like." Frank wandered over to a side table and ran a finger over a briefcase that stood on top. "Use this for work do you?"

"It's just a prop to make me look brainy. I never have anything in it."

Frank flicked open the lock and opened up the case. It was empty. "It's certainly roomy. I wonder how many twenty pound notes you could fit inside this."

Mickey shifted his weight from one foot to the other. "A lot, I guess."

"Two hundred and ten thousand pounds' worth if you want to know."

Mickey set his drink down on the table. "So it was you that followed me to the gym. Or one of your mates anyway."

"Might have been. What were you doing handing over that much money to Dave Casey?"

"You won't believe it was gym membership then?"

"You could have bought the gym for that amount."

"I was paying off my brother's debt. He'd borrowed the money off Casey. Stupid of him, I agree, but there you have it."

"Wish I had a brother like you." Frank smiled.

"He's going to pay me back."

Frank nodded. "Your Mum's car still hasn't turned up?"

"You tell me. What do you think are the chances?"

"We're pulling out all the stops to find it. Should still turn up, eventually."

"Good," said Mickey.

"It'll be interesting to see how the bodywork is."

"How do you mean?"

"Whether there are any bumps on the front," said Frank. "Where the car ran someone over."

Mickey laughed. "Gordon Bennet! You think I ran over Vanni in my Mum's car. You're off your rocker. I'm the one with the twenty-stone bodyguard."

Mickey went to refill Frank's glass, but Frank put his hand up to stop him. Mickey filled his own.

Frank found a diary beside the phone and started flicking through it.

"Oi! That's private," said Mickey.

"Just curious as to how busy you City people are. You hear all this about working eighty-hour weeks. Just wondering how often you manage to get down the pub."

"Most nights after work. Though in a way that's also work. Talking shop."

"How about drinks with friends or family; a genuine social pint?"

"Hardly ever."

"I thought you were in the pub with your brother on the night Ben Stein died and again the night Vanni Gamberoni was run over?"

Frank flicked through to November thirtieth and December ninth. The entries for both had 'drink with Marcus'.

Mickey took the diary off Frank and put it back in its slot beside the phone.

"I've given you all that information already."

Frank could see the blood rising in Mickey's cheeks. Something was wrong with the alibis. Frank was sure of that. Strange how Mickey lost it on the alibis when he was so cool over everything else.

"Odd all the same," Frank pressed. "You just said that you hardly ever go out for a pint. And yet, the two nights in question you were at the pub with your brother."

Mickey said nothing.

Frank set down his wine glass. "Well I'd better be going. Thanks for your time." He moved towards the door, but turned just as he was reaching for the handle and looked down to Mickey's running shoes, dumped behind the coat stand. He bent down to pick them up.

"Aesics are a good make," said Frank.

"They do the job."

"Size nine."

"Someone's got to be."

"Ever had a pair of the Gel Cumulus?"

"I don't really take much notice. I just go to the shop and take what they recommend."

"The Gel Cumulus are red and white. Ever had a pair of them?"

"You asked me this the other day. I presume they are the ones that match the footprints found at Ben's house?"

"Perhaps."

"Well even if I ever did have a pair, they weren't my footprints. I wasn't there that night."

"That's right." Frank placed the shoes back on the floor. "That was one of your rare nights out. In the pub with your brother."

Frank opened the door and passed out to the street. "That was very helpful, Mr Summer."

Mickey shook his head. "You've really got it in for me haven't you? But you're off track. Way off track. The killer is out there somewhere. On the loose."

Frank nodded to the door. "Then you'd best put that wood in its hole and lock it behind you."

47

A week until Christmas and the markets were quietly winding down to the year end. Nobody wanted to take risks and further damage what had been a bad yearly performance for most funds. But Mickey rang round his clients anyway, with some of the better ideas from the strategy team's year-ahead report. Always going that little bit further was what gave Mickey the edge over the competition.

It was late in the morning before he had time to think about other matters. When he did, he remembered Sir Stanley had not yet delivered the new contracts for the lock-in group. He hurried off the floor and called Ruth in Personnel, but her phone was answered by her secretary.

"Ruth is tied up all day," she informed him.

"Wouldn't a muzzle be a better idea?" asked Mickey. "Then she could at least get around the office. Seriously, Debbie, I need to talk to her, right now."

"She said she wasn't to be disturbed for anything."

"What's she doing that's so important?"

"Graduate trainee interviews."

"Graduate interviews? Come on, you can interrupt those."

"Ruth places great store in presenting the bank in the best possible light to graduates."

Mickey smacked his forehead. "What is your idea of a good night out, Debbie?"

"Why? Are you asking me out?"

"I will if it gets me in to see Ruth."

"I'm not sure Max would be happy about that."

"All right. So, what's a good night out for you and Max?"

"We normally go out to a restaurant for dinner."

"Dinner for two it is then. Any restaurant you like. Provided you get me in to see Ruth right now."

"That's a bribe."

"It's a reward for your hard work in managing the diary. Come on. I only need five minutes."

Silence. Mickey imagined cogs turning in Debbie's mind.

"We like Ubon."

"Ubon it is then," said Mickey.

It was another three before Ruth came on the phone. "This better be very important, Mickey. Graduates are the future of this firm."

"But I'm the present," said Mickey. "And I'm worried about becoming the past. So, where are the new contracts?”

"Relax. I have them in front of me.”

"I'll be there in two minutes.”

"Sir Stanley wants to hand them out individually.”

"Well he'd better meet me at your desk.”

48

Helen Summer had a homely face. She wore no paint or powder that Frank could see and she probably looked the better for it. She'd insisted on meeting in the open air and Frank had suggested Green Park. As they wandered along the footpaths she explained the story behind the planting of London's plane trees and the conversation drifted onto global warming and the environment. She was as 'new age' as Mickey had suggested and she was a breath of fresh air. Frank wondered how she had survived in London for as long as five years. And how she had survived living with Mickey for more than a few days.

With the pleasantries over, Frank eased into some personal questions about Mickey.

"Is he ever angry or aggressive?” asked Frank.

"Not to me,” she said.

"Never? We've all got a temper sometimes.”

"Well …”

Frank waited a moment, but she'd stopped. "Well what?”

"No, you'll get the wrong impression.”

"So he is sometimes aggressive?”

"Not aggressive,” she countered. "But when he's had too much to drink he can be a bit unreasonable.”

"Does he get angry then, threatening perhaps?”

"He never threatened me. He just gets defensive when he's drunk. Doesn't accept he's had enough to drink. That's what I'm talking about.”

"Do you think he drinks too much then?”

She sighed. "I don't know. Probably. It's the culture. They all drink too much.”

"And when he's drunk, then he gets angry?"

"Not with me."

"But with strangers then. You've seen him get angry? Aggressive?"

She frowned. "He might get angry about bad service in a restaurant or people pushing in the queue, when usually he'd just let those things go."

"So does he get into fights because of incidents like that?"

She stopped walking and folded her arms. "I don't understand where this conversation is going. You said I could help you find out if Mickey is in danger. That's why I came to talk."

"That's right," said Frank. "I'm trying to understand if he had made any enemies."

"No you're not. You're trying to find out if Mickey had something to do with the deaths aren't you?"

"I'm looking at every possibility," admitted Frank.

"Well you're completely wrong. Mickey wouldn't hurt a fly."

"Maybe not a fly. But he wasn't so concerned about hitting a boy with a baseball bat when he was a teenager."

She looked surprised.

"He was expelled from school," explained Frank. "For persistent fighting. Didn't you know?"

The wide eyes told him she didn't.

"Mickey came from a rough background," she said. "He's done well to escape it."

"And you know about his father?"

She nodded silently.

"A murderer. A violent man by definition. He probably didn't treat Mickey well. So it wouldn't be surprising if Mickey did grow up violent and aggressive. Wouldn't even be his fault really, would it?"

"I don't know." She looked down at her boots. "All these things you're saying. It's not the Mickey Summer I know."

"But do any of us really know Mickey Summer?"

49

While Ruth fished through the pile of envelopes, Mickey picked up a photo of what he guessed was her daughter in graduation clobber. "She looks the spit of you, Ruth. Is she going to follow Mum into the City?"

"I hope she'll find something better to do with her life," replied Ruth.

"I bet you didn't say that to any of the graduates."

She smiled, found Mickey's envelope and handed it over.

He flicked through the contract until he found the new clause to the effect that in the event of death the beneficiary would now be the next of kin. For clarity, the new contract specifically stated that money already in the moat pool from the old contractual arrangement would be honoured.

Mickey concentrated hard on the legal double-speak until he was satisfied all was in order. "I presume that's the only change?"

Ruth shifted position. "Sir Stanley has made a couple of other minor changes."

"Minor?" Mickey skimmed over the pages. "Is that minor like in Asia minor, which is actually very large? Where are these minor changes?"

"The second paragraph on page four is what you should look at."

Mickey had to read it twice to believe it. The lock-in, instead of being paid in cash as in the original contract, was now going to be paid in shares and options.

He read on. The strike price of the options was not set at a discount. It was simply set so that if the share price didn't move he could sell his options on January second and realise the same amount of money as if he'd just got cash. Of course if the share price rose between now and then he stood to make even more money. But if the shares fell, he could lose out big time.

"Is this a rum and coke?"

"A what?"

"A joke. Ruth. Seriously."

"No, it's not a joke."

"I don't want to gamble on Royal Shire Bank's share price over the next fortnight. It could easily fall another ten per cent and then my options would be underwater."

"It's not a fortnight," said Ruth. "Check the date."

He did. He couldn't believe it. The payment date wasn't the coming January second but the one after. It had been moved out by a year. He would have to stay at work for another year to get his money. That wasn't what they'd agreed in the Ritz.

"Sir Stanley must be mad." Mickey slipped the contract back in its envelope and pushed it over the table. "I'm not signing that."

"Don't be so hasty." Ruth pushed the contract back towards Mickey. "Take it away. Talk it through with your wife tonight."

Mickey wondered how Ruth knew he was seeing Helen that evening. Then he realised she was just making an assumption. Normal husbands did see their wives in the evening.

"I don't need to talk it through with my wife. I'm not signing."

"Then let Sir Stanley explain how it works. He's thought it all out."

"I'm sure he has. So have I."

Mickey picked up the contract and dropped it into Ruth's waste bin.

50

Mickey had always liked the Punch and Judy because of the terrace overlooking the buskers below in Covent Garden. But this was the first sub-zero night of winter and he shivered in the wind. Further along the terrace, a party of theatre goers, dressed in tails and bow ties, huddled tight as emperor penguins.

Mickey looked down at the busker. A Harlequin juggling skittles.

"He's only juggling three," said Karim. "I can do that."

"Even the pigeons think it's crap," agreed Mickey.

He looked to see which act was up next and was encouraged to see a ten-foot monocycle resting against one of the pillars of St Paul's Church. Above it, the blue and gold clock told him that Helen was already fifteen minutes late.

His gaze drifted down and he saw her picking her way through the crowded street. She was wearing a red jacket, black tights and boots. Mickey had always liked her in red.

He straightened his tie and brushed his jacket collar. "Action stations."

"I'll leave you to it then." Karim withdrew inside the main bar and took a seat at the end of a table already occupied by three women in tinsel and heavy make-up.

Mickey watched the door. He could feel his heart beating. He suddenly remembered the Love Stone. And that he hadn't brought it. It had only been partly an accident. He hadn't really wanted Helen to take it away. They'd bought it together on honeymoon as a symbol of their love for each other. Now she wanted it as a cure for her bad circulation. It didn't seem right.

She appeared in the doorway, smiling. Her cheeks still red from the cold. Her wide blue eyes looked straight at Mickey. He smiled but she blanked him then looked away. He realised she wasn't wearing her glasses. She was blind as a bat without them. He waved an arm and she peered at whatever blur she could make out and waved back.

She forced her way through. "Hi!"

"Hi."

Helen offered a cheek for a kiss. "Sorry I'm late. I got stuck in Christmas shoppers on Bond Street. Couldn't move."

Mickey pointed to the bottle on the table. "I've got some Chianti, or we can go to the bar if you fancy something else."

"You know I love Chianti, thanks."

"We first drank it on honeymoon in Tuscany, remember."

"Yes. Yes I do."

Mickey poured out a second glass. "So how are you?"

"I'm fine. More importantly how are you? What on earth is going on at Royal Shire?"

"Nobody seems to know," said Mickey.

"Is it as dangerous as it sounds?"

"I've got a bodyguard."

"Really?" She looked around.

Mickey pointed inside. "See the big geezer being ignored by the girls at the table. That's him."

Helen swayed from side to side, peering through the crowd. "Isn't that the chauffeur man?"

"That's the one. Karim."

She returned Karim's wave. "Is he qualified to be a body-guard?"

"He's a black-belt in Ikebana."

"I've not heard of that one."

"It's the Japanese martial art of flower arranging. Anyone messes with me and he'll wrap them in orchids."

"You don't take anything seriously do you, Mickey?"

She looked worried and Mickey wanted to put her at ease.

"He's ex-army. And he's built like a rhino and is a good bloke who I don't mind having around all day. He's moved into the flat. Plus he's got a gun."

"A gun? Isn't that dangerous?"

"Given that four of my colleagues have snuffed it, I reckon it's more dangerous not to have one. The other good thing is that the police are now treating it as a murder enquiry."

Helen nearly choked on her wine. "This is all supposed to be good news?"

"It makes it unlikely anyone will try another move."

"Actually, I know the police are involved," she said. "I met this policeman. I forget his name."

"DI Brighouse I bet." Mickey took a sip of wine.

"That's it."

"What did he want?" asked Mickey.

"He asked me why we split up. What you were like to live with. I think he was fishing to see whether you were ever violent to me."

"I presume you told him I wasn't," said Mickey.

The pause was a second too long.

"Well?"

"I did admit you had a temper when you were drunk."

"Great. Brighouse will have loved that. What else did you tell him?"

"Nothing. I didn't really feel comfortable talking about it."

They gazed back down at the mono-cyclist who had replaced

145

the Harlequin. He circled round a member of the crowd who was lying down on the ground between two ramps. Then he turned in, raced up one ramp, flew into the air and sailed over the man. As the bike landed on the other ramp the crowd roared and the pigeons rose into the air.

Helen turned back to Mickey. "Do you really think the killings were done by these anti-capitalist demonstrators? I went to the demo at St Paul's earlier. They seem harmless enough."

"I don't think it is one of them. I think it's one of us. One of the lock-in group."

Helen's eyes widened. "Who would even think like that?"

"Could be any of them. My money is on Sir Stanley."

"You can't be serious! He's a Knight of the Realm."

"Yeah, and the police don't think he did it either. Too well educated. They're looking lower down the qualifications table."

Helen ran a finger round the rim of her wine glass. "The police think it's you don't they?"

"DI Brighouse seems to."

"Why?"

"Dad, I guess."

"But that's nothing to do with you, is it? I mean killing isn't genetic is it?"

"I don't know," said Mickey. "But even if it is, do you really think I could be described as violent?"

"No. No I don't think you are the type to … you know, kill."

"You don't *think* I'm the type to kill. Surely you can do better than that. You are the person who knows me better than anyone."

"You hear stories though," said Helen. "You know, about wives who never knew their husbands were paedophiles and terrible things like that."

"Well thanks for that ringing endorsement. Did you offer that thought to Brighouse?" Mickey finished another glass. Bloody hell, even his wife didn't trust him. "So anyway," he said, feeling suddenly confrontational. "What did you want to meet up about?"

Helen nodded as if she'd been expecting the question. She looked down at her crossed hands. "The timing isn't great with everything else that's going on but …"

146

"But what?"

"Well, we can't carry on as we are. Can we?"

Mickey's stomach tightened. He wished he hadn't asked. "If you want more time to …"

"No, Mickey, I want a divorce."

Mickey felt as if someone had punched him on the side of the head. He set his glass down on the shelf and clasped the railing.

"Why?" he asked, though he knew it was a stupid question.

Helen's right arm crossed over to clasp her shoulder. "I'm not made for this city life, Mickey. I need a simple life. I'm sorry. It's not your fault."

"How about if we moved out of London and …"

"It's no use, Mickey."

"I'm serious. Remember Whitwell farm? I've put an offer in to buy it. I really have. I was going to tell you as soon as it was a done deal. What do you think of that?"

She started to smile and then she sighed. "It's not about where we live, Mickey. It's the lifestyle."

"We'll change it. I'll change."

She shook her head. "You're not the problem, Mickey. It's me that can't cope. I'm sorry." There was an awkward silence. For once, Mickey couldn't think what to say. "I think I'd better get going," she said eventually, avoiding eye contact.

"If you have to."

"I'm sorry it's turned out this way."

Mickey sighed. "Right."

"Will you be OK on your own?"

"I'm not on my own am I? I've got Karim. Muslims make great drinking partners because you get the whole bottle to yourself."

She leant down to pick up her handbag. "I don't suppose you remembered to bring along the crystal did you?"

"I forgot. I am sorry."

"Perhaps you could post it up to me?"

"I'll bring it up to you as soon as I can."

"It'll be fine in the post. Goodbye." She softly kissed the top of Mickey's head. The smell of perfume lingered as she walked away.

51

Inject another five billion to save Royal Shire Bank, or let it go under. The choice was simple but the arguments had been going round in circles through the night. The UK government didn't want to inject more money into a bank that was inevitably going to be American-owned one day. They wanted State Financial to inject the capital and take majority control now. But of course State Financial's balance sheet was shot to pieces like every other bank. They'd have to get the US government to stump up the money. But how would the president explain why he was using US taxpayer's money to bail out a British bank?

Round and round the garden.

Sometimes Stanley had been present in the room, and at other times, no doubt when they were considering letting the bank go under, he had been asked to step outside. That had allowed him space for the odd cat-nap. Nevertheless, by six in the morning, he was exhausted.

"I'm afraid it's getting close to decision time," he said, cutting into another argument on irrelevant detail, with the big decision still not made. "Someone needs to make a statement before the market opens. Otherwise our share price will fall into a death spiral."

"It would be easier for us to make a statement if you had managed to sort out the lock-in payments," said the chancellor.

"I'm working on it."

"Work harder," he snapped. "We can't give you five billion pounds of cash and see a good part of it walk out the door in bonuses two weeks later."

"I've cut the bonus pool down to the muscle."

"But not the lock-ins."

"The lock-ins are not bonuses," Stanley said quietly.

"Don't start on that again." The chancellor's voice quivered as he tried to contain his anger. "These are your people. Make them see reason."

"I have a plan to deal with that." Stanley smiled. "Meanwhile the stock market is about to open and investors are expecting an announcement. What are we going to say?"

The chancellor turned to Robert Swan, his favourite investment banker. "What do you think, Robert?"

"We have no choice. We have to save the bank. We have to announce an injection now. Stanley then has a fortnight to work on the lock-ins in order to save us from the embarrassment of the inevitable headlines."

"And," the chancellor looked directly at Stanley, "To save your title."

* * *

Sir Stanley was twenty minutes late and some of those waiting in the boardroom were restless. Not Mickey. Even if he hadn't had a volcanic hangover he wouldn't have felt much like working. He found himself doodling Helen's name and then Whitwell. Was he just kidding himself or could the farmhouse bring Helen back? Her eyes had lit up when he'd mentioned it in the Punch and Judy. If he could just get her to come and see it, once it was bought, and beg her to give it a go. One last chance.

He realised he had scribbled through the paper onto the Boardroom table. As he tried to rub the ink marks out of the wood he had the germ of an idea. He would carve a name plaque for the farm and give her that as a Christmas present. Something from the heart. That might just do the trick.

His thoughts were interrupted by the arrival of Sir Stanley, who took his seat without apology. His two bodyguards stood behind. "Thank you all for coming. Now I've just about got fifteen minutes before I have to leave for a meeting."

"Is there a problem?" asked Turrell. "Our share price is off ten percent. There are rumours all over the market."

"I can't discuss that. Let's get on to matters in hand. I trust you have all read the new contracts?"

Heads nodded around the table.

"So are there any questions?" asked Sir Stanley.

"It's all very clear," said Carrick. "I'm ready to sign."

"And me," said Weil.

"Thank you William and Zac." Sir Stanley looked round the

table. "Is anybody not happy with the new contract?"

The eyes flitted again. It seemed nobody was going to speak. Mickey cleared his throat, but Vincent beat him to it. His skin glistened and he lowered his eyes as he spoke.

"I wonder whether it would be possible to make the strike price for the options lower. Given that the share price keeps falling, and there are rumours of another capital injection, we need a cushion."

"That just isn't going to be possible. I've had to clear this with the Government and they don't want to give even more value away. I happen to think the shares are cheap right now. You should all do very well out of this."

Vincent screwed up his face. "I think the shares are still overvalued. They might even be worthless for all we know."

"I can't get a lower strike price," said Sir Stanley. "Any other comments?"

Mickey looked around the table, but nobody appeared ready to speak. So Mickey stood up. He pictured Helen standing at the entrance to Whitwell farm, beside the name plaque that he had carved. "I don't want to wait another year for money that is due me in a few days. I don't see why you went and changed it anyway."

"It's very simple. If the killer is in this room, I don't want him to be able to just walk away with the money."

The circle muttered support.

"But what about those of us that are innocent?" asked Mickey. "We're being put through the wringer as it is, and now we're going to be penalised by having to wait another year."

"You still get your money, just a year later. If the share price rises then you'll make even more."

More muttered approval and nodding of heads.

"A year is still a long time to wait for the cash," said Mickey. Even if Helen could be persuaded to wait another year, he was pretty certain the vendors of Whitwell farm would not be so understanding.

"Do you have some pressing need?" asked Sir Stanley. "Something that can't wait a year?"

He did, but his marriage wasn't any of their business.

"We're in the middle of a recession," said Mickey. "We could all do with the cash."

"You could always try your money-lending friend," said Sir Stanley with a wry smile. So much for police confidentiality. Sir Stanley and the Chief Constable had clearly been talking.

"Of course," said Mickey, "deferring the payments by another year and paying in shares and options also helps your numbers for this year and rebuilds the equity base."

"That's how I was able to sell it to the Treasury." Sir Stanley looked at his watch. "Any more questions?" They shook their heads. "Well, if you can hand your signed contracts back to Ruth then we can all get back to work. There's still business to be brought in before the year is out."

"I won't be signing," Mickey called out, more loudly than he'd intended. He lowered his voice. "I'll just stick with the old contract."

"That is your prerogative."

"I'm not signing either," said Nav, looking up from his Blackberry. "I'd rather have cash in a fortnight than options in a year."

"Fine."

"I'm also not sure," said Vincent.

"But they can't do that," said Percy. "They can't decide unilaterally. It would invalidate our new contracts."

"Percy's right," said Carrick. "Unless all eight of us sign the new contract it doesn't work."

"So what do you suggest we do?" asked Sir Stanley through gritted teeth.

"Go back to the Treasury and try again," said Mickey.

"I can't." Sir Stanley glared at Mickey, and then his eyes softened. "Come on Mickey. Do the right thing. Do it for all of our sakes."

"I'm not signing."

"And neither am I," said Nav.

"Then we may as well all stick with our existing contracts," said Carrick. "I just hope we all make it through the next fortnight. Alive."

52

The Victorian terrace reminded Frank of his childhood home. Mrs Summer set out a teapot and matching china cups. She took the one with the chipped rim for herself then poured the tea and milk.

Frank chatted a while about the weather, then explained that he wanted to talk about Mickey's childhood.

"Why would I talk to you about that?" she asked.

"I'm a police officer involved in a major enquiry, Mrs Summer. The question is: why wouldn't you talk to me?"

"I don't owe the police any favours. Not after what they did to our Tommy. Put away for murder. He shouldn't have gone to prison at all."

"I'm sure it must have been very difficult for you."

She opened her mouth to say something, but seemed to think better of it and settled back in the chair again. "So what do you want to know about our Mickey? I don't see how I can tell you anything that he can't tell you his self."

"You'll remember different things and see some things from a different point of view."

"Like what things?"

"Mickey must have been around nine when his brother went away to boarding school. Am I right?"

She looked away. "That's right."

"I take it Marcus was the brighter of the two then?"

"No, he was the lucky one. Winning the scholarship. But Mickey was a bright lad as well."

"But Mickey left school without any qualifications."

"It was a bad school and Mickey got in with a bad crowd. It didn't help when his dad moved away."

Moved away? Interesting euphemism for prison. "Mickey got into a lot of trouble didn't he?"

"Nothing serious. Just teenage boys messing around."

"It was a bit more than messing around." Frank took a sip of his tea. "He put someone in hospital."

"Casey wasn't put in hospital. He just went for an X-ray and they kept him in overnight as a precaution."

"It was still assault."

"Casey was asking for it. He wouldn't stop teasing Mickey about his dad. Mickey just stood up for himself."

"With a baseball bat?"

"Casey was two years older than Mickey. What was Mickey supposed to do?"

"Fighting continued after school didn't it? After Mickey was expelled."

"Look. I know where you're going and you've got it wrong. Mickey has a heart of gold."

Frank decided to back off a little. On the mantelpiece was a photo of the dad with the two boys, probably aged six and ten. "The boys take after their father."

She followed his gaze. "He'd be very proud of them now. To think those two little monkeys grew up to be money men in the City."

"Any grandchildren on the horizon?"

Mrs Summer didn't answer.

"Mickey's separated isn't he?"

"You said you wanted to talk about his childhood."

"Do you know why the marriage has broken down?"

Mrs Summer shrugged. "She never was right for Mickey."

"When did the fighting start then?"

She frowned. "They never did fight, so far as I know."

"Arguments then."

"Not arguments either. She just don't like his lifestyle."

"What doesn't she like about it?"

"The pace of it mainly. The long hours. London."

"The heavy drinking?" asked Frank.

"What heavy drinking?"

"Mickey likes a drink or two doesn't he?"

Mrs Summer set down her cup. "I'm not talking to you anymore. You're just looking for bad things to say about my son. But you've got him wrong. Mickey is as honest as the day is long."

* * *

153

Mickey lay the hammer and chisel down in the pile of shavings on the kitchen floor. He took a few steps back from the work bench to admire his handiwork. Not bad, even if he said so himself. Not bad at all. The letter 'W' was a bit wonky but that proved it hadn't been machine made. Gave it character, that's what Helen would say. All it needed now was a coat of varnish. It would be the cheapest Christmas present he'd ever given. But in Helen's eyes, because it was made from the heart, it was priceless. At least, that was the theory.

* * *

Eddie took a sharp turn into a street market in full swing, dropping down to first gear as traders and shoppers spilled off the pavements into the road.

"Is this really a short cut?" asked Frank, bracing his arm against the door.

"I know these streets like the back of my hand," replied Eddie.

"I didn't ask how well you knew the street, I asked whether this is a short cut."

"Trust me." Eddie smiled.

Frank turned his attention back to his notes and the profile he had sketched for Mickey Summer. Inside a bubble entitled 'violence' he wrote: 'expelled for fighting', 'baseball bat' and 'cat'.

"So this neighbour you saw is prepared to testify about the cat?" he asked Eddie.

"Absolutely. Even though it was a long time ago she still wants justice."

"Is she a credible witness?"

"Eighty-two, but still making sense." Eddie braked hard as a woman suddenly walked a pushchair out into the road.

Frank hated being in the passenger seat, but he wanted the driving time to think. "And did she actually see Mickey Summer burn the cat?"

"She saw the two brothers running off down the alley. Then she found the cat still in flames. There was nothing she could do but watch it burn and then she buried it. She went round to the mum but the kids denied it of course. She's never forgotten."

"But she didn't actually see Mickey burn the cat. So she couldn't testify to that in court?"

"Not as such."

"More flipping circumstantial evidence." Frank placed a question mark beside the 'cat' and drifted down the page: gambler, heavy drinker, separated, argumentative when drunk. "We need more from the wife."

"She's refusing to see us again. And she says if it came to court she wouldn't testify against Mickey."

"We'll see about that."

"Do you think he's put on the frighteners?" asked Eddie.

"If he's capable of murder he's capable of that."

Frank put the pen and pad in his coat pocket. If Mickey Summer was their man then he'd give himself away eventually. One way or another, consciously or otherwise, criminals want their handicraft to be recognised by someone who appreciates it. That was basic human nature.

53

Mickey pointed to a brightly-lit curry house on the other side of Brick Lane. "How about that one?"

Marcus shook his head. "I've been recommended this new Balti restaurant."

"They all come out the same in the morning," said Mickey.

Marcus walked on. "Come on, it'll be worth the effort."

Mickey stuffed his cold hands in his trouser pockets and followed. He'd had three pints of beer on an empty stomach and was starving. He also felt vulnerable without a bodyguard, especially on Brick Lane, with its sweetmeat shops, sari boutiques and Bengali graffiti. But that couldn't be helped now. Karim had understandably had to rush off to see his mum when he got the call from the hospital.

A figure emerged from a side street. Mickey jumped back and then relaxed as a bemused old man in Kurta pyjamas walked past.

Marcus laughed. "You're jumping at shadows."

"I'll give you one more minute to find this place. Then I'm going into the first curry house we see." Mickey meant it.

They walked on a short distance and then Marcus stopped. "This is it."

In the doorway Mickey cast an eye round the room. At the nearest table were four suits without ties, talking about the England cricket tour. At another, with wrapping paper and birthday cards littered among the plates, sat a party of older women. The only other customers were a young couple holding hands across the table. It looked safe enough.

Mickey followed Marcus to the table and they ordered at once. As they tucked into their onion baji starters Mickey described the terms of the new contract Sir Stanley had offered.

Marcus agreed he'd done the right thing in not signing. "We need cash now. Besides. If the murderer isn't one of the lock-in group, but is actually one of the sixty million of Her Majesty's subjects who hate bankers, then there's no point in changing the contract."

"That's true," said Mickey.

"And we still don't know if anyone *has* been murdered."

"You're not still saying it could all be bad luck, are you?"

"From what you say," said Marcus, "The police don't appear to have any proof."

"Come off it Marcus."

Marcus wiped his eyes with his serviette. "The point is that there is little or nothing to be gained by changing your contract. But an awful lot to be lost. Plus you only have a fortnight to go."

"Right now a fortnight seems like a long time," said Mickey. "I'm getting a crick in my neck from watching my back."

"Good. You need to stay alert just to be on the safe side. You're careful about letting people know your movements now, aren't you?"

"Manita keeps it as confidential as she can."

"Well I think we can trust her," said Marcus. "And you always have a bodyguard. Other than tonight of course. Are you sure we shouldn't fix for someone to replace Karim?"

"Nah. I've got my big brother to look after me." Mickey thought about the call Karim had received from the nursing home. "I hope his old dear is all right. He was in a right old panic when he ran off."

Mickey suddenly noticed a tall, thick-set man pressing his face against the restaurant window, one hand covering the glare from the street light. "What's that geezer looking at?"

"He's just checking out the restaurant. Relax."

"You're the one who got me thinking about it all again."

Mickey's gaze fell on an internet café across the road where another bloke was reading the paper. "Nobby-No-Mates over there in the café was looking right at me, till I caught him staring."

"You're a good looking man."

"Seriously."

"Mickey, relax! Look, if there is a killer, then surely it wouldn't make sense for him to strike again now, with the police all over the case and everyone with a bodyguard."

"Everyone except me," added Mickey.

"Let me ring up for a replacement for Karim then."

Mickey shook his head. "Don't bother. I'm all right really."

The main course arrived, sizzling in metal pans. Mickey's mouth caught fire as he tried his food. He pushed the pan back over to Marcus. "Try some of this."

"No thanks. Last time I had one of your curries was your stag do and I spent the entire wedding day on the lavatory."

Mickey pulled the dish back. "No pain, no gain."

"Talking of which. What did Helen have to say for herself the other night?"

Mickey hesitated. He wasn't ready to tell anyone she'd asked for a divorce; even his brother. And he was still hopeful he could change her mind. "Nothing much."

"Why did she want to see you?"

"She was worried about me."

"Shows she still cares."

Mickey stabbed a prawn with his fork. "Let's change the subject."

"All right. Let's discuss the only genuinely important issue in the world right now, which is the matter of you coming on board Summer Securities."

"Marcus, I don't know. I just don't know about anything anymore."

"I understand. You've got a lot on your plate. But the thing is, Mickey, I really need to know, one way or the other."

"Give me one more day."

"One more. But if you haven't decided by then I'm cutting you out. And this time I am serious."

* * *

Summer and his brother headed off towards Liverpool Street. Frank followed on foot, a hundred metres or so behind, with Eddie further back in the car. Frank had always enjoyed hands-on policing. It was one of the reasons he was not so bothered about being constantly passed over for promotion. Didn't want to spend the rest of his career behind a desk.

They moved down the row of neat, red-brick Huguenot's houses on Fournier Street, then passed the white spire of Christ Church. As they crossed Commercial Street, Frank noted that they were in the City of London and therefore no longer in Met territory. Suddenly a BMW screeched round a corner and stopped twenty metres in front of the Summer brothers, its engine running and lights full on. Frank instinctively knew that something was wrong.

As the Summer brothers drew up beside the car, its doors flew open and three men jumped out. They wore balaclavas, dark clothes and each held a baseball bat.

Frank grabbed his radio. "This is DI Brighouse, urgent assistance needed on Gun Street. I've got three men with baseball bats attacking the Summer brothers. Need back up now."

As Frank sprinted forward, the baseball bats started swinging. "Police officer! Back off!" he screamed.

Two of the gang looked to the ringleader. He motioned them to continue the assault on the Summers and he stepped forward to confront Frank. He raised his bat over his head. As he swung it down, Frank stepped inside and chopped hard with the bone of his forearm into the bicep.

One of the other two now left the Summers and turned on Frank, swinging a bat in a plane that took in his head. He had no choice but to block it with his arm. Hard wood cracked on bone but Frank was close enough to get in a kick that bought him space. The ringleader had recovered his bat and the two of them came forward together.

"I'm a police officer," shouted Frank.

They hesitated.

Frank saw Mickey Summer behind them, grappling with the third man. His brother was flat out on the pavement.

Eddie's car squealed round the corner, siren whooping, and the gang turned and ran to the BMW, smashing both Eddie's headlights as they passed. Frank pelted after them. He was much quicker over the ground, but still got to the car too late. He noted the registration as it did a three-point turn and disappeared, then he called the number through on the radio. He turned back to the Summer brothers. Mickey was kneeling down beside his brother, about to lift him up.

"Leave him," Frank called out. "Could be a head injury."

Frank knelt down and checked for a pulse. It was strong enough but he didn't like the blood pouring from his head. "Eddie, call an ambulance."

"Is he going to be all right?" asked Mickey.

"I'm not a doctor, but he's conscious."

Mickey looked back up the road. "We could 'ave been killed."

"Where was your bodyguard?" asked Frank.

"Had to go visit his sick mother. Last-minute thing. Just as well you were following us."

Frank felt his arm where it had taken the bat.

"Are you hurt?" asked Mickey.

"Don't reckon anything is broken. You know who those guys were?"

"No idea," said Mickey. "Will you catch them? You got the number plate."

"We'll find the car," said Frank. "Finding the blokes might be trickier."

159

54

The nurse took the thermometer out of Marcus' mouth and held it at eye level.

Mickey tried to see the reading. "How is it?"

"Normal." She placed two fingers on Marcus' wrist, glanced at her watch and began counting in silence.

Mickey watched her breasts rise and fall with her breathing, then remembered Veronica's warning about staring and looked back at her eyes.

"How is his pulse?" asked Mickey.

"Fine."

Mickey watched her make a careful note on the clipboard. "Do you enjoy your work?"

"Why do you ask?"

"I'm just interested. Thinking of a career change."

"Don't make me laugh," said Marcus. "It hurts."

"Mostly I enjoy it," said the nurse.

"What do you like about it?" asked Mickey.

"I like working with people, and I'm constantly learning. It's very rewarding."

"Good money then?"

"Oh sure. I just bought my second Porsche. I mean it's rewarding to see people get well again."

Mickey nodded. "I envy you. Doing a real job."

"Working in the City's not a real job then?"

"Can't speak for all of it, but sometimes I don't feel like I'm doing a real job. I don't make anything or do anything real for anyone. I just shuffle piles of money around."

"He loves it really," said Marcus. "He's just playing for sympathy."

"Well I've got to get on." She backed to the door.

"See you later." Mickey waved.

She gave him a half wave and left the room.

"I've always had a soft spot for nurses." Mickey picked up the clipboard and checked the readings. "Your pulse is actually up, you know?"

"Stop worrying. I've got a cracked rib, that's all."

"And you got a bang on the head."

"The scan showed nothing."

"That's what worries me. It should have shown a brain."

"Funny ha-ha. I'll be discharged as soon as the registrar comes back on duty." He looked hopefully at the door and then back to Mickey. "Anyway. How are you feeling?"

"Just bruises." He stretched his back until he could feel the ache. "We got off lightly. Those boys meant to kill us."

"I know. You're going to have to be much more careful, Mickey. You're in real danger."

A siren warbled outside and Mickey stepped to the window to watch an ambulance heading east along Whitechapel Road. "I can't remember if I've already said this, but thanks."

"For what?"

"For standing with me."

"I didn't do anything. I just stood around as a punch bag."

Mickey smiled. "You were pretty useless as it happens. But at least you stood your ground. You didn't run off, even though it wasn't your fight."

"Of course I didn't run off. You're my brother."

"It's at times like this you realise blood runs thicker than water. And I've been thinking about what happens next. You know, after Royal Shire Bank. I am going to join you."

"That's brilliant."

"We need to stick together. Besides, I'm sick of busting a gut to make profits for an employer that don't appreciate me. I want to work for my own firm. Even if it is a basket case."

Marcus winced with pain as he stuck out a hand. "It's not a basket case. We'll take the City by storm."

55

Frank hadn't expected a medal for saving the Summer brothers but neither had he expected to be on the receiving end of a rollocking from DCS Armstrong.

"So when you saw Mickey Summer was without a bodyguard,

why didn't you offer him police protection?"

"I didn't think of it, Sir."

"Didn't think of it," repeated Armstrong. "What did you think of?"

"I wondered if he was planning something and didn't want anyone watching."

"Did you consider his personal safety at all?"

"I was in surveillance mode. I've been working on the assumption that Mickey Summer is a murder suspect."

"He is also a potential victim."

"Sir."

Armstrong unfolded his arms and placed his hands on the table. "Fortunately Summer hasn't made a complaint. Quite the opposite in fact. He's passed on his thanks for your brave intervention up through to your Chief Constable. So back at the ranch you'll be looking good. But here on my team, your card is marked. I don't want any more cock-ups."

"Noted," Frank responded, finding the patronising tone more than a little annoying.

"So give me an update on Mickey Summer."

"Well. Looking at him as a potential victim, Sir, he's out of hospital with just a cut on his cheek and his brother has been discharged as well. He got a cracked rib and a cut eyebrow but the head is fine. He's doubled up on his bodyguards so he has twenty-four-hour protection. And he's going to be a lot more careful about his movements."

"No more late-night curries in Brick Lane then," said Armstrong.

"No. Then looking at him as prime suspect, he has means, method and motive, but we've still got only circumstantial. Size nine feet, car used in the hit and run matches his mum's missing car, his dodgy alibis and all the rest."

"But we've still not turned up anything concrete."

"Something will turn up," said Frank. "A bill record, a CCTV picture, something."

"If Mickey Summer's our man, you mean?"

"No doubt in my mind."

"Even after what happened last night?"

"Look, I don't know for sure. It could be that Mickey was nearly number five. But Mickey Summer is still my prime suspect."

56

In spite of everything that had happened, or perhaps because of it, and the need to raise morale, Sir Stanley had given the go ahead for the Royal Shire Christmas party. Mickey's bodyguards weren't keen on him attending and he was in no mood to party with four colleagues dead. But he decided duty required he at least show his face. One drink, just to show willing.

A jazz band was playing something vaguely familiar as he handed his coat to the cloakroom attendant. He looked around to see which group to join, and was surprised to see his brother approaching.

"Gate-crasher. What are you doing here?"

"I won't be stopping long," said Marcus. "Can't think of anything more hideous than a Royal Shire Christmas party. But I needed you to get this and I didn't trust a courier."

He handed Mickey an envelope before moving away into the crowd. Mickey guessed it was the paperwork for his joining Summer Securities. He didn't want anyone seeing that, so he stuffed it into his inside jacket pocket, as cheers and whistles rose on the other side of the room. It was the comedian Weil had hired as entertainment. He started his act with a few predictable digs at City bonuses, but then made the mistake of overestimating the audience's interest in politics, and the show went downhill fast. He finished to muted applause and people went back to their conversations.

Richard Turrell, looking the worse for wear despite it being early still, staggered over to Mickey and jabbed a finger in his chest. "I hear you had a little altercation, Mickey."

"I was nearly killed," said Mickey. "If that's what you mean."

"Hurt, were you?"

Mickey shrugged. "No need to send me flowers if that's what you're thinking."

"Is there anything under that sticking plaster?"

"Yeah," said Mickey. "Me."

"Looks like you got off lightly, if you want my opinion."

"I don't."

Mickey turned to move away but Turrell pulled him back. "My money is still on you, Mickey."

"What are you getting at?"

"I'm with the police."

Mickey finally realised what Turrell was saying. "You're with the police now are you? A career change is probably just what you need mate. You always was a crap broker."

"No-one's been tricked by your set up in Brick Lane."

"So you think I set that up do you? My brother was put in hospital. So how do you explain that?"

"I saw him here earlier. Looked fine. Is he in on it as well?"

Mickey squared up to Turrell but Karim stepped between them.

"Easy gents," he said.

Angus from the warrants desk pulled up beside Mickey and whispered in his ear. "Richard's been on a booze cruise on the Thames all afternoon with Investit. He doesn't know what he's saying."

"Hands up," Turrell shouted across the room. "All those who agree with the police that Mickey Summer is the Royal Shire killer."

"Now you really are bang out of order." Mickey pulled back his fist but Karim caught his arm, turned him round and marched him towards the exit.

"Everyone saw that," shouted Turrell. "Mickey attacked me. The police might not be able to get you for murder but we'll at least get you for attacking a colleague. Better bring a bin bag to work in the morning."

Mickey was desperate to have a go at him but Karim forced him towards the exit. Just before the cloakrooms he was pulled to one side by Percy Hetherington. "Don't take any notice of Turrell. He's an idiot."

"He's not even that smart," said Mickey.

"How are you after Brick Lane then? Not too badly hurt I

164

hope."

"I'm alive," said Mickey. "And that's a result."

"I think we can safely assume you won't be going out without your bodyguard again." Percy motioned to two unshaven men standing at the bar with orange juices. "I'm taking no chances either."

"Should do the job," said Mickey.

"We all need to be very, very careful. Only a matter of days now."

57

The dancer's starch-blond hair fell to the mirrored floor and her breasts wobbled like pink jelly. As she swung around the pole Percy began to wonder at her blank expression and pale skin. He was gaining the firm impression that she was actually not human but some form of very life-like robot.

He glanced at the other girls sitting half-dressed at the bar. He realised they were robots too. It was simply staggering what they could do nowadays with machinery and cosmetics. Beautiful and with movements as natural as a real person. He wondered how far the engineering had gone.

He caught himself slipping off the seat. He sat upright, blinking hard to keep himself alert. Then he realised he had been hallucinating again. The cocaine he'd picked up at the party must have been laced with something interesting. The music stopped and the dancer sat down.

Percy turned to his bodyguards. "This is more fun than your usual assignments I bet."

"It's different," said one.

The other said nothing. They were proving to be rather tiresome company. Percy resolved to find another pair in the morning. He glanced around the room to double check there was nobody in there he knew. In the good old days he didn't need to care who was watching. But the Americans disapproved of exotic dancing. Said it demeaned women. At first they pressurised Sir Stanley into banning it just for clients, which was a damn shame as it had always been an easy win. But then Sir Stanley had ruled that employees could not even go in their own free time. Bloody imposition. Still, Percy had only a matter of days now of being treated like a child, then the rest of his life could begin.

The dancer caught his eye and Percy waved her over. He gave a gentle nudge to the bodyguards who took a second or two to understand, then shuffled along to the next table. She took a seat next to Percy, who slipped a note into her leg garter. "Beautiful dancing. What's your name?"

She picked out the money and put it into a heart-shaped purse. "My name is Danute," she said in some heavy East European accent.

The waiter appeared. "What would you like to drink?"

"Vodka and orange," said Danute.

Percy placed a hand over his own glass. He was feeling whoozy enough already. He slid a little closer to Danute. "You're new here aren't you?"

"I am starting last week."

Percy thought her accent endearing. "Which country are you from?"

"Poland."

"Lovely country. There are a lot of you Polish over here. Things not so good back in Poland then?"

"We make good money here and then go home to Poland."

"I see." Percy slipped a hand onto Danute's knee. "I know a way you could make some good money tonight."

Danute moved his hand away firmly.

He slipped it back on. "How much money would you like to send home to Poland?"

"Only dancing." She stood up quickly. "I am dancer."

Percy watched her walk away. The bodyguards returned. Not a great switch. He suddenly felt very tired. He didn't have time for courtship games. He decided to try elsewhere. But first he needed a pick-me-up.

"Just popping to the little boy's room," he said. "No need for you to come with me."

166

Before the bodyguards had time to object, Percy headed for the disabled toilet. He locked the door and fixed himself a long line. He was fizzing as he came back into the room. His heart pounded in rhythm with the strobe light as another girl took the stage. He felt amazing.

"Come on," he shouted at the bodyguards.

He took a moment to re-orientate himself in the direction of Dean Street. The cold air helped his shortness of breath but his head was spinning badly and he realised he might have overdone it back in the toilets. Still, nothing he couldn't handle. The army training told him to keep moving and sweat it off. Left, right, left, right …

In the distance he could see the lights of Gerrard Street around the red pagoda dragon. Suddenly it rose into the air and flew towards him, looping above his head before returning to its nest. He realised he was tripping again. He stood to attention as his heart flip-flopped, while overhead the street lights flittered like fireflies. Acid rain sizzled on his head and bounced off the streets. He lost his balance and steadied himself on a parked car.

"Are you all right?" The bodyguard's voice came from far away. The pounding in Percy's chest grew painful now. This wasn't normal. His heart skipped another beat.

"Help me!" he shouted, as he fell to his knees.

One of the bodyguards grabbed him under his arms and lowered him into the recovery position.

"Stay still and relax. Just breathe normally." The bodyguard pulled out his phone. "Ambulance needed. Suspected heart attack on Dean Street, Soho." He then dialled a different number. "DI Brighouse? Percy Hetherington has been taken ill on Dean Street. Looks like a heart attack. I've called an ambulance."

"It's too late," Percy rasped. "They've got me as well."

"Who's got you?" asked the bodyguard.

Percy's eyes were rolling in his head. "Whoever …"

"Don't worry about that now," said the bodyguard. "Just concentrate on breathing normally. There's an ambulance on its way."

* * *

The ambulance was just pulling away as Frank turned into Dean Street. The lights were flashing, which was a good sign. He said a quick prayer as he pulled up beside some police tape. The bodyguards were still there, arguing over something. They stopped as Frank climbed out of the car.

"How is he?" asked Frank.

"Not good."

"Did he walk into the ambulance?"

"Carried. Unconscious."

"Where had you come from?"

"The Starlight Strip. Round the corner."

"Jump in."

Frank drove them round to the strip joint. A bug-eyed police van was parked outside and a group of leggy girls were gathered on the steps. A uniform was taking their names and addresses as Frank walked up.

"Constable McGregor, Charing Cross. I'm the first responder."

"DI Brighouse. What have you got then?"

The constable opened his notebook. "The man's name is Percival Hetherington. He collapsed two hundred metres up the road after leaving here. Looks like a straightforward overdose on cocaine to me, but the bodyguard told me to treat the club as a crime scene."

"If the victim dies it's a murder scene."

"Murder?"

"That's right, son. So cordon everything off and sanitise it. Then call forensics. Have you tracked down everyone who was inside at the time?"

"I've got a good idea, thanks to the girls and Mr Zanib, the manager."

Frank turned to a man who was leaning against the wall, chewing his nails. "Did you know the man who was taken ill? Had he been in before?"

Zanib nodded. "They recognised him."

Frank turned to the girls. "He was a regular then?"

One of the girls stepped forward. "Been coming for years. Bit of a creep, but polite and a big tipper."

He could afford to be, thought Frank. "Anything peculiar about him tonight?"

"Not especially. He was sniffing around Danute." The girl pointed to a tiny blonde girl, shivering despite the coat round her shoulder.

Frank studied her face. "How old are you, love?"

She glanced nervously at Zanib before answering. "Twenty-one."

She was sixteen at most. This wasn't Frank's patch but he would chase it up later. "Did he speak to you?"

"I had drink with him."

"What was his manner like?"

"His man?"

The other girls laughed.

"Did he appear drunk or drugged?"

"I don't know about this."

"Did anyone see anything unusual?" Frank looked around at the eclectic mix of women and girls around him. They all shook their heads.

"Thanks, ladies." Frank turned back to the constable. "What else have you got?"

He looked back to his notes. "They've given me good descriptions of nine punters who were in at the time. There's CCTV covering the entrances. We're getting a copy."

"Good. I'll take a quick look inside." Frank walked up the pink-carpeted stairs into the darkened interior with its mirrored dance floor.

"Where were you sitting?" he asked one of the bodyguards.

"The corner booth."

"And did he have any other company?"

"Not since the party."

"What party?"

"He went to a staff Christmas party earlier in the evening," said the bodyguard. "We did advise against."

"Did you now?" said Frank. "And did you give him any advice on the legality of taking class-A drugs?"

"Didn't really think that was any of our business."

"Do you know where he got the drugs?"

"I think he was a regular user. But in any case, in the toilet at the party it was being handed out like peanuts."

"And you didn't think to stop that either," said Frank.

"We're bodyguards, not policemen."

That was so often the problem, thought Frank. Everyone thought it was someone else's job to speak out. "I'll probably need to talk to you both tomorrow, but that's all for tonight."

"We'll get off to the hospital," said one of the bodyguards. "And for what it's worth, we're sorry. I mean for letting our guard down."

"Not as sorry as Percy Hetherington might be," said Frank.

They shuffled off, resuming their argument as they returned to the street. Frank followed them out and checked the uniforms were on top of things, then he went back to the car.

"Control, this is DI Brighouse. Percy Hetherington has been taken by ambulance from Dean Street. Can you tell me to which hospital?"

"Roger, DI Brighouse. He's been taken to UCH."

"Thanks."

"Just to let you know, DI Brighouse. Percival Hetherington was DOA."

58

DCS Armstrong arrived at the station dressed in a dinner jacket and had evidently been at some posh do when he'd got the call. "You've brought Summer in?" he asked without preamble.

"Sir. Ready to interview."

"I'll sit in with you."

Frank was surprised at the suggestion. "If you like."

"I don't like, DI Brighouse. I don't like that we've got five people dead and nobody under arrest. So if Mickey Summer is our man I want to make damn sure we nail him."

Nothing like having your hand held, thought Frank. But he'd

probably do the same if he were in Armstrong's position. "Ready when you are then, Sir."

Frank led the way into the interview room, where Mickey Summer was sitting back in his chair, legs crossed, cool as you like in jeans and sweatshirt. Beside him was a severe, yet attractive looking lawyer, presumably the one Eddie had seen Mickey with the other day. Frank zipped through the formalities and then dived straight in.

"So let's go back to the beginning. The night Daniel Goldcup died. Whose idea was it to go to the Dickens Inn?"

Mickey looked at Veronica and then back to Frank. "You said you wanted to talk about Percy. See if I noticed anything odd about him at the Christmas party."

"We'll come to that in due course," said Frank. "First I'd like to talk about Daniel Goldcup."

"We're right back at square one aren't we? You still think I've got something to do with all this, don't you? Look mate, I'm the one in danger here. You should be protecting me instead of bringing me in for questioning."

"Just doing my job. I'm sure you understand."

"I've got nothing to do with Percy's death. I was only at the party for a quick drink. I spoke to Percy there, but that was all."

"As I said, we'll come on to that later. So whose idea was it to go to the Dickens?"

Mickey sighed. "I can't remember. We often go to the Dickens. It's out of Canary Wharf which is good, but not so far that people are put off going on their way home."

"Your secretary booked a cordoned off area of the bar. That would suggest to me that it was your idea."

"That would suggest to me that it was my secretary's idea," Mickey corrected him.

"How much did Daniel have to drink that night?"

"Oh I am sorry. I forgot to keep tabs on his drinking."

"The autopsy shows he was four times over the legal driving limit."

"So why ask me if you already know?"

"Were you aware that he was drinking heavily?"

"Too Olivered myself to notice."

"Did you fill up his glass at any stage?"

"Rude not to."

"You made sure he had plenty to drink didn't you?"

"Didn't need to. Daniel was a big boy."

"It was your card behind the bar wasn't it. You paid for everyone's drinks. Why did you do that?"

"I was the most senior person there. That's how it goes."

"I think you wanted control of the drinks, so it didn't look odd when you poured out drinks for people. And all that was designed to make sure Daniel left that pub drunk."

"It wasn't like that at all."

Frank put his elbows on the table and pressed his fingertips together. He'd long since forgotten the theory but it was meant to open up an obstructive interviewee. "You left the pub at the same time as Daniel. Why was that?"

"Just did, that's all."

"Your driver says you went to your car and put your briefcase in and then you went back to talk to Daniel."

"I went back to the pub to pick up my card. I'd left it behind the bar. I bumped into Daniel when I went back. I offered him a lift, but he wanted to walk."

"So you let him walk. And then you followed him, didn't you?"

"I went into the pub and paid for the drinks."

"And then you followed Daniel."

Mickey shook his head. "It might be easier if I tell you what I actually did, rather than you tell me what you hope I did. I went to the pub to pay for the drinks, then I went straight back to the car."

"Your driver says you were gone ten minutes. It shouldn't take ten minutes to pay for the drinks."

"That's what I said when they finally got it done. But you can't get the staff these days."

Frank was silent for a moment. "Ten minutes would be long enough to walk up on to the bridge and push a drunken man over the side."

"I wouldn't know mate. I've never tried."

"I think you have."

Mickey turned to Veronica. "How much more of this do I have to take? I came here to help find out what happened to Percy. To help try and find out who really is behind this, before someone else gets killed. Someone like me."

"You don't have to answer any of DI Brighouse's questions," said Veronica. "You came on a voluntary basis."

"For which we're very grateful," intervened Armstrong. "And I would appreciate it if you would continue to answer the questions."

Mickey turned back to Frank. "Listen mate, I paid for the drinks, left the pub and went home. End of."

"Turning to December ninth then," said Frank, "The night Vanni Gamberoni was run over, you claim you were in the Plough and Harrow that night with your brother."

Mickey hesitated. "Maybe."

"Maybe," repeated Frank. "You're not sure then?"

"I am sure. I was in the Plough and Harrow."

Frank shook his head. "You weren't in the Plough and Harrow that night, were you?"

"Yes I was. You saw it in my diary."

Frank laughed. "I don't buy your little diary trick, Mickey. You put that entry in for my sake, didn't you? But you never went to the pub."

"Says who?"

Frank noticed the averted eyes and flushed cheeks. Mickey was lying. He was lying about everything, probably, but for some reason he couldn't hide it about the pub alibi. "Says the pub landlord. He remembers seeing your brother, and he was on his own."

"We look alike," said Mickey.

"Everyone we've spoken to who remembers seeing your brother, remembers that he was on his own."

Mickey's cheeks reddened further and he turned to Veronica. "Could I have a word in private?"

She looked at Frank. "Could I have a moment with my client?"

"Of course. Interview suspended at eleven thirty four."

173

* * *

Once outside the interview room, Armstrong dragged Frank a few yards down the corridor. "What's this about these other witnesses in the pub? When did that come up?"

"It didn't, Sir."

"So you've just lied to him," said Armstrong.

"I said everyone who remembers seeing his brother sees it the same way as the landlord. It is also the case that the landlord is everyone who remembers seeing his brother."

Armstrong closed his eyes and took a deep breath. "DI Brighouse. As of right now, you are very far out on a very thin limb of a very tall tree. And if you fall I'm not going to catch you. Understood?"

"Understood, Sir."

* * *

The interview room door opened and Veronica beckoned them back in. Frank took his seat anxiously.

"My client would like to amend his answers to his whereabouts on the nights of November thirtieth and December ninth," she said, before turning to Mickey.

He cleared his throat. "I was at home in the Royal Docks both nights."

"So, why did you say you were in the pub?" asked Frank, trying to conceal his satisfaction at finally getting inside Mickey's cocky defence.

"It was my brother's idea. He figured I needed a stronger alibi than being home alone."

"Why did he think you needed an alibi at all?" asked Frank. "Why not just tell the truth?"

"Because you've been suspicious of me since day one."

"So what else have you lied about?" asked Frank.

"Nothing."

"So you weren't in the pub on the ninth," said Frank. "You actually started the evening at home in the Royal Docks. That much we

174

can agree on. And then you drove to Hadley Wood."

"I didn't."

"You drove there in your mum's car didn't you?"

Mickey shook his head but said nothing.

Armstrong jumped in. "You're doing the right thing, Mickey. Telling us the truth. Don't stop now. Tell us what happened."

"I never went to Hadley Wood that night. Like I told you, I stayed at home."

"How long would it take to drive from the Royal Docks to Hadley Wood at night?" asked Frank.

Mickey shrugged. "An hour?"

"I did the trip in thirty minutes."

"You don't have to worry about speed cameras, mate."

"So, you could have got there, run over Vanni and got home again, all in under an hour."

"But I didn't."

"You could also have driven over to Woodford Green the night Ben died."

"Could've been Prime Minister," said Mickey. "Could've played for England. Could've done all sorts of things. But, I didn't."

"You like running don't you?" asked Frank.

"Not sure I like it. I do it to keep the tyre off."

"Me too," said Frank. "And you use Aesics shoes don't you, because they fit the best?"

"I thought that was Everest double glazing?"

Frank smiled but ignored the joke. "Have you ever owned a pair of Gel Cumulus size nine?"

"I told you before: I don't know. I just buy what the shop assistant tells me."

"And the assistant would probably advise you to buy Gel Cumulus nine, because they have a specially built-up instep for people with fallen arches." Frank paused. "That's a condition you suffer from isn't it?"

"It's not exactly held me back," said Mickey.

"So you buy shoes that correct for that?"

"Usually."

"And what size shoes do you wear?"

"Nine," said Mickey. "As you already know."

"And we also know that the footprints in Ben's garden were made by a pair of size nine Gel Cumulus," said Frank. "They were yours weren't they, Mickey?"

Mickey shook his head and looked to the ceiling. "This is barmy."

"How would you describe your financial position?"

"You going to offer me financial advice next?"

"Not my area of expertise," said Frank. "But I know enough about it to spot that your finances are in a bit of a mess. Aren't they?"

"Nothing that the Bank of England couldn't sort out."

"Why did you need to take out a loan from an East End loan shark like Dave Casey? You did that because you're in a mess aren't you."

"It was my brother who took out the loan," said Mickey. "I was paying it back for him."

"That's not what Dave Casey told us. He said it was you that took out the loan."

"He got the wrong end of the stick." Mickey could hardly believe that he was having to justify the ins and outs of Dave Casey's intellect. "Casey never was the sharpest tool in the shed."

"Come on, Mickey, admit it, the money was borrowed by you to pay off a huge gambling debt wasn't it?"

"I don't gamble."

"But you're a member of the Claremont Club."

"I was, but I quit. I haven't been a member for a year."

"But you were gambling at the Claremont on December third with Alistair Beers."

"I wasn't gambling. That was my brother."

"Your brother again! So Alistair got the wrong end of the stick just like Dave Casey."

"My brother was in the middle of what he thought was a good hand and he asked me to chip in to help him out."

Frank passed a plastic pouch with two notes in over the table. "You wrote these promissory notes for Alistair. It's your writing isn't it?"

Mickey looked through the plastic, nodded and sighed.

"Suspect has identified his promissory notes, exhibit sixteen."

Mickey noted the use of the word suspect and handed the pouch back.

"I understand you're separated from your wife," said Frank.

"Yes."

"Are you expecting a divorce?"

Mickey didn't answer at first. "Yes. She's probably filing for a divorce in the New Year."

Mickey and Veronica exchanged glances and Frank felt that the lawyer showed more than just a professional interest in the news.

"How long have you been married?"

"Three years."

"Not long."

"Long enough for her."

"Did you have any long-term relationships before that?" asked Frank.

"Not especially."

"Is that because you find it difficult forming long-term relationships?"

Mickey glanced at Veronica.

She fiddled with her hair.

"What are you getting at?" asked Mickey.

"I'm wondering about your state of mind, Mickey. You see, you come across as a bit of a joker, happy-go-lucky. But I think that's a front. I think you find it difficult to keep relationships with people. That's why you can murder your colleagues without showing any emotion."

Mickey slapped his hands on the table and jumped to his feet. "I've had enough of this! Instead of harassing me, why don't you get out there and find out who the killer really is?"

"Sit down," said Frank, delighted that Mickey was finally losing his cool.

Mickey remained on his feet for a few seconds and then sank back into his chair. "Have you forgotten I was nearly killed in Brick Lane? You were there for God's sake."

"I've told you before not to swear in my company," said Frank.

"Sorry," said Mickey, sarcastically. "I forgot you were the sensitive type."

"You arranged that incident in Brick Lane to throw us off the trail, didn't you, Mickey?"

Mickey laughed. "You're wasted in the police. With speculation like that you should be running a hedge fund."

"I'll speculate some more if you like."

"I'm not sure I like any of this."

"I think sometime this year you realised that the City gravy train has run out of track and these golden handcuffs are going to be your last big pay day. And yet it wasn't a big enough bonus to support a lifestyle that included high stakes gambling, especially with your wife about to divorce you and take half your money. So you decided to increase that last big pay day didn't you, Mickey? A spur of the moment thing at first, when you followed a drunken Daniel Goldcup up onto Tower Bridge and pushed him in …"

"I never …"

"And when you got away with killing Daniel," continued Frank, "You went round to Ben Stein's house. You got lucky again and he had a heart attack. What I'm wondering is whether you found him dead or was it the shock of seeing you that killed him?"

"I've never killed anyone."

"Next, you ran over Vanni Gamberoni in your Mum's car and hid the car somewhere. Then you poisoned Benaifa and then last night you slipped Percy Hetherington some bad drugs. You were never going to get away with it though, Mickey. And now you've been rumbled."

"The only rumbling I can hear is your brain dreaming up this story, because you haven't done your job and found the real killer. Five dead and you're obviously none the wiser. What's your plan? Wait until there are eleven dead and then you'll know who the killer is?"

"Why don't you tell us who it is?" said Frank.

Mickey turned to Veronica. "I've had enough of this. Can I go?"

"We have covered this ground already," she said. "My client has answered all your questions. You have presented no evidence linking him to the crimes, other than highly circumstantial. So, unless you have new lines of enquiry to explore, or you want to charge my client, we'd like to leave."

Frank thought about it for a few seconds and then turned to the tape recorder. "Interview terminated at four forty-nine."

Mickey stood up.

"Before you go," said Frank. "There's someone you need to meet."

Frank left the room and returned with the Special Branch Protection officer he'd fixed up earlier.

"This is Sergeant Sinclair. I'm assigning him and a colleague of his to look after you."

"No offence mate, but I'm happy with the back warmers I've already got."

"Sinclair is in addition to your own bodyguards. The state will pay."

"It ain't the money that bothers me."

"I insist," said Frank.

"Why the change of heart?" asked Mickey. "A minute ago you accused me of murder."

"If you're innocent, then we have a duty to protect you." Frank leant right into Mickey's face. "But, if you *are* involved, then I want to know exactly where you are, twenty-four seven."

* * *

Frank and Armstrong walked back to the incident room together. "What did you make of him, Sir?" asked Frank.

"I really don't know," said Armstrong. "He looks very shaky on some things but the rest of the time he bats back hard, full of confidence."

Frank poured a cup of water from the dispenser. "I think he's starting to crack. Next breakthrough we get will tip him over."

"Have forensics come back on Percy Hetherington?"

"Just before we went in to the interview," said Frank. He picked up the report from his desk. "Cause of death is arrhythmia following an overdose of atropine."

179

"I thought he'd OD'd on cocaine?" asked Armstrong.

"It had been cut with atropine," said Frank. "In small doses it's a kick. But in high doses it's fatal."

"So, he was taking dodgy gear. Have we any reports of others at the party getting ill?"

"Hetherington's cocaine was different from what we found at the party. Forensics has matched it to a shipment that came in from the Netherlands last year."

"I remember that now," said Armstrong. "Caused five deaths before we got it off the streets."

"Looks like you didn't get rid of it all," said Frank. "Question is: where did Mickey Summer get hold of some?"

"Could be it was Percy Hetherington's own supply," said Armstrong. "Just an accident."

"Do you really think this is just another accident, Sir? Five in a row?"

"No," said Armstrong. "It's murder number five. And we better solve this before we have number six."

59

The flag was down as the taxi passed Buckingham Palace.

"No point calling in for a cuppa then," said Mickey, trying to lighten the atmosphere.

Veronica said nothing. She'd hardly spoken since they'd left the police station.

"Sorry for that false alibi business," continued Mickey.

"Best not to talk about it now," she said.

Mickey caught a smirk on Sinclair's face, then looked back to Veronica. "What do you think Brighouse will do next?"

"He'll keep digging until he finds something to go on."

"But there isn't anything."

"There's always something. They'll look deeper into your personal life. And for sure they'll go back over your father's case. So you should be prepared. Get your facts clear about why he murdered the teacher."

"It wasn't murder. It …"

"The court found him guilty of murder," Veronica interrupted. "It doesn't do any good to argue otherwise."

"Sorry. But if you call it murder most people just picture my dad as a killer, a monster. But he was a man. Just a normal dad who played with us, built sandcastles on Southend beach, threw us over his shoulders in the swimming pool and all that sort of stuff. He was our Dad. Lovely. Normal. Not a murderer."

"Was he ever violent?" she asked.

"No. He was a gentle giant. He never got into fights. The killing came out of the blue."

"So what did happen? As far as you know."

Mickey was reluctant to talk with Sinclair in the cab, but he didn't have any choice. "He killed a teacher at Marcus' school. They had an argument. Dad punched the teacher. The teacher fell down and smacked his head on the concrete. Never regained consciousness."

Mickey had a picture in his mind of the teacher on the ground with his dad standing over the body. It was a picture he'd seen so many times over the years that it had become real. "The prosecution claimed Dad went up there with the intention of hurting the teacher and so it was murder, not manslaughter. Dad did himself no favours by refusing to explain his actions or show any remorse. So the jury bought it and gave him a life sentence."

"What had the argument been about?"

"Marcus had been having a bad time at school," said Mickey. "He'd come home during term time and said he wasn't going back. I guess Dad blamed the form teacher for not looking after Marcus."

"Have you never asked him?"

Mickey turned to face her. Of course, she didn't know. "No. He killed himself in prison."

"Sorry. I'm very sorry."

"It weren't your fault."

They continued in silence as the taxi worked its way through a packed Piccadilly.

"I was twelve at the time," Mickey said eventually.

"That must have been tough for you."

"I have to admit I went off the rails a bit. Dropped out of school. Mixed with the wrong people. I really don't know what mess I'd be in now if it weren't for Marcus."

"Marcus?"

"He pulled me out of it. Told me that Dad would be disappointed if I didn't make something out of my life. So Marcus got me a job in the Royal Shire post room. From there I managed to talk myself onto the trading floor. I had to work twice as hard as everyone else to make up for not having the qualifications, but I soon realised I had a knack for sales trading. After that I never looked back. I think Dad would be proud of how far I've come." He looked up at the grey sky as they sped along Embankment. "Won't be so pleased about the mess I'm in right now though."

They drew up to Temple Gardens and Veronica asked the driver to pull over. The cab squealed to a halt.

"It would be useful to get more background on your father," she said. "Try to discover what the argument was about. I'm sure it is going to come up again. Talk to Marcus and your mother. Perhaps visit the school."

"I'll see what I can find out." Mickey had been meaning to do that for some time in any case. He opened the door for Veronica. "Are you doing anything tomorrow night?"

She stopped half in and half out of the cab. "Why?"

"I got two tickets to see the new Casablanca show." He fished two tickets from his wallet and showed them to her. "Play it again Sam, and all that."

Veronica climbed out and stood on the pavement. "The way things have developed I need to keep things strictly professional."

"I understand." The alibi mess had done it.

"I'm sorry," she said as she pushed the door closed.

The cab pulled away and Mickey spotted Sinclair smothering a smile.

"Did I miss something funny?" asked Mickey.

"You've been trying it on with your brief. That was never going to go anywhere, mate."

"Have you got a girlfriend?" asked Mickey.

"I wish. Been married ten years."

"What are you doing tomorrow night?"

"Nothing special. Why?"

Mickey passed over the tickets. "Take the missus out for a treat. Married to you, she'll probably need one."

Mickey had a sudden urge to call Helen. But after their last meeting he doubted she'd fancy a chat. Besides, he wasn't sure she believed in him anymore. Was there anybody left who did?

* * *

The taxi dropped them next to the old stone building of Lincoln's Inn Library and they walked the short distance over the gravel courtyard to the solicitor's offices.

Karim waited at reception while Mickey and Sinclair passed through a metal detector and body search, before a secretary led them to the meeting room. Inside, Marcus was waiting with some pin-striped lawyer.

Sinclair checked the room over and looked into the anti-chamber. Satisfied, he moved over to stand with his back to the door.

"I'm afraid this meeting is private and confidential," said Marcus. "You'll have to wait outside."

Sinclair stood his ground.

"I'm not in any danger from my brother," said Mickey.

Sinclair shrugged, then nodded and went out into the corridor. Marcus closed the door after him.

"Your new bodyguard is very thorough."

"Police protection officer," explained Mickey.

"Good. About time they started looking after you."

"It's not what it seems. I'm in a lot of trouble, Marcus."

"I know. I've heard about Percy. There can be no doubt about it now, Mickey. You're in mortal danger."

"That's not the trouble I'm talking about. The police seem convinced I'm the killer."

"Surely they've given up on that, after what happened to us in Brick Lane."

"They think I fixed that up."

"That's ridiculous."

"And they also now know my alibis were false."

"How did they find that out?"

"I told them. I had to. DI Brighouse could tell I was lying."

Marcus tapped his fingers on the desk. "Never mind. They can't send you to prison for lying. And they'll realise eventually that you didn't kill anyone."

"Let's hope I'm still alive when they do," said Mickey.

"I second that. Now, to business. You haven't told anyone why you're here have you?"

"I haven't even told myself," said Mickey. "If Sir Stanley finds out I'm joining a competitor he'll pull my lock-in."

"Ipso facto."

"The Romans left centuries ago, Marcus. Let's stick to English."

"Pardon my education. To continue in the vernacular then. I presume you've read the contract and are happy with it?"

Mickey shook his head. "I still reckon the price is all wrong."

"You're coming in at the same share price everyone else did."

"They bought in before you went into loss."

"I think you'll find we've made a small but tidy profit of one hundred and eighty thousand pounds this year," said Marcus.

"Not on a cash basis." Mickey pulled out the copy of the financials and turned to the balance sheet. "Unless I'm missing something, it looks like you lost well over a million when we're talking about real money. The folding kind."

"That's about right. The main difference between the P&L and cash are simply trade debtors. Clients who owe us commission but who won't give us the cash until the New Year, when they re-organise their commission lists. You know how it works, Mickey."

"I still don't see how you can book them as income now."

"Matching income against costs for the period incurred. Leave the accounting to those who understand it, Mickey."

Mickey shrugged. "Maybe it is OK on an accounting basis then. But it don't change the fact that you're bleeding cash."

Marcus folded his arms and leant back in his chair. "Look, if you've changed your mind about joining me then just admit it."

184

"I'll sign up," said Mickey. "I told you after Brick Lane I'd do that. I just want to be sure about what I'm signing up for."

"The business is sound, Mickey. Trust me."

Mickey sighed. With all the trouble elsewhere in his life he didn't really have the energy to argue over the financial figures. And Marcus was the analyst after all.

"All right. Give me a pen."

The lawyer took one from his inside pocket and handed it to Mickey. He signed beside the pencilled 'X'.

Marcus whipped up the signed contract and put it in his briefcase. "Ordinarily, this would warrant a glass of bubbly, but I'm afraid I need to get straight round to the bank with this."

"Not the Dave Casey bank?"

"Coutts," said Marcus. "Bankers to the Queen, and now to Summer Securities."

60

Sinclair let out a low whistle as they drove past manicured playing fields up to a dark stone building.

"Looks more like a castle than a school," he said.

There were few children around, as it was the end of term. Those that were walking round were casually dressed. Mickey tried to picture the school as it would have been in term time, with hundreds of children in uniform. A far cry from his playground days. He couldn't help but feel a pang of jealousy and wonder how things might have turned out for him if he'd won the scholarship instead of Marcus.

Karim pulled into a parking space. Mickey and Sinclair stepped out and walked up the steps to the main entrance. They passed through the open oak doors into a stone corridor that formed one side of a quadrangle. Paintings of past headmasters hung from the panelled walls. Not a smile among them.

Neither had the present headmaster, who greeted them with handshakes before leading them into his office. Mickey took a wooden seat, which offered up a carved rose right into the small of his back. The Headmaster sat on a nice leather number behind his desk.

"Thanks for seeing me so close to Christmas," said Mickey.

The head smiled. "I could hardly refuse. You said it was a matter of life and death."

"It could be. Have you been following the City killings story in the press?"

"Loosely." The Head sipped his tea. "Five bankers have died mysteriously and the police think anti-capitalists may be responsible."

"That's right. I work for the same firm. So I'm in the line of fire. At the same time, I'm also under suspicion because of who my father is. Do you remember Tommy Summer?"

The Head lowered his head to peer over the top of his spectacles. "Of course."

"That's what I want to talk about. What happened that day?"

The Head stood up and walked over to the window which looked out over the playing fields.

"What happened is a matter of record, Mr Summer. Your father murdered one of our teachers. Mr Ranger. It was a terrible, terrible business and an awful shock for everyone."

Mickey wondered if he had made a mistake in coming. "Do you mind telling me what you remember about it?"

The Head turned round, removed his glasses and placed them in a case that he slipped into his pocket.

"Ranger was your brother's form master," he said. "Your brother had been having a difficult time and his grades had slipped dramatically. He was skipping classes and then he ran home. Your father came up to discuss your brother's difficulties with Mr Ranger. The conversation became heated and your father hit him. Mr Ranger fell and hit his head on the pavement. He died of a brain haemorrhage."

"Poor bloke," said Mickey, genuinely sad at the story, even though he knew it so well.

"I appreciate your sympathy. It's more than your father showed. He left Ranger dying on the floor when he could have called for help. As I understand it, he never showed any remorse for what he'd done, and that counted against him at trial."

"That's what I don't understand. Dad wouldn't have just thumped some geezer because his kid was underperforming at school. There must have been a better reason."

"None that I know of."

"What can you tell me about Mr Ranger?"

"He came to us from a very good private school in Boston. I forget the name but …"

"He was American then?" interrupted Mickey. "So what was he like?"

"I was in my probationary year. I hardly knew him."

"Do you think Ranger might have been giving Marcus a hard time?" asked Mickey.

"Why do you ask?"

"I'm just trying to think of a reason for my Dad to hit him."

"Look, what happened was terribly tragic but it was a long time ago. I really think it's best left alone."

"I'll do just that," said Mickey, who sensed he was on to something. "I'll walk away and not say a Dickey about any of this to anyone. Once I understand what happened."

"I'm afraid I can't help you."

Mickey had to know the truth. "I've a mate who's a journo. He'd love to dig around a story of boarding school teachers bullying their pupils. Always makes good copy, no matter how long ago it happened. Probably turn up some present day stuff at the same time."

"Are you blackmailing me, Mr Summer?"

"I just want to know the truth. The police think my dad was a psycho. They think it runs in my blood. But I think my dad must have had a reason for hitting this teacher."

The Head took a deep breath and closed his eyes. "In those days the school still approved of corporal punishment. And Ranger did have a reputation for being rather free with this. I think he possibly had been a bit rough on your brother."

"You mean he'd been beating him up," said Mickey.

"Over-zealous, is how I would put it."

"Bullying."

"I think we are just trading semantics now."

Mickey's heart began to race. "So if he were hitting Marcus, then it were no wonder my dad hit the geezer. He deserved a good sorting."

"I don't know whether or not he deserved a 'good sorting'," said the Head. "But he certainly didn't deserve to die."

61

Christmas Eve in the City was usually slow. Those that bothered to go in for the half day could enjoy a quiet morning of trading, then off to the pub at twelve. But everyone was in at Royal Shire Bank because Sir Stanley had chosen that day to announce bonuses, so that the inevitable negative headlines would be buried under last-minute Christmas shopping.

Mickey stopped outside the glass door to the trading floor and rearranged the pile of envelopes that he had brought back from Personnel; envelopes that contained the letters informing each of his team their bonus.

Manita was waiting at her desk. "Are you ready to go?"

"As soon as you get hold of body armour and a helmet."

"Is it going to be really bad then?" she asked.

"It's not even going to be that good."

Mickey went into his office and took Ole's envelope off the pile. He checked that the letter inside referred to him. Personnel had once stuffed the wrong letters into the envelopes and the line manager had handed them out without checking, causing a riot. As he sat waiting for Ole, he checked the note he had made during his appraisal: 'Claims he's getting calls.' This is going to get messy, thought Mickey.

Ole stopped in the doorway, his jacket on, looking pale. "Is it worth coming in?"

"Course it is, Ole. Most people aren't getting a bonus at all. You're one of the lucky ones."

Mickey opened the envelope and turned the paper round for Ole to see.

Ole frowned. "It's only thirty thousand."

"That's a good result, mate."

"It's down on last year. I expected to be well up."

"The average is down sixty percent, Ole."

"How much of the bonus is in cash?"

"None. It's all in deferred stock."

"No cash?"

"Not this year. The government insisted."

"And the shares get awarded after paying fifty percent tax, I suppose."

"Until they make me Chancellor, I can't do anything about the tax rate."

Ole crossed his arms and sat back. "But you're all right aren't you, because of your lock-in?"

"I'm not here to talk about me."

"Stuff you, Mickey. And the rest of you lock-in bastards. To be honest I'm not bothered that you all seem to be dying."

Mickey was taken aback by Ole's anger, but he refused to rise to it. "I don't have to justify my lock-in to you, Ole. You were still in nappies when I was putting in the work that earned me that."

"And then you're going to walk aren't you? After your lock-in is paid you'll be clearing off."

Mickey couldn't deny it, but he also couldn't admit it. "Also none of your business, Ole. Now, do you want this bonus or not? I've got plenty of other takers for it."

Ole picked up his letter and left without another word. The rest of the morning continued in similar fashion. Individuals entered and left the room in varying degrees of anxiety and anger. By eleven o'clock Mickey was finished, in every sense of the word. He needed to get out of the building.

* * *

Canary Wharf's underground shopping mall was heaving with last-minute Christmas shoppers. Even with his bodyguards, Mickey was anxious about being in such a crowd. The killer could jump out at any moment. But he reasoned that if someone did try to kill him it probably wouldn't be out in the open. More likely to be another 'accident'. That thought wasn't much comfort.

He wandered round the mall, window shopping. He'd got Mum's, Helen's and Manita's presents sorted, and he and Marcus had long ago made a pact to skip gifts. Sadly there wasn't really anyone else for him to buy for.

Everyone seemed to moan about Christmas shopping, especially those with kids, but Mickey would love to have a big family to buy presents for, to wrap them up and pile them under a tree. All those smiles on Christmas morning. Maybe someday. Maybe one Christmas morning in Whitwell farm he would play out that scene for real.

He shook his head. Dream on Mickey. More likely, the way things were turning out, he'd be opening Christmas presents in a prison cell for many years to come.

His thoughts turned to the trip to Woodhouse School. At least that had gone well. It had been worthwhile. He now knew his Dad had good reason for hitting Mr Ranger. So he'd be sticking that on DI Brighouse next time they met.

He came to a bookshop and, hoping he might find something of interest, he drifted inside. The shop was doing heavy trade in coffee-table picture books, reviews of the year, Christmas quiz books and the usual end-of-year junk.

Mickey spotted the true-crime section and suddenly had an idea. He turned his head to one side and started reading the spines.

"What are you looking for?" asked Sinclair, clearly intrigued.

"Ideas on how to do my sixth murder." Mickey slapped a hand to his mouth. "Oops, I've given the game away ain't I."

Sinclair grunted something, then started to run his own eye along the titles.

"What are you looking for then?" asked Mickey.

"There's a new book out on London gangs where I get a mention."

"So that's what you did before you joined the Old Bill?"

Mickey eventually found a book focusing on the profiles of murderers. He was pleased to discover that, according to the author, almost everyone was capable of a single murder. Given the right circumstances and background emotions, most humans could kill: in rage, or envy, or self-defence.

So even if the prosecution had been right and his dad had gone up to Woodhouse intent on murder, he had been displaying the sort of abnormal behaviour that any 'normal' human was capable of in extreme circumstances; such as discovering that a teacher is bullying your son.

Mickey would have got worked up about that himself. It didn't make either him or his dad a psychopath.

That, Mickey discovered as he read on, was another business altogether. It required a special type of personality to kill repeatedly. It seemed that psychopaths were manufactured by experience. Usually it took sustained and serious abuse to twist an otherwise normal person into a psychopath. The abuse left them with an ability to kill without feeling any remorse.

Surprisingly though, the doctors didn't consider it to be a mental illness. The psychopath knew that what he was doing was wrong. He just didn't care.

Mickey was particularly drawn to a section detailing the personality profile of a typical psychopath. Interpersonally, the typical psychopath is grandiose, egocentric, manipulative, dominant and forceful.

A woman beside him coughed and Mickey realised he was blocking the shelves.

"Sorry love."

He checked his watch. Time for a change of venue.

* * *

With bodyguards in tow, Mickey hurried to the bookshop café, settled into a leather settee with an espresso and returned to the psychopath profile. He read that they display shallow emotions which are highly changeable and are unable to form long-lasting bonds with other people.

Now Mickey understood Frank's line of questioning about his relationships. What a plonker. It was Helen that ran out on him. He did want their marriage to work. He read on.

Apparently these psychos have few principles and no empathy. Principles? He liked to think he had a few. He stuck up for the underdog. He'd supported the Hammers for long enough. As for empathy, he wasn't exactly sure what that meant, but he understood others' feelings. That's why he was a good man-manager wasn't it? There were others in the lock-in group who better fitted the profile. Weil had no principles. Carrick had no empathy. Nav was an emotionless robot.

"Found it," Sinclair shouted. He pointed a stumpy finger at the middle of the page and read aloud. "We'd been getting grief off this copper by the name of Sinclair, so we had to switch venues."

Sinclair looked up for some response.

"Is that it?" asked Mickey.

"I didn't say it was a big mention."

"Don't bother chasing the royalties," said Mickey.

He sipped his coffee, which by now was cold, and went back to his book. He read the list again: grandiose, egocentric, manipulative, dominant, forceful, highly changeable emotions, no long-lasting bonds, no principles, no empathy.

Any of the lock-in group at times displayed some of the characteristics of a psychopath. Then again, so did pretty well anyone in the City. It seemed finance was staffed by psychopaths. That would explain a lot.

He checked his watch and realised he needed to catch the close of trading.

* * *

When he got back on the floor, Manita waved him over urgently. She hustled him into his office and closed the door.

"I got a phone call from that Dave Casey bloke. He called me on my personal mobile."

"What did he say?" asked Mickey.

"More importantly, how did he know my number?" she asked. "I only give it out to friends."

"I don't know. I didn't give him it. What did he say?"

She looked over her shoulder to check Sinclair was out of earshot. "He says he's got something important to tell you. He wants you to go round to see him. But he says you need to come on your own, without the bodyguards and with your mobile turned off, so the police can't track you."

"Without the bodyguards? Are you sure he insisted on that?"

"Yes," said Manita. "What are you going to do?"

62

The incident room had been emptying steadily since midday, as people took the afternoon off to make last-minute Christmas arrangements. It always puzzled Frank how stressed people got; faces dragged down by shopping and preparations. Christmas was a feast day, to be enjoyed.

But for once, even Frank couldn't look forward to it. Not with five unsolved murders and rumours that DI Hunt had asked to take over Frank's line of investigation on Mickey Summer. Armstrong had apparently said no. But he wouldn't support Frank indefinitely.

Frank needed a breakthrough.

"Let's call it a day," said Eddie, for the second time.

"You go," said Frank. "I'm just pulling together some stuff to take home."

"You're not going to work on Christmas Day, are you?"

"I might be able to sneak in a bit, while Julia and the kids are watching a film."

"I don't understand you. You won't work Sundays but you'll work Christmas Day, which is the biggest religious day of them all."

"Easter and Good Friday are more important than Christmas," Frank corrected him. "Christmas isn't as big a deal as everyone makes out. And of course it was originally a Pagan festival."

"Well it's a big deal to me. So I'm off down the Six Bells." Eddie switched off his computer and picked up his bag.

"Do that," said Frank. "Armstrong's buying apparently."

"Are you coming on down?"

"Not me."

"Come on Frank. It's almost Christmas."

"There are five families that won't be enjoying Christmas this year," said Frank.

"That's not our fault though is it? We didn't kill anyone."

"But we didn't protect them."

Eddie set his bag back down on the desk. "You said our job is to solve crime."

"We haven't done that either."

"We will do. We're ninety-nine percent done. We've got a mountain of evidence."

"But it's all circumstantial," said Frank, who had spent hours sifting through the increasingly large file, so that he knew it all off by heart. "How smart would you say Mickey Summer is?"

Eddie shrugged. "Smart enough."

"So why would a smart enough guy push Daniel Goldcup off the bridge just minutes after having a drink with him? Why let everyone know he was there?"

"I'd say it's pretty good cover."

"Why would a smart enough guy traipse through Ben Stein's rose beds then walk all over his white carpet?"

"Nervous. Mind on other things."

"And why take the Star of David?"

"To make it look like a burglary."

"But there was no need. It looked like a heart attack. Why use your Mum's car to run over your next victim? Why not hire one?"

"That one is easy," said Eddie. "No records of you hiring a car."

"Isn't it easier to buy one for cash? And why give Percy Hetherington bad drugs at a party instead of on the quiet? Why poison the woman at a lunch you're attending? Why put yourself at the scene of crime every time? It's as if he wants us to know it was him."

"Maybe that's what it is," said Eddie. "Textbook case of the criminal seeking attention."

"Nah."

"I don't see what you're getting at, Sir. The simple answer to all your questions is that Mickey Summer was at the scene of the crime every time because he killed them. That's why we've got so much circumstantial."

"I think we're missing something," said Frank.

"Well, we're not going to find it on Christmas Eve. Last offer. Come for a pint."

"Honestly, I'm fine. You go on."

Eddie shrugged. "I wish you a Merry Christmas then."

"And a happy one to you, Eddie."

63

Mickey closed the meeting room door, turned off his mobile and turned to Manita.

"Right then. I'm ready to go."

Manita shook her head. "I'm really not convinced this is a good idea, Mickey. It's dangerous going anywhere without your bodyguards. Let alone going to see this strange man."

Mickey wasn't mad keen on the idea either, but Casey had insisted he go alone and he was desperate to find out what Casey had for him. "I won't be without them for long."

"Are you sure you're not up to something illegal?"

"Cross my heart and hope to dye my hair ginger."

"I'm still not sure about it."

"Don't worry. I'll just slip out onto the walkway and I'll be back before you know it."

"And what am I supposed to do in the meantime?" asked Manita.

"Just stay in the room. Make a bit of noise every now and then. Talk to yourself. Make some phone calls. Improvise."

"What if Sinclair comes in to check on you? What do I tell him?"

"Then tell him the truth. Tell him I walked out onto the walkway saying I may be some time. Captain Oates and all that."

She sighed, then shrugged her shoulders. "All right."

Mickey crossed over the room and opened the glass door onto

the outside walkway. A rush of cold air lifted the papers off the desk and Manita slapped them back down again.

Mickey pressed a finger to his lips. "Shssh!"

"Sorry," she said. "And for goodness sake be careful out there. Keep away from the edge."

"Too right I will. I don't fancy the express ride to the ground floor." He closed the window gently and pulled his jacket tight against the wind. The walkway was about three metres wide and was bordered by two wires, one at knee height and the other at chest height. They didn't look particularly robust and Mickey didn't fancy relying on them to stop him falling off. He shook his head clear. He had to stop thinking about that. He hated heights.

He needed to walk by a half-dozen meeting rooms to get round to the other side of the building. Fortunately, the people in the first room were so wrapped up in their business that they didn't see him. Neither did the woman in the next room who was working on her laptop with her back to the window. But as he approached the third window he was spotted. It was some boys from fixed income. Mickey winked at them, then bent down to pick up an imaginary wet cloth which he wrung out as he whistled and pretended to clean the windows.

He didn't get a laugh, but then people in fixed income stopped laughing a long time ago. They turned back to their meeting and Mickey walked on, relieved that they hadn't asked any questions. He came to the corner and as soon as he rounded it he was hit by a gust of wind. With nothing to hold on to Mickey was thrown back out to the edge of the walkway. He grabbed the top wire with both hands. It held. He looked down at the cars and street-lights way below. His head started to spin. He shut his eyes. If he slipped through the wires the next stop was the pavement, hundreds of feet below. Accident number six. And Brighouse would probably still suspect Mickey.

He tightened his grip. The wind suddenly dropped. He pushed off from the wire, ran over to the side of the building and hugged the window.

On the other side, Valerie from Human Resources looked to be fielding an angry complaint from a member of staff. No prizes for guessing what that was about. Her mouth dropped when she saw Mickey. He pointed to the door handle.

Valerie rounded the table and opened the door. "What are you doing out there, Mickey?"

"Trying to get in."

"You shouldn't be out there at all in these high winds."

"Let me in then."

She opened the door fully and Mickey stepped into the room. "'Scuse me for interrupting," he said to the man. "Bonus not up to scratch?"

"None of your business," he said.

"Happy Christmas anyway," said Mickey.

He winked at Valerie, opened the door as quietly as possible and stepped into the corridor.

Aware that Sinclair was sitting round the corner only fifty metres away, Mickey held his breath and crept to the fire escape. His security pass let him through the door to the internal stairs and he took them two at a time all the way down to the underground parking. Then he ran out into the street and down to the taxi rank.

* * *

The receptionist at Casey's Gym looked up from her magazine. "You again."

"And you again," said Mickey. "That's a double co-incidence."

"If you're looking for Dave, he ain't in."

"When will he be back?"

"Dunno."

"I'll wait."

"Suit yourself."

Mickey took a seat and picked up a bodybuilding glossy. He flicked through pages of veins and muscles but was soon bored. He dropped the magazine and moved to check his phone before remembering he'd switched it off as instructed. No bodyguard and no phone. He turned to look at the meat-heads pumping iron in the gym and suddenly felt very vulnerable. It was another ten minutes before Casey finally arrived.

"Nice of you to turn up," said Mickey.

"Come into my office," replied Casey.

He led the way through the gym and into the room behind a one-way mirror. He took a seat behind his desk.

"So, what's the big secret?" asked Mickey.

"I thought you might like to know who jumped you the other day near Brick Lane."

"Too right," said Mickey. "Who was it?"

"What's this information worth to you then?"

Mickey shook his head. "You're a legend, Casey. A thousand pounds?"

Casey laughed. "That's loose change for you, Mickey. Let's make it ten."

"Bloody Hell! OK, ten then."

Casey smiled. "Cash."

"Agreed. So who was it?"

Casey nodded into the gym at the big black guy that Mickey recognised from his last visit. "It was Winston and a couple of his mates."

Mickey turned to look at Winston doing bench presses. He now noticed a bandage and realised it was probably covering the bite mark he'd left in the leg.

"How do you know it was him?"

"I paid him to do it."

Mickey swung back round to Casey. "What the hell did you do that for?"

"Because someone paid me to get a job done on you."

"Who?" Mickey's mind was racing.

Casey fixed Mickey a stare. "So it really wasn't you then?"

"Of course not. My brother was nearly killed for God's sake."

"We had to make it look realistic."

"I don't get this," said Mickey, sitting down. "Why are you telling me this? What's to stop me going to the police with this? I took a bite out of someone's leg, right where Winston has a fresh bandage. I'll bet the police could find an imprint of my teeth."

Casey shook his head. "I wouldn't recommend that. The police already suspect me and they think you put me up to it. If you confirm it was me they'll be all over you."

"How do you know what the police think?"

"That DI Brighouse was round here earlier. Asking if I had any ideas who jumped you in Brick Lane."

Brighouse again. He was obviously not going to stop until he had Mickey behind bars.

"What did you tell him?" Mickey asked.

Casey held a hand up as a stop then pointed through the window back into the gym. "There's two hundred kilos on that bar."

Mickey turned to see Winston psyching up for a lift. He took three quick breaths then snatched the bar. Veins bulged as he lifted it over his head.

"So what did you tell him?" Mickey asked a second time.

"I don't talk to filth on principle do I? But he knows you paid me two hundred and ten thousand pounds the other day. He thinks that was advance payment for jumping you in Brick Lane. He really does think you are the killer, Mickey."

"What else do you know about this then?" asked Mickey. "Tell me."

Casey crossed his arms and leant back in his chair. "This courier drops off an envelope with ten grand cash in it and a letter saying I get another ten when the job is done. Instructions are to jump you and make it look like we wanted to kill you but not to do any serious damage."

"Why are you telling me all this?"

Casey sniffed. "I think you're innocent."

Mickey was surprised at how relieved he was to hear Casey say that out loud. "I am."

"So, someone is setting you up for murder."

"Do you have any idea who?"

Casey shrugged. "Someone who knows about our relationship. Someone well connected to the police. Maybe even someone in the police."

"The police?"

"How else would they be able to get away with it for so long?"

64

Christmas morning. Breakfast alone. Just a bodyguard and a hangover for company. Mickey regretted finishing the second bottle of wine when he'd got in the night before, but his mind had been racing with what Casey had told him. And this morning it had picked up where it left off. There could be no doubt now. Someone was trying to frame him for the murders. And they were doing a bloody good job of it.

Mickey moved to the window and looked out on a dockside that was as empty as the Hammer's trophy cabinet. Light drizzle fell on the grey water. At least he was alive though. Poor Daniel and Vanni and the others. And all their families, getting up for Christmas with a loved-one missing. Going through the motions just to keep their minds off it.

Mickey hadn't bothered going through the motions. Hadn't even got a tree this year. And he didn't have any presents to put under it. Nothing even from Helen. Just a card, though she never was big on Christmas presents. She normally just drew him a painting or made up a poem. She hadn't bothered with that this year.

He hoped Helen liked his present for her. It had been a pain carving out the letters for Whitwell Farm. Cut his finger at one point as well. All just because she liked hand-made presents. Bonkers. Though, if truth be told, he'd actually surprised himself by the end and had started to enjoy it. He felt proud of making something with his hands. Helen was always saying how everyone has a little bit of creativity in them. That was what was missing in a lot of lives. Could be she had a point. At the very least she should appreciate the effort.

But he was also worried it might backfire. She might think he was being too pushy, banging on about the farm. She could be angry that the present had an ulterior motive. But what did he have to lose?

He decided to put on a Christmas compilation disc. He turned the volume low while he shaved and showered. He dressed smartly for the sake of his mum. He was tempted to have an early beer but fought the urge, fixed a coffee and went back to the window.

It had stopped raining and a low sun struggled through the clouds. An old man was walking a brute of a dog. This inspired Mickey to walk to his mum's. It would help him relax and the exercise wouldn't go amiss. Sinclair wasn't big on the walk idea so he followed in the car, kerb crawling about twenty metres behind. Mickey felt like an extra in some gangster movie.

65

"Not that way!" Frank called to his kids, who were sliding away down a pavement.

"This is the way home," replied Billy.

"But we want to go over the fields," said Frank. "Make a walk of it, so you've got room for your turkey."

"We want to get home," said Billy. "It's freezing."

"I know. It's a brilliant Christmas morning, isn't it."

"And we want to open our presents. Please, Dad."

Frank turned to Julia. "What do you want to do?"

"It is bitterly cold," she said. "And we are all dressed for church rather than the Arctic."

"Fair weather walkers," said Frank. He put an arm around Julia and followed in the children's footsteps.

"That was an interesting point the priest made today," said Julia.

Frank hadn't really listened to the sermon. He'd been replaying the last interview with Mickey Summer. Couldn't get it out of his head how cool he was in his denials. "What point was that then?"

"About Jesus being either mad, bad or telling the truth."

"Run that by me again."

"Weren't you listening?" asked Julia.

"Not exactly. Go on. What was his point?"

"Well it is recorded fact that Jesus, the man, repeatedly claimed to be the son of God, didn't he?"

"That was the gist of it," said Frank.

"So there are only three possibilities. He could have been delusional. A mad-man who believed he was the son of God. Or he could have been a bad man. A sane con-man who tricked everyone and pretended he was the son of God for whatever reason."

"But he was neither," said Frank. "Wouldn't have had the following he had if he was mad or bad."

"Precisely. Everything else we know about his life shows he was a wise and kind man. So the only other possibility about his claim to be the son of God is that he was telling the truth."

Frank stopped in his tracks.

"Do you like it?" asked Julia.

"Like what?"

She frowned. "Have you been listening?"

"Possibly not," said Frank. "Possibly not well enough."

66

The long walk managed to clear Mickey's head and give him an appetite for lunch. His mum had set out the usual crimbo spread: mash, roast potatoes and Yorkshire puddings; carrots, sprouts, onions and peppers; bread sauce, gravy, red currant jelly and sitting centre piece, a huge turkey. Given there was only Marcus, Mickey and his mum at the table, she would be finishing off turkey leftovers for weeks to come.

"Are you sure we shouldn't invite that policeman in, Mickey? It don't seem right him sitting out there on Christmas Day."

"He told me he doesn't do Christmas, which is why he's working today. Leave him out there."

"All the same, I'm going to take him out some food."

She piled up a plate and took it out to the car.

Mickey turned to Marcus. "If I tell you something, I want you to promise me you won't go to the police with it."

Marcus raised an eyebrow. "What is it?"

"I found out that it was Dave Casey who jumped us the other day in Brick Lane."

Marcus put his drink down. "What? How do you know?"

"Casey told me."

"But you paid off all the money didn't you? You didn't mess it up?"

"It's nothing to do with the loan," said Mickey. "He was paid to jump us. Instructions were to make it look realistic but not actually kill us."

"Bloody hell. Did he say who paid him?"

"He's got no idea."

"Well that is outrageous. Of course we have to tell the police. He nearly killed me."

"No." Mickey held up a hand. "The police are already suspicious that he did it. They think I fixed it up to throw them off the trail. If I tell them, it'll just confirm their suspicions."

Marcus rubbed his head where the bandage had been replaced with a sticking plaster. "So was it you then?"

"Of course it weren't, you idiot."

Marcus put his hand on Mickey's shoulder. "Look, Mickey, if it was you I understand. And I won't tell the police. I just need to know."

"No, it weren't me. What do you think I am, Marcus, gone radio rental? I think it was Sir Stanley."

"Sir Stanley?" repeated Marcus. "Why would he do that?"

"I think he's behind the whole thing. The five murders."

"Are you out of your mind, Mickey?"

"Hear me out. Who else knows everyone in the lock-in group well enough to plan each murder so that it looks like an accident? He's also got the most to gain from frightening us all into signing his new contract. It gets him out of the headlines."

Marcus frowned while he thought it through a moment. "But why would he choose you to take the blame?"

"I reckon he must have known about Dad. He's best friends with the Chief Constable, ain't he? He probably mentioned it sometime and then Sir Stanley chose me as his fall guy. He made sure I was always around when the killings happen. He also blocked my promotion to make it look like I had an extra motive."

Marcus nodded slowly. "Bit far-fetched. But possible."

"And he knew about me paying the loan off to Dave Casey. He mentioned it the other day. Must have been his Chief Constable friend keeping him in the loop again. So it would have been easy enough for him to drop off an envelope round at Dave Casey's with a message to jump on us. All that being designed to further the suspicions of DI Brighouse. A double bluff."

Marcus puffed out his cheeks. "What are you going to do about it?"

"I'm going to give my theory about Sir Stanley to DI Brighouse for starters. I'm also going to tell him something else I've discovered."

"You've obviously had a busy couple of days."

Mickey hesitated. He suspected this was going to be upsetting for Marcus. "I went up to Woodhouse School. I found out why Dad hit that teacher."

Marcus took a gulp of wine. "What did you find out?"

"About Ranger. About the bullying."

"Is that what they told you?"

"Yes. So I understand why Dad hit the bloke. I also understand why you've had it in for Americans all these years."

Marcus turned to look out the window. Mum was passing the plate of food to Sinclair through the open car door.

Mickey let the silence hang a while. "The point is, now I can show Brighouse that Dad had good reason. He wasn't some out-of-control killer. And neither am I."

"Mum's coming," said Marcus. "Change the subject."

She came back smiling. "It didn't feel right him sitting out there with his sandwiches, while we tuck into a feast."

"You're a saint, Mum," said Marcus.

"You're right about the feast in any case," said Mickey. "You've done us proud."

"I've done my best. I'm sure you get prettier looking meals in your posh City restaurants, but home cooking is better for you."

"Too right, Mum." Marcus stood over the turkey ready to carve. He sliced off some breast and served them all, Mum first of course.

"Are you feeling all right, Mickey?" his Mum asked, passing the potatoes. "You don't seem yourself."

"I can't celebrate like a normal Christmas when those others are dead," replied Mickey. Not to mention the fact that someone was trying to kill him and frame him for murder at the same time.

"Try and cheer up, for Mum's sake," said Marcus.

"I am trying," said Mickey. "But I can't just pretend nothing has happened."

"Let's change the subject. Whose is that spanking new camper van along the street mother?"

"The Donahue's," she replied. "He just retired. They're driving to Andorra in the spring."

"Nice," said Marcus. "Though not my cup of tea of course. Far too small."

"Andorra?" joked Mickey.

"I meant the camper van," said Marcus. "Though it applies to both I guess."

"Daniel Goldcup planned to take his wife around the world when he retired," said Mickey, unable to stop himself sinking into negative thoughts again. "He won't be travelling anywhere now, will he?"

"Who's Daniel Goldcup?" asked Mum.

"He's the colleague of Mickey's who jumped into the Thames." Marcus glared at Mickey.

"Oh dear." His Mum clasped a hand to her mouth.

"Let's keep the conversation on more pleasant topics," said Marcus. "What do we think the Queen will have to say?"

"Well it's not been a great year for her has it?" His mum suddenly set down her cutlery and looked at Mickey. "You're not right are you?" She placed her hand to his forehead. "It's all this stress and worry. You need a break from work."

Mickey loved the feel of her hand on his head. But he knew Marcus was right, he needed to make more of an effort. Couldn't spoil Mum's Christmas. He sat up in his chair and knocked back half a glass of wine.

"I'll be taking a break soon enough," he said. "I'm moving firms."

"Oh dear."

"It's nothing to worry about."

"Mickey's coming to work with me." Marcus helped himself to more potatoes. "We're going to rename the firm Summer Securities."

"Well that is good news." She beamed. "The two of you working together."

Mickey nodded, "It'll be a family firm. We can get you a job there if you like, Mum."

"What would I do?"

"Trade Eurobonds," said Mickey. "Run the derivatives. You choose."

"Don't be silly." She smiled, obviously pleased that her two boys got on so well that they were going to work together.

"So what will you do with your garden leave, Mickey?" asked Marcus.

"Take a holiday for sure. Any ideas Mum? You can come with me."

She smiled. "I'd love to."

"That's a great idea," said Marcus. "I'll join you. At least for a few days."

"It's been a long time since we had a family holiday," said Mum.

"We should go somewhere special," said Marcus. "How about the Maldives? Warm sea, white sand."

Mum frowned. "I don't want to travel far."

"I forgot you're afraid of flying," said Marcus.

"She's afraid of crashing," Mickey corrected him. "Ain't that right, Mum? You've got no problem with flying."

"I stand corrected. You drive her somewhere then, Mickey."

"I'm up for that. What do you think, Mum?"

She smiled. "I can't wait."

67

"It's your move, Dad."

Frank shook his mind clear of Mickey Summer and focused on the chess board. Billy's queen was bang in line with his bishop. It would kill Billy's chances if he took his queen but it had to be done. Harsh lessons in life and all that. He moved his hand towards the piece …

"You can't move your bishop, Dad," said Billy. "You're in check, remember."

"Sorry. I forgot."

"Come on then."

"Give me a second to think."

"You've taken about ten hours already," said Billy.

"I got distracted. I'm on the case now." Frank started to work through the possibilities to get out of check. He might have to lose the bishop to Billy's queen. And then Billy's queen would also be right in amongst it. He'd be able to pick off his pieces one by one.

"Come on, Dad."

"Sorry." Frank gave the bishop up for dead and concentrated on saving his king and queen. There was only one move which left both safe so he took it.

Billy jumped his knight into a gap Frank hadn't spotted.

"Check mate!"

Frank looked for a get out but couldn't find one. "It is check mate."

"Have I really won?"

"Yep. Clever lad."

Billy's eyes lit up and he ran out into the garden to tell the others. Frank was pleased for Billy, even if it had been less a case of him winning the game and more Frank losing it. He'd been so distracted by Mickey Summer that he'd completely missed the knight.

He thought again about what Julia had said. He wondered whether Summer, like Jesus, was mad or bad, or whether he was just telling the truth. But what about all the circumstantial evidence against him? He walked over to the dying fire and threw on some fresh logs. They'd come from the wood pile in the back yard and were too large and damp to catch fire. But as Frank sat back in his chair, thick grey smoke began to waft up into the chimney.

He'd been distracted by all the circumstantial. He'd assumed that where there's smoke there's fire. Trouble was, sometimes, where there's smoke, there's simply smoke.

* * *

Mickey sat by the phone all evening, hoping, keeping himself awake with red wine and channel hopping.

But at five-past midnight he realised that Helen was not going to ring so he turned off the TV, puffed up his pillows and knocked out the light. Of course she might have just forgotten to ring. Might not have got his phone messages. More likely her silence was her way of showing disapproval at the carving and the not so subtle attempt to persuade her to give Whitwell Farm a chance. It had back-fired.

He'd probably made her even more determined to push ahead with a divorce in the New Year. He lay down in bed and closed his eyes. Let it be. He was tired of fighting it.

68

Frank wanted to run his idea by someone who would appreciate that this was simply him thinking aloud, rather than clutching at straws. So he took Eddie over the road to a greasy-spoon café that served weak coffee and strong tea.

"What if Mickey Summer is telling the truth?" said Frank. "What if he's innocent and the real killer is setting him up? What if it's someone who knew about Mickey's dad and knew we'd find out, and decided to set Mickey up as the fall guy?"

"It's possible," said Eddie after a moment's reflection. "But not probable. Too difficult to organise."

"D'you reckon? Wouldn't be too difficult for any of his colleagues to organise the killings around Mickey's diary. And they could easily have seen what type and size of shoes Mickey used down the gym, and worn the same when they went round to Ben Stein's house."

"But what about the money he paid Dave Casey?"

"Paying off a loan," said Frank. "Just as he said."

"And the gambling habit and the divorce?"

"Neither are crimes."

"So why did he give us false alibis?" asked Eddie.

"He was frightened," said Frank. "Because he knew we'd find

out about his dad."

"And what about the Brick Lane set-up then?"

"That wasn't Mickey either. That was also the killer playing sweet and making us extra suspicious of Mickey."

"You mean like a double bluff? Bit too clever that."

"It's all been a bit too clever," said Frank. "That's another thing that makes me doubt it's been Mickey Summer. He's not daft, but neither is he the sharpest tool in the shed."

"What about the car then?" asked Eddie. "How did the killer get hold of Mickey's mum's car?"

"We don't know his mum's car was used. All we know for sure is that a black car was used in the hit and run. We don't even know that it was a Golf."

Eddie grimaced as he pushed away his half-full cup of coffee. "So what are you going to do about it?"

Frank was about to answer when his phone rang.

It was Hunt. "We've got it, Sir."

"Got what?" asked Frank.

"We've found the mother's Golf."

"I'll be right back." Frank picked up his jacket and turned to Eddie. "Come on."

"So what are you going to do about it?" asked Eddie, as they walked out the café. "I mean about this new theory."

"Forget it," said Frank. "I was just thinking aloud."

* * *

Frank jogged down the street and thanked the Lord he hadn't tried out his theory on DI Hunt, or worse still, DCS Armstrong. Arriving back in the incident room, the buzz was clearly more than the usual post-Christmas chatter.

DI Hunt hurried over to Frank. "We've got him now!"

"Where did you find the car?" asked Frank.

"On the A111, near Hadley Wood. December ninth."

Hunt pulled a picture out of a folder and Frank suddenly realised the car had only turned up in CCTV pictures and not physically. "Let's have a look," he said, trying to hide his disappointment. Hunt handed over the picture and Frank checked the date and time. "So it fits perfectly the timing of Vanni Gamberoni being run down. Given there are no markings on the bonnet it must have been taken just before."

"On his way there," agreed Hunt.

"But you can't make out the driver's face."

"We don't need to," said Hunt. "We know its Mickey Summer."

"You need to check the rest of the film. See if you can get his face."

Hunt shook his head. "This is the best we can get."

"Well done anyway." Frank sighed as he handed back the photo. "But it's just more flipping circumstantial."

"It's better than nothing," said Hunt. "We haul Summer in and show him the photo. He's bound to crack."

Frank suspected otherwise. But what did he know? Seemed like he couldn't tell one end of Mickey Summer from the other. Maybe it was time to let someone else take over. He suspected Armstrong would think the same thing if he didn't get a breakthrough with this next interview. "Let's bring him in again."

69

The markets were quiet and there was no sign of the traditional year-end rally. Those who were in were sorting through their admin backlogs and reading books they'd got as Christmas presents.

Glen pulled back an elastic band and fired a paper pellet in the direction of the sales desk. He didn't look to see who he'd hit. "This is deadly," he announced without a hint of irony. "We might as well nip down to All Bar One. What do you think, Mickey?"

"Not for me."

He wasn't in the mood for socialising. His mind was screwed up enough without adding alcohol to the mix.

"Why not?" asked Glen.

"Got a lot on my mind. But you go get a drink. Stop you bothering me."

Glen didn't wait for a second invitation. He picked up his jacket and called across the desk. "Drinky-poos anyone!"

The desk emptied in short order. Mickey closed his eyes and listened to the quiet hum of computers for a moment. He thought about ringing Helen. But what was the point? She'd made her position clear. She wanted a divorce. She wasn't interested in giving the dream home a chance.

A light glowed on his dealer board. He regretted taking the call when he discovered it was DI Brighouse.

"Inspector."

"Mr Summer, I'd like you to come down to the station."

"Why's that then?"

"I want to ask you a few questions."

"Look, I don't want to be difficult," said Mickey. "But I'm bored of answering the same old questions. My lawyer said last time that if you haven't got any fresh evidence then leave me alone. Otherwise its harassment."

That was the word Frank had been worried about. The last thing he needed was to be responsible for the Met being sued for harassment. "We have got fresh evidence, Mr Summer. We've got your mum's stolen car."

"Really? And?"

"And I'd like you to come down to the station so I can ask you a few questions."

*　*　*

Frank switched on the recording equipment and turned to the microphone. "This is a recorded interview at Snow Hill Police Station. I am DI Frank Brighouse and present with me is DCS Armstrong." He nodded at Mickey and Veronica. "Could you identify yourselves please?"

"Mickey Summer."

Frank stared at Mickey. He was definitely not his usual cocky self. He looked anxious. He was fidgety. Maybe he was ready to finally crack.

"Veronica Edwards, solicitor for Mr Summer."

Frank went through the usual drill. "You do not have to say anything. But it may harm your defence if you do not mention when questioned something which you later rely on in court. Anything you do say may be given in court as evidence. You are not under arrest and are free to leave the station at any time. Is that clear?"

"Crystal," said Mickey.

Frank cleared his throat. "Now that we've found the car it's time to come clean, Mickey. Tell us everything you know about the murders and we will make sure it counts in your favour when it comes to court."

"I've already told you everything."

"I don't think you have," said Frank. "So I'm giving you a chance to confess. It will be easier for you if you do so."

"Nothing to confess, mate."

Frank placed a black-and-white photograph on the table, facing Mickey.

"This photograph was taken by a CCTV camera near Hadley Wood on December ninth. You recognise the car don't you? It's your mother's Golf. The one that was supposedly stolen."

"I can't tell if that is mum's car but I'll take your word for it."

"It's her registration plate."

"It'll be her car then," said Mickey.

"And that's you behind the wheel isn't it?"

"No it's not. You can't see the face anyway."

"The photo was taken shortly before Vanni Gamberoni was run over," continued Frank. "A black Golf fits the spec of the car used. We can tell you see, from the height of the bonnet, the size of the wheel tread, the paint scratches; they all match. Think about that a moment, Mickey."

"You told me all that before. I told you I don't know about bonnet heights and all that. But I know for certain it's not me driving that car."

"So who do you think it was?"

"I suppose it's whoever nicked my mum's car. So have you found it then?"

Frank ignored the question. "So this thief who took your mother's car just happens to be driving round Hadley Wood the night Vanni Gamberoni is run over."

"Looks that way."

Frank shook his head. "We've had too many coincidences already, Mickey. It was you driving. So tell me, where have you hidden the car?"

"The only time I drove it, I left it outside my mum's house, on her birthday."

"We're going to find the car. We've got every available resource on it. It won't take long. And when we do, we'll be able to show that it knocked down Gamberoni and that is was you driving."

"Have you thought about another possibility?" asked Mickey. "That someone else has done the killings. And set them all up to look like it was me, including nicking my Mum's car? Someone who is well connected to the police and so able to know how the inquiry is progressing and what buttons to push to keep your suspicions focused on me."

"Who might that be?" asked Frank, intrigued to know whether Summer had a candidate.

"The person who has most to gain from what's happened. Not financial gain. But something more valuable to him than money. His reputation."

"Don't keep us in suspense, Mickey."

"Sir Stanley."

Frank laughed.

"Why are you laughing?" asked Mickey.

"Because we ruled him out in the first ten minutes. He was out of the country when Daniel Goldcup died and he has perfect alibis for the others. Unlike you, I should point out."

"He could have paid a hit man," said Mickey.

"Forget it," snapped Frank. "We're not going to be distracted by this."

Frank took the picture back from Mickey and put it inside its envelope. He bridged his hands under his chin.

"I've been talking to your mum, Mickey. She explained how you had a rough time as a child after your dad went to prison for murder."

"Yeah, well I've found out something for you to stick in your pipe and smoke, Sherlock. That teacher had been bullying my brother. That's why my dad hit him."

Frank wasn't to be distracted. "Your school work collapsed, you got into fights, mixed with the wrong …"

"I know the story," interrupted Mickey. "I was there."

"She remembers how you were so upset you often wet the bed."

"Not that it matters," said Mickey, "but that was my brother. He'd been so embarrassed he paid me a pound a time to pretend it was me. We swapped over the mattresses and I took the earache from Mum."

"Well, I guess we'll have to check that story out with your brother."

"He wasn't the only kid who ever wet his bed." Mickey turned to Veronica. "Look, this is all bonkers. It's just going over the same old ground. How much more of it do I have to take?"

Veronica sat forward in her seat. "We do appear to be no further forward, DI Brighouse. The only new material you have is a photograph of Mickey's mother's car which you have failed to show has any relevance to my client. So, are you going to bring a charge?"

Frank hesitated. They weren't ready for that. And she knew it. "Not yet," he conceded.

Veronica closed her notebook. "So, this interview has come to an end."

Mickey stood up with her.

"We'll find the car," said Frank.

"I hope you do," said Mickey.

"Oh, and don't be in too much of a hurry to spend that lock-in of yours."

"You want a share of it now as well?"

"Not a share," said Frank. "I might take it all off you. Confiscate the lot."

70

A heavy mist soaked their faces as they walked up the street, on the look-out for taxis. Sinclair kept a couple of paces back so Mickey felt relatively free to talk.

"Can the police really seize my money?" he asked.

Veronica wiped a flick of wet hair from her eyes. "They can seize the assets of anyone they suspect of committing crime."

"They only need to *suspect!* Well then, I can kiss my lock-in good-bye."

Veronica flagged a cab, which failed to stop. "Don't worry. I'm pretty sure DI Brighouse was bluffing."

"How do you know?"

"He's frustrated that he can't hang anything on you, so he mentioned seizing assets to show he's still in charge of the situation."

"So if Brighouse wants to show he's the boss he'll go ahead and seize my money, if he can."

"He'd have to convince a civil court the balance of probability suggests you have benefited from the proceeds of crime. Even then it would only be temporary. They have to give the assets back if they can't actually prove your guilt."

"If they can't actually prove my guilt. You sound as if you think I am guilty."

"When they can't prove your guilt, then."

Mickey stopped her in her tracks. "Veronica, if you don't believe I'm innocent, then I don't want you on my team."

She took a long time before answering. "I told you when we first met, I do my job professionally and without prejudice. What you need to understand is that it doesn't matter how much you protest your innocence to the police, there is a mass of circumstantial evidence building up against you. If your mother's car does turn out to have been involved in the hit and run, then you're in real trouble."

"I didn't do it, Veronica. I'm not a killer. And by the way, neither was my dad. I found out what happened. The teacher had been bullying Marcus so bad that he'd run away from the school. That's why dad hit him."

A cab pulled up and Veronica climbed into the back seat. "We should meet early in the New Year and you can tell me all about that. In the meantime, call me immediately if the police ask to see you again."

"Don't worry," said Mickey. He didn't want her to leave before he'd convinced her of his innocence, but he realised he couldn't do that. But at least he wanted to leave on a more friendly tone. "Doing anything special to see in the New Year?"

She hesitated. "I'm going to a riverboat party on the Thames, with my old university friends. And you?"

"Stopping at home with my new security friend," said Mickey, glancing at Sinclair. "Enjoy your party."

He shut the door and the cab drew away. Mickey felt very alone. He knew that New Year's Eve traffic across London to the Wharf would be a nightmare, so he headed for the nearest tube station. At a news-stand, he read the headline on the Standard: 'Police Arrest City Killer.' Beside the headline was his picture.

* * *

Back in the incident room, Frank walked up to the white board and placed a question mark beside the 'bedwetting' entry.

"We need to check that one out again with the mother and brother," he said. "If they can confirm it was Mickey that wet his bed, that would come in very handy."

"What is it about bedwetting anyway?" asked Eddie. "I don't get it."

"Didn't you study the homicidal triad in training?"

"Rings a bell," said Eddie, unconvincingly.

"Not a very loud one though," said Frank. "It's a common pattern of childhood behaviour in psychopaths. Cruelty to animals, pyromania and continued bedwetting after the age of ten."

"And we already know from Mrs Sidnall that Mickey burnt her cat," said Eddie. "So that's two in one, I guess."

"Bedwetting completes the triad," said Frank. "It's only a theory of course. But it's another piece of the mosaic."

"And how do you think the mosaic is coming on?" asked Eddie.

"Nicely. Very nicely indeed."

* * *

Mickey imagined people's reactions when they read the headline. People who knew him and who might give him the benefit of the doubt, and the majority who didn't, and wouldn't. He turned his phone on and checked his messages. He wondered if anyone had seen it yet.

The first was from Manita. "Hi Mickey, can you give me a call. Everyone's asking me what's going on."

Next Glen. "Hello darling. Those silly policemen are on the wrong track again I see. Give me a call when you get a moment."

People obviously had seen the headlines. There were seven more messages. He didn't want to listen to them. He dialled his mum, but only got the answerphone. "Mum, its Mickey. Just ringing to say, don't believe what's in the papers. I've not done anything wrong. I've got nothing to do with these murders. Speak soon. Love you Mum."

He was about to call Helen when his phone rang. It was Manita. "Are you all right, Mickey?"

"I'm fine."

"The Standard says you've been arrested?"

"I went in for questioning. That's all."

"Everyone is talking about it."

Mickey could imagine. "Stick out a global email from me saying I was not arrested. I have not been charged. And I have done nothing wrong."

"I'll get it out straight away," she said. "The phone has been ringing non-stop. Are you coming back to the office?"

"I was going to. I'm stood outside the tube now." Mickey checked his watch. "But now that I'm on the front page of the Standard accused of murdering five people …"

"Perhaps you should just go home."

"You're a mind reader," said Mickey.

He desperately wanted to get behind closed doors with the phone off the hook. But first there was something he had to check out.

71

As Mickey and Sinclair approached the entrance to Summer Research, two men in fluorescent bibs were taking down the old sign, whilst at their feet, wrapped in bubble wrap, was the new sign for 'Summer Securities'.

Passing through reception onto the trading floor, Mickey was struck by how few people were in the office. It was always quiet between Christmas and New Year, but as he looked around he realised that half the work stations were decked out with new equipment but empty of any personal belongings. They were unused. Marcus had clearly over-expanded. No wonder the business was bleeding cash.

Outside Marcus's office his PA, Michelle, looked up from a copy of the Evening Standard and did a double take.

"That's right," said Mickey. "I'm not in prison."

"I didn't believe it anyway," she said, standing up to take a peck on the cheek.

"Wish there were more like you, Michelle. Good Christmas?"

"A quiet one. It's difficult to celebrate anything with redundancies in the air."

"Tell me about it. It's difficult to celebrate when your colleagues are being killed around you."

She slapped a hand to her mouth. "I'm sorry, Mickey. You've got more to worry about than me. It's terrible what's been happening."

She looked Sinclair up and down then turned back to Mickey. "Can I ask you a question?"

"I'm already married, Michelle but thanks for thinking of me."

She laughed. "Is it true that you're going to invest in the business?"

"Sshh!"

"Sorry."

Mickey was both shocked and angry that Marcus had been so indiscreet. But of course it wasn't Michelle's fault. "That is a totally hush-hush, what-the-Queen-wears-in-bed, category-ten, state secret. Understand?"

"Of course, Mickey. I really hope you do. Marcus says we just need to keep going a couple more months and then we will …"

She broke off at a disturbance in Marcus' office. Inside, some plum-faced analyst was shouting.

"No points for guessing what he's mad about," said Mickey.

"The lack of bonus," she said. "Like yours truly."

The door flung open and the man stormed out. He stopped when he saw Mickey. "Does Royal Shire Bank need a retail analyst, Mickey?"

"Not at the minute."

"Put the word around for me, will you. I'm leaving this dump."

"It's a free market," called Marcus, from inside the office. "There are plenty of others who'd be happy to take your seat."

"Oh yeah, like they're queuing up," he yelled as he stormed over to his desk, grabbed his jacket and headed for the exit.

Marcus waved Mickey into the office. He was holding a copy of the Standard. "What's this all about?"

"Ignore it," said Mickey. "They're making it up."

"So you weren't arrested."

"I wouldn't be here if I was."

"Now you see why I don't read the rag." Marcus waved at the analyst, who was looking back over his shoulder as he reached the exit. "Don't worry about Julian by the way. He'll be all right once he's calmed down. He knew it was a gamble coming here. They all did. But our white knight is about to ride to the rescue, aren't you, Mickey?"

"How come Michelle knows about it?" asked Mickey.

"She knows everything. Did you see the new Summer Securities sign on your way in?"

"They were just putting it up," said Mickey. "I also saw the banks of empty desks. I'm wondering how much those are costing you?"

"Infrastructure spending. They'll be filled in due course."

"No wonder you're bleeding cash."

"Don't worry about it." Marcus pointed to a corner office on the other side of the floor. "I'm fitting out that office over there for you. What do you think?"

"I probably don't need an office," said Mickey. Now that it was his own money there would probably be a few things done differently. "I haven't come about that anyway, Marcus. I want a straight answer from you on something."

Marcus walked over to a cabinet and squeezed a plastic Santa. It began to sing 'Merry Christmas'.

"Christmas present from the Telecom team," he said. "See,

not everyone round here is as disgruntled as Julian." He laughed. "You'll like the Telecom team, Mickey. They do a sheet with daily trading ideas ..."

"Shut up will you. And let me tell you what I just found out at the police station."

Marcus sat down. "What?"

"Sir Stanley was out of the country when Daniel was killed and he has cast-iron alibis for the other times."

"And?"

"And so I don't reckon he's got anything to do with the killings."

Marcus nodded. "Good. It upset me to think he was behind this. He's a knight of the realm, after all."

"But it means it also weren't Sir Stanley who got Dave Casey to jump us."

"That follows."

"So guess what else follows?"

Marcus frowned. "You've lost me now."

"It must have been you."

"Me?! You're off your head little brother."

Mickey studied Marcus in silence for a moment. He'd always been a brilliant liar.

"Who else would have thought of using Dave Casey?" asked Mickey.

Marcus shrugged and rolled a paperweight globe around on his desk. "I really don't know."

"It was you that paid him weren't it?"

Marcus made as if he was about to protest. Then he dropped his hands and smiled. "OK, I admit it. Of course it was me."

"Bloody hell, Marcus. What did you do that for?"

"Why do you think?" asked Marcus. "To get Brighouse off your back."

"Why didn't you tell me about it?"

Marcus laughed. "Have you ever been able to keep a secret, Mickey? If you didn't actually tell the whole City, your body language is so transparent that Brighouse would have read it anyway."

"I can't believe you did that. And I thought you were meant to be the intelligent one."

"No harm done is there. Except to me. I'm the one who got whacked, remember."

"No harm done?" asked Mickey. "Only that the police didn't believe it was for real. It's made them even more suspicious of me."

"I was only trying to help."

"Well it didn't work, Marcus. It's like your alibi idea. They found out those were false too. The killer don't need to frame me for the murders. You're doing a fine job for him."

Marcus rubbed his forehead. "I am sorry, Mickey. It just seemed like a simple way to throw the police off you."

"I'll have to tell them the truth."

"Don't be ridiculous."

"It's best to come clean. Like I have done on the alibis."

"No way," said Marcus. "They're already suspicious. If you admit I fixed that up, they'll just think I'm in cahoots with you."

Mickey sighed. "Well, what the hell shall I do then?"

"Just let it drop."

Mickey looked at Marcus. His anger slowly subsided. "All right. But I don't want any more of your help. Seriously, no more stuff behind my back."

"Promise. Besides, you have less than forty-eight hours to go, and then you'll get your lock-in and be in the clear. In the meantime, you just keep your head down and stick close to your bodyguard." Marcus checked his watch. "I've got to run. New Year's Eve party back in Oxford to get to. What are you doing tonight?"

"Keeping my head down and sticking close to my bodyguard."

72

Beer in the fridge, a bottle of red on the coffee table, assorted bags of nibbles piled on the sofa and a hundred or so TV channels to flick through. Mickey had just decided that a New Year's Eve 'in' might not be so bad after all, when the doorbell rang.

"Were you expecting anyone?" asked Sinclair, walking off to answer the door.

"Only the Queen to run her New Year's honours list by me," said Mickey, but his joking couldn't hide his anxiety.

He set down his wine, rubbed his hands on his knees then got to his feet. He turned to face the door then relaxed when he heard a woman's voice. He walked through into the hallway. It was Veronica, in heels and a green ball gown.

"Let me guess," said Mickey. "You've no money for a taxi so you've come to borrow my pumpkin."

"Not quite," she said. "My river cruise party starts from St Catherine's pier. When I realised how close it was to your house I thought I'd pop in to wish you a Happy New Year."

"Well Happy New Year to you," said Mickey. "Can I get you a drink?"

"No, I won't come in."

"Understood. Don't want to miss the boat."

There was a moment's silence in which Mickey sensed Veronica wanted to say something else.

"Also," she said eventually. "I wanted to tell you that I do believe you're innocent."

"Thanks a million." Mickey felt suddenly elated. "That means a lot. Are you sure you haven't got time for one quick drink? It is New Year's Eve and I can't go out."

She checked her watch. "I suppose the boat doesn't sail until eight."

"Good call," said Mickey, leading her through to the living room. "I can only offer you red wine. I wasn't expecting company."

She took a glass and walked over to the window. "The towers are actually quite stunning at night, aren't they?"

"Thinking of flying into them at night now?" asked Mickey.

She laughed. "The Docks are pretty too. All those boats ready to sail off to faraway places."

"Most of them never seem to move," said Mickey. "Just parked there by bankers as luxury tax breaks, from what I can tell. But I do enjoy the sound of the rigging in the wind at night. That's very calming."

"Yes, it is all quite different from the nine-to-five Canary Wharf that everyone thinks of."

Mickey laughed. "More like five to nine than nine to five."

"Yes, you do work long hours. I think people forget that."

"Don't worry. I'm not looking for sympathy for bankers."

"That's just as well."

Mickey started scrolling through his MP3 player. "What's your music taste?"

"Pretty eclectic."

"I ain't got any of theirs," said Mickey. "How about a bit of classical?"

"Why not?"

He only had the classical on there for Helen. Hadn't played any since she left. Veronica nodded her appreciation as the music started. "Somehow I didn't think you would like classical music."

"What did you think I'd like? Music hall? Down at the Old Bull and Bush, and all that."

She laughed. "I don't know really. I just didn't think you'd be into Vivaldi."

"Viv who?" asked Mickey. "I thought this was the chocolate advert."

"It's Winter from Vivaldi's Four Seasons."

"It was an advert first," said Mickey. "This Viv Aldi geezer must have done a cover version."

"I never quite know whether you're being serious."

"Neither do I." Mickey smiled. "But here's a serious question: fancy a knees-up? You're dressed right for it."

"It's hardly the right music for a knees-up," said Veronica.

"A bit of Strictly Come Dancing then. I've always wanted to give it a go. Come on. And then I'll let you go catch your boat."

"I'm really not a dancer," said Veronica. "I've got two left feet."

"Then you'll balance out my two right feet." Mickey took the glass from her hand and pulled her into the middle of the room. He placed his other hand on her waist. "Any idea what we do next?"

Veronica placed her free hand on his shoulder. "We step: one, two, three – one, two, three …"

"One, two, three …" repeated Mickey as they moved off.

"That's all there is to it," she said. "Just counting."

"I never went to university remember."

She laughed. "Why do you always put yourself down?"

"That way I don't have so far to fall."

Mickey followed Veronica's lead and, taking care not to tread on her toes, they were soon making steady progress round the room. He heard the doorbell ring but didn't let the interruption break their rhythm. Sinclair would get it. He didn't want to interrupt this for anything.

"I reckon we're not doing too badly," he said. "The judges are pencilling us in for nines and tens."

Veronica laughed and Mickey held her more tightly as they upped the tempo and careered around the room. They slowed again as the violins faded, but Mickey held her just as tightly. She lifted back her head and they held each other's gaze.

Their lips met.

A cough from the other side of the room broke the silence.

Helen was standing in the doorway.

73

Stanley had drunk too much champagne and was becoming more and more irritated by the overly-enthusiastic applause for the winner of each charity bid. In previous years he'd have been bidding with the best of them. He'd always been keen to give something back to the community. No longer. That community was now calling for his title and his lock-in. Well they could have one or the other. And then go to hell.

He wandered out onto the veranda, turned his back on the ever-present bodyguards and lit a cigar.

"I thought you'd given up, Stanley."

He was about to tell the interloper to mind his own damn business, when he realised it was the Chief Constable. "It's New Year's Eve, Anthony. Join me?"

"Gave up on the Millennium," said Anthony. "So, how are you bearing up?"

Stanley sighed. "I'll be glad when it's all over."

"Just forty-eight hours and you'll be in the clear."

"Are you still confident of that?" asked Stanley.

"We're as sure as we can be that the murderer's motivation is financial. So, once the payments have been made, you should have nothing to worry about."

"If only my worries would end when the lock-ins are paid." Stanley tugged on the cigar and blew a small pall of smoke. "But that's when they really begin."

"I don't follow."

"They want me to step down, old boy."

"Retire?" asked Anthony.

"Fall on my sword."

"But why now?"

Stanley flicked some ash over the stone railing. "Apparently the press are ready to run the RSB scandal on the front pages on bonus day. You can imagine the story. A venerable institution brought to its knees by casino bankers, who then continue to pay themselves multi-million pound bonuses. And is it any wonder someone decided to take justice into their own hands?"

"That's scandalous. We'll take a very dim view of anything suggesting approval for vigilantism."

"They'll print what they want."

"You're right," accepted Anthony. "So, you're the scapegoat."

"Precisely. Still, perhaps I'm better off out of it."

"You can take your money and start again elsewhere," suggested Anthony.

"Oh, I'll have to pay back the money," said Stanley.

"They can't make you do that."

"No they can't make me. But if I don't I'll suffer the same fate as Freddie. I'll be stripped of my title, vilified for the rest of my life and never see the inside of a boardroom again."

Cheers and clapping rose inside the gallery, as another auction went to the highest bidder.

"Do you know how many millions I've given to charity over the years?" asked Stanley.

"A great deal, I'm sure," said Anthony.

225

"And of course, memories are very short. Who remembers that I made Royal Shire Bank what it is? Even if it does need some state support right now, it's still a company employing thirty thousand."

"Absolutely."

"When I started it was adrift in a backwater, utterly uncompetitive, with nothing to pitch for business other than tradition and past glories. I dragged it back up to the top table of investment banking. I made it a world-class bank again. Me."

"I know, Stanley. That's why you won the knighthood of course."

"Too damn right. For services to banking. And my only crime was not to have seen the credit crunch coming. Just like ninety-nine percent of people in finance."

"And a hundred percent of people outside," added Anthony.

"And so it needs a capital injection. A portion of the taxes we contributed over the years. We've still been a net contributor to the Chancellor's coffers."

"I'm sure."

"I gave this country one last chance to compete with the American banks," continued Stanley, who was growing ever more indignant. "And it could still be done. The government could buy out State Financial, give me free reign to build Royal Shire back up again, and we could again have a British bank able to compete on the world stage."

"I'm sure you're right."

"But they don't have the vision, you see. These politicians who have never run a business. They'll take the easy option. Playing to the galleries. They'll carry on bashing bankers until all the good ones have gone. State Financial will take over what's left of Royal Shire. And one day they'll discover Britain has no financial services industry left. There will be an almighty hullabaloo. Only by then it will be too late."

"Isn't that worth fighting for?" asked Anthony. "Give it one last push."

"I've tried everything," said Stanley. "Believe me. You don't know how hard I've tried."

74

Veronica turned to see what Mickey was staring at.

"This is my wife, Helen," said Mickey. "And this is Veronica. My lawyer. We were just having a dance, for a bit of a laugh. Come in!"

Helen blushed. "I can see I've called at a bad time."

"Not at all, Mrs Summer," said Veronica. "I was just leaving. Got a boat to catch. Seriously. New Year's Eve party on the Thames."

Helen didn't reply. She just looked down at her flat shoes as Veronica clipped passed in her heels.

Sinclair showed her out.

"That really is my lawyer," said Mickey.

"I suppose it's none of my business anymore," said Helen. "She's very pretty."

"There's nothing going on between us. We were just having a dance."

"It looked to be a little more than a dance." Helen took a deep breath. "Look, I shouldn't have come."

"Yes you should," said Mickey. "Let me take your coat."

"I won't stop. I've got a party to get to as well. Though nothing quite so glamorous as your friend's. Just round at my Aunt Barbara's in Clapham."

"I didn't think you were big on New Year's Eve parties."

"It's a joint do, to celebrate her fiftieth. And it's something of a three-line-whip."

"Where are you staying the night?" asked Mickey.

"There." She checked her watch. "Actually, I really had better get going. The tubes will be a crush if I leave it any later."

"Why don't you stop for a drink and then I'll drive you over."

She shook her head. "No thanks."

"Why did you come?" asked Mickey.

She looked back down at her feet. "I just thought that, as I was in London I should pop in to wish you a Happy New Year. I'm sorry I didn't call you on Christmas Day. I'm a bit confused about things. Not thinking straight."

"Join the club."

"I also wanted to pick up the rose quartz, if that's all right?"

Mickey looked over at it. He didn't want her to take it. But he wasn't going to make a fuss. "It's all yours."

She walked over and put in her handbag. "Thanks."

"Any other reason you came?"

"To check you were all right of course."

"I'm half left," said Mickey.

"Seriously, Mickey. I'm worried you might be killed."

"Me too." He was pleased she was worried. That at least was something. He checked his watch. "The lock-in gets paid in about forty hours. Everything will be sorted then."

"Do you really think so?" Helen shook her head. "I don't think money has ever sorted anything. It seems to always bring trouble."

"That's as maybe, but the point is that once it's paid I'll be safe. And in the meantime I'm lying low."

"I'm glad about that."

"Did you have a good Christmas?" he asked, hoping to prompt a response to his present.

"Yes thanks. It was very quiet."

"So was mine," said Mickey. "Went round Mum's."

"Is she OK?"

"She's fine. What did you think of my present then? I made it myself."

"I appreciated that. It's very good. You could have a second career as a sculptor."

"I'll change my name to Mickey Angelo."

They stood in silence a while.

"The offer's still there in any case," said Mickey. "A fresh start on Whitwell Farm. If you think you can give us another try."

"Are you sure you want to? You look like you're doing fine without me."

"Of course," said Mickey. Then he realised what she was getting at. "There's nothing happening between me and that lawyer. That was just, I don't know, a spur of the moment thing."

Helen smiled and buttoned up her coat. "I'd better be going. Happy New Year."

75

A few minutes before midnight, people started scurrying around the house to fetch drinks and re-unite with partners and friends before countdown. Frank found Julia in the living room.

The party host raised his glass and shouted. "Here's wishing everyone a happy and peaceful New Year."

"What about prosperous?" shouted someone.

"Prosperous is having a decade off," said Frank.

Julia smiled, took Frank's hand and squeezed it gently. "I'll settle for happy and peaceful."

Frank kissed her forehead.

"Ten, nine, eight …" the crowd began to count down.

All eyes now turned to the face of Big Ben on the TV screen. "Five, four, three, two, one."

The chimes rang out.

"Happy New Year!"

Glasses chinked, smiles broke out and then everything was drowned out by the thunder claps of nearby fireworks ripping open the night sky with yellow, red and green flashes.

There was a cheer, mostly of relief, when the fireworks eventually stopped and someone started up with Auld Lang Syne. The party united in song and hand clasps.

Frank's phone started pinging with incoming text messages.

"You're very popular," said Julia.

"They'll all just be from work."

Frank pulled up the messages. "Eddie: Greetings from the North Pole."

"Is he really at the North Pole?"

"He's in Scotland. But to a Londoner like Eddie it's the same thing. The next one is from a Scot, Angus, you know, the pathologist."

"What does he say?"

"Happy New Cheers."

"Quite funny," said Julia.

"It is for a pathologist."

Frank saw that the next message was from Mickey Summer.

"Happy New Year Frank. Hope for both our sakes you crack this case soon."

"More of the same," said Frank putting the phone back in his pocket and turning to look at the party. "That was some firework display wasn't it? Must have been a few grand gone up in smoke there."

"Who was that last message from?" asked Julia.

"No-one in particular."

"Who was it from?"

"Mickey Summer."

"What does he want?" she asked.

"Wants me to get on and crack the case."

"The cheek of it."

"I just don't know," said Frank. "I can't tell whether he's guilty or not. Maybe I'm losing my touch."

76

Mickey woke on the couch about three in the morning, unable to stop his brain churning. It was not looking good. He was a prisoner in his own home, fearing for his life, but at the same time he was the prime suspect in five murders, with a mountain of evidence pointing to him. The more he thought through that evidence, the more he realised what a great job someone had done in framing him. And if the police found Mum's car and it did turn out to have been the one that ran down Vanni, then it was game set and match over. Even the biggest mouth in the City couldn't talk his way out of that.

Mickey finally fell asleep just as the sun came up. When he woke again it was lunchtime. He couldn't bear the thought of spending another day hiding in his room, so despite protests from the bodyguards, and the fact that he wasn't especially hungry, he decided to go out for a pint and a bite.

The Duke of Wellington was the nearest pub serving food on New Year's Day. It was dimly lit and smelt of spilt beer on the worn carpet. Sinclair and Karim sat at the bar, neither of them drinking. Mickey sat by the window with a pint, pie and chips, working through the report and accounts for Summer Research. After all, if he did manage to escape death and prison he would move to Marcus's shop in the New Year, so he needed to get his head round the business. It soon became clear that the published report and accounts looked very different from the management accounts that Marcus had shown him. And they made for scary reading.

Not only had Marcus been booking commission promises as real income, he'd also been depreciating IT expenditure over ridiculously long periods and capitalising consultancy fees. There was also a string of unexplained provision reversals. This all helped give the appearance of a business making a profit. But when Mickey carefully constructed a cashflow analysis from the movement in the balance sheet he realised Summer Research had been bleeding cash every year, to the tune of two or three million pounds.

Bottom line was, the accounts were a total fiction.

Mickey set down his pint and stared out the window at a darkening sky. What sort of mess had he got himself into?

He went back to the accounts and turned to the auditor's report. There were no qualifications to the accounts, just a big loopy signature from someone at Deloutes Accountants. He relaxed a little. If Deloutes were happy then maybe it wasn't such a fiddle after all. But when he read the name of the accountants again he realised it was a slightly different spelling from the big accountancy firm he'd first assumed. He decided, as he had nothing else to do, that he might as well check it out. He spotted a phone mounted on the wall beside the bar and picked up the yellow pages.

"I hear this is a cracking read," he said.

"Belter," replied the barman.

Mickey flicked through to Chartered Accountants. The big names had half-page advertising spreads filled with beautiful people. Deloutes had just a phone number and an address. He scribbled it down on the back of a beer mat.

"Come on boys," he said to Sinclair and Karim.

Twenty minutes later they arrived at a run-down office block behind Euston Station. He pressed the buzzer, but wasn't surprised to get no answer on New Year's Day. After pressing another half dozen buttons he got lucky.

"Who is it?"

"All right, mate?" said Mickey. "I want to get in to Deloutes Accountants. But their buzzer ain't working."

There was a short purr and Mickey pushed the door open. He stepped inside and studied the office block plan. Deloutes was on the second floor.

He took the stairs and stopped at the door with a nameplate for RJ Deloutes, FCA, MAAT.

Through the broken glass panel he looked inside. It was just the one room with two desks facing each other. Presumably one for RJ and the other for the secretary. There were books and papers strewn everywhere. An ashtray sat on the table overflowing with fag ends. Not exactly one of the Big Four.

Marcus had paid some back-street bean counter to cook his books.

77

The relaxation room in the gym had no windows and low lighting. Marcus was sitting on a chaise longue, wrapped like a Roman emperor in a white dressing gown and towels. He raised an arm in acknowledgement of Mickey, but didn't turn his head so as not to disturb his face pack.

He barely moved his lips as he spoke. "I know I look ridiculous. But it's fantastic. You should try one yourself."

Mickey shook his head.

"Go on. I'll call over the …"

"I didn't come for a facial, Marcus."

"How about a sauna then, or a massage?"

"Shut up."

"You need something to relax you. The stress is showing in that twitch in your eyelid."

"It's not bloody surprising I'm stressed, is it?"

Marcus sat up slowly and took a sip of water through a straw. "What's troubling you now?"

"Apart from worrying about getting killed and being suspected of murder, I've just been round to your accountants and that was the scariest thing of all."

"*Our* accountants," corrected Marcus. "I'm surprised he was working on New Year's Day."

"I'm surprised he's working at all. Bloody hell, Marcus how much did you pay him to fiddle your accounts?"

"I'm not sure what you're implying, Mickey. I don't recall the fee, but he wasn't expensive."

"You know what I'm getting at. No real accountant would have signed off those accounts. They're a joke, Marcus. Summer Research is losing millions."

"Let's not go over all this again," said Marcus, patting the white face pack. "Of course I've got cash flow constraints."

"Constraints! Is that what you call your black hole?"

"That's why I need your capital injection." Marcus frowned as his pack cracked. He unwrapped a hot towel and wiped his face clean.

"The thing is, Marcus, I don't care so much about the fact the business is losing money. What I really care about is you lying to me. And those management accounts you showed me were even more of a lie than the real ones."

"They weren't a lie, Mickey. They just weren't the whole truth. Anyway, what do you really care about it? The money you're investing isn't really yours anyway. It's only the extra money that went into the moat pool."

"Do you think that makes me feel better?" asked Mickey. "It's money that should have gone to Vanni and Dan and the others."

"Let's face it, Mickey, they don't need it now."

"But it still doesn't feel right using their money this way. I feel like you've cheated them as well."

"It's too late to worry about that now, Mickey. The contract you signed was irrevocable."

"Stuff the contract, Marcus, you lied to me. So I'm having a rethink."

"I think you'll find that won't stand up in court, Mickey."

"Maybe I'll go check that out with a lawyer."

"Look, don't blow it now, Mickey, not after we've come so far. Not after all the effort I've put in to get you here."

"Effort you put in? What effort."

Marcus hesitated. "Persuading you to come. Putting the contract together."

Mickey suddenly had a hunch that the 'effort' referred to more than just putting together a contract.

"It was you. You scuppered my promotion so I would join you. You spread the rumour I was leaving and you complained to Sir Stanley about Amsterdam. It was you."

"Of course not."

But Mickey suspected his brother was lying. "You sod, Marcus. You knew what that promotion meant to me."

"It wasn't me." Marcus raised the palms of his hands. "But in any case you really wouldn't have enjoyed being Head of Equities at Royal Shire Bank. You'll have much more fun building a business with me. Trust me."

"Trust you! Don't make me laugh."

78

Frank could smell the alcohol the moment the headmaster entered the room. He'd obviously enjoyed a tipple too many with his New Year's Day lunch.

"I really appreciate you seeing me like this," said Frank.

"Not at all," replied the headmaster. "Always happy to help the police."

Frank explained why he'd come in a little more detail than he'd given over the phone.

"Marcus Summer's brother came a few days ago, asking the very same thing," said the headmaster.

"So I understand. So can you tell me what you know about events that day?"

"I know only the basic facts. That Tommy Summer hit Mr

Ranger during an argument. He fell over, hit his head on the pavement and died of a brain haemorrhage."

"And do you know what the argument was about?"

"Mr Summer never told us. He never explained his actions."

"I understand you told Mickey Summer that his brother was being bullied by Mr Ranger."

The headmaster flushed. "I didn't say that. Mickey Summer jumped to that conclusion."

"It's important I understand exactly what happened," said Frank, sitting forward in his seat and fixing the headmaster with a stare. "So, in your opinion, had Mr Ranger been bullying Marcus Summer?"

The headmaster wiped the back of his hand on his mouth. "Yes, I think probably Mr Ranger had been pushing Marcus too hard. But that was because Marcus wasn't performing. He'd been the brightest boy in the class and then his work just collapsed."

"What did you put that down to?"

"I didn't really think about it. I was newly qualified at the time. But I remember being impressed when I first arrived at the school, by Marcus' sharp brain and bright personality. He was a delight to teach. But for some reason he started to go into his shell. His class-work deteriorated sharply. He became angry and unruly. If he hadn't left he'd probably have been expelled for causing the fires."

"What fires?"

"He set fire to the gym," explained the headmaster. "He'd already set fire to a wastepaper basket in his room, and to the bins behind the kitchens. He'd become a danger to the other pupils."

"What can you tell me about Mr Ranger?"

"I didn't really know him."

"But you think he might have bullied Marcus," said Frank. "Was he aggressive?"

The headmaster nodded. "He was a big man. He was a bit too free with the corporal punishment, I think."

"Was he a happy man?"

"I couldn't say. I didn't really know much about him. Nobody did, really. He kept very much to himself."

"Bit of a loner then?" asked Frank.

"You might say that."

"Married?"

"I don't think so."

"Girlfriend?"

"Not that I knew about. When you live in, as Mr Ranger did, then it's difficult to make relationships outside of the school."

Frank nodded. "In that case do you think Ranger might have looked to make relationships inside the school?"

The head crossed his arms. "I don't know what you mean."

"I mean, did he try and make relationships with the boys?" Frank stared at the headmaster.

"Absolutely not."

"Can you be so sure, if you didn't really know him?"

"I can't be sure, but there's absolutely nothing to support that suggestion."

"Nothing?" said Frank. "One of the boys in his care underwent a severe personality change, probably as a result of being bullied by Mr Ranger. The school didn't do anything about it, and so he told his dad who was so angry about what he'd heard that he came up and hit that teacher. Hit him so hard he fell to the pavement and died. And why didn't the dad show any remorse? Why did he refuse to talk about it? Because Mr Ranger had broken the oldest taboo. Hadn't he? Well, am I right?"

The headmaster walked over to the window and stared out at the playing fields.

"All right," he said eventually. "There were rumours about Ranger and his interest in the boys. But whether the rumours were true or not, I really don't know."

"You mean you didn't *want* to know," said Frank. "Did the school investigate?"

"Ranger was dead. So what was the point?"

"A man was in prison for murder when he shouldn't have been."

The headmaster frowned. "You're the policeman, Inspector Brighouse, but I'm not sure if the knowledge that Mr Ranger had been abusing Marcus Summer would have changed the verdict. Surely it would simply have demonstrated motive. Murder is still murder, regardless of what Mr Ranger may or may not have done."

79

The gunshots grew louder as they drove the mile from the lodge to the shoot. Stepping out of the car the salvos became almost continuous, and the smell of discharge so strong, that Mickey wondered whether it could really be safe.

Then a horn sounded and the shooting stopped. From the leafless trees the hunters emerged with guns broken, laughing and bragging about their exploits as they crunched over the frozen ground. They gathered round the back of a Landrover. Sir Stanley pulled out a walnut drawer full of glasses, drinks and cigars. He helped himself to a whisky, then raised a bushy grey eyebrow as he caught sight of Mickey.

The loader who had driven Mickey up whispered in Sir Stanley's ear and he nodded and set down his drink.

"You have five minutes until the next drive, gentlemen," he called as he walked over, accompanied by a bodyguard.

"Happy New Year, Mickey."

"And you, Sir Stanley. Sorry for disturbing your shoot. Having any luck?"

"I've bagged a duck and a partridge. Now what brings you out here?"

"A few weeks back someone told you that I was planning to leave Royal Shire. I really need to know who told you that."

"It was said in strictest confidence."

"The thing is, I think I know who told you," said Mickey. "And he was doing it because he had his own agenda. He wanted you to think I was leaving so that you didn't promote me."

"As I said …"

"It was my brother wasn't it?"

Sir Stanley studied Mickey a while. "I'll answer your question honestly, if you answer one of mine honestly."

237

"Deal."

"*Are* you planning to leave the bank?"

Mickey hesitated. If he knew, then Sir Stanley might pull his lock-in payment.

"Don't worry," said Sir Stanley who must have guessed what he was thinking. "I'll honour your contract."

Mickey studied Sir Stanley closely and realised he was still the honourable gent he'd always been. He was old school, a man of his word.

"I probably am going to leave," said Mickey. "After everything that's happened, I need a change of scenery."

"You're not the only one, Mickey," Sir Stanley winked.

"You too?"

"Now we both have a secret to keep."

"It's safe with me," said Mickey. Even he could keep a secret for twenty four-hours. Just. "So, was it my brother who shopped me?"

"Yes, it was Marcus. He told a mutual acquaintance, ostensibly in strictest confidence, but with the certainty that I would be informed."

"And did Marcus tell you about the Dutch business?"

"That was an anonymous letter," said Sir Stanley. "Purporting to be from a client. But there was no such client. It could well have been from Marcus. It was the sort of dirty trick he used to get up to only too often: anonymous letters, off-the-record briefings to journalists – that sort of thing was Marcus' hallmark. Could I give you some advice, Mickey?"

"I'm sure you could."

"Leave Royal Shire if you must. But don't go and work with your brother. He's really not to be trusted."

"Why do you say that?" asked Mickey, who suddenly felt a sense of loyalty to his brother. "You trusted him enough to offer him a lock-in contract, so he can't have been all bad."

"Marcus was never offered a lock-in," said Sir Stanley, with a wry smile.

"What are you talking about? Course he was."

Stanley shook his head. "Your brother upset a lot of people at the bank and I took the view that it would solve a few issues and give us a fresh start if he left. Moreover, after everything he'd said over the years about the Americans, I knew he couldn't possibly have worked with our new friends. So Marcus agreed to leave without any compensation and without making any trouble, so long as we let him go with his pride intact. That meant him pretending he had been a key individual and had been awarded a lock-in. I never told anyone he had been given a lock-in, but I didn't disabuse people of that opinion."

"Bloody hell, I never knew." Mickey now wondered how many other lies his brother had told him.

Sir Stanley checked his watch. "Now, unless there's anything else you want to ask me …?"

"Well, I suppose, as we're almost there, I might as well know," said Mickey. "How much is my share of the lock-in going to be?"

Sir Stanley leant closer and whispered in Mickey's ear, to the discomfort of both sets of bodyguards, who shuffled about anxiously. "Twenty-million pounds, Mickey. So if you are planning on resigning, make sure you wait until after tomorrow!"

80

It was a bad day to be an employee of Royal Shire Bank. The newspapers had led with the billion pounds to be paid out that day, to the greedy parasites at the failed bank. Special anger was reserved for the dirtiest dozen in the lock-in group, whose number had been whittled down by one of their own.

So there was none of the usual excitement of bonus day. Of course many were not getting a bonus at all, and they felt as if they'd worked the whole year under false pretences.

For those who were getting one, it would be sharply down on what they expected, and much less than they could get for their services elsewhere. Their disappointment was tempered by the reality that any bonus was better than none. However, in such uncertain times, nobody really trusted what was written on the letters they'd received on Christmas Eve. Until the money was in the bank account, nothing was taken for granted.

So the mood was edgy.

There was also an undercurrent that Mickey had never experienced before. People avoided him as he walked to his desk; turning away or side-stepping to another route so their paths didn't cross.

The greetings from his team were not quite as welcoming as usual. And as he waited for his screens to come on he looked to other desks. The eyes he met flicked away. They believed the headlines. He thought once more whether the best thing to do would be to just slip away quietly. But that had never been his style. He put on his jacket and walked across the floor to the podium.

He blew on the microphone. "If I could have your attention please. I know some of you are surprised to see me. Some of you think I was involved in the deaths and I don't blame you for thinking that. The suggestion is there in black and white in your papers ain't it?"

He looked around the floor and saw the faces of people he used to think were friends. "But I'm telling you straight. I ain't got nothing to do with it. The other thing I want everyone to hear from me is that I've just quit the firm."

A gasp cut through the room, followed closely by hurried whispers as people speculated that Mickey had thrown away his lock-in by resigning before it was paid.

"I have many reasons," he continued. "Sure I was disappointed at not being promoted. Sure I'm fed up with the constant banker bashing just like you all are. There is also a personal twist for me, because someone I trusted tried to trick me into giving them a share of my bonus. But bloody hell guys. Five people are dead. Five people we all cared about. And it looks like they've been killed because of money. I've learnt over the last few horrible weeks that money is not everything. In fact it can be the worst thing of all. So I'm leaving mine on the table." He waved. "Best of luck."

Leaving the room in stunned silence, he hurried into a lift. As it descended he watched the floor numbers count down from twenty, through every million he was throwing away, all the way down to zero. His legs felt weak as he walked out into the lobby.

But as he exited into the cold air of the Wharf, he knew he'd done the right thing. Marcus wouldn't get a penny out of his trickery. And as for Whitwell Farm. Well, he'd lost Helen anyway. Why would he need a farm now?

81

Marcus insisted on meeting in one of the City's few remaining sawdust taverns. Mickey found him reading the FT at an upturned barrel that served as a table.

"Where have you been?" whispered Marcus. "Is everything all right? I've been calling you for the past hour."

"I walked," said Mickey.

"You walked here from Canary Wharf? Why?"

"Because I wanted to."

Sinclair had kerb-crawled beside Mickey again, much to his annoyance.

"Well you're here now." Marcus poured Mickey a glass of wine. "It should really be champers but I did too much of that on New Year's Eve. What did you get up to?"

"Stopped at home."

"I heard about your resignation," said Marcus. "It's all over the market. Word is that Sir Stanley is going to fall on his sword. Shame if you ask me."

Mickey said nothing.

"Everyone is wondering where you're going next," continued Marcus. "It'll be fun making the announcement."

"There won't be any announcement." Mickey shook his head. Marcus still didn't get it. "I'm not joining you, Marcus."

"Still feeling angry about the accounts?"

"I spoke to Sir Stanley. He said it was you who fed him the rumour I was leaving and that it was probably you who made the complaint about Amsterdam."

"Did he say that? And I told Carrick in strictest confidence. I thought he was a man of honour."

"What would you know about it?" said Mickey.

"Look, I had to be cruel to be kind, Mickey. You need to move on. I'm not surprised you're angry now, but you'll come round, eventually." Marcus took a drink of wine. "So, the lock-ins must have been paid earlier than expected, if you resigned this morning."

"I resigned before they were paid."

Marcus opened his mouth, caught his breath then shook his head. "That was very risky. They might have pulled the payment." He shrugged and leant closer. "Still, it doesn't matter now I suppose. So tell me. How much did we get?"

"Nothing."

"Don't tease me."

"We got nothing, Marcus."

"I can't afford any delay on this, Mickey. The money needs to be in the account today. Coutts are expecting it."

"You haven't been listening, Marcus. I said I resigned. This morning. Before the lock-in was paid."

"I know. But … Oh God no … they didn't pull it. They can't do that. We'll sue."

"I forfeited it on purpose."

Marcus flashed a panicked smile. "This is a joke, right?"

"Can you see anyone laughing?"

"You'll have to go back, Mickey and tell them it was a mistake."

"The mistake was yours, Marcus. For lying and scheming against your own brother."

Marcus screwed up his eyes. "I don't understand. You're not really, really telling me that you've just thrown away, what, twenty million pounds?"

"Now you've got it."

"I don't believe it."

"I think you do."

Marcus wrapped his arms round his body and rocked gently back and forth. "No. No. No."

"Do you honestly believe I would let you ruin my career and trick me into propping up your broken business with the blood money from my dead friends?"

"I'm finished," sobbed Marcus. "Without that money the business will fold."

Mickey said nothing.

"There must be some way for you to get the money back."

"The money has gone," said Mickey.

Marcus stood up, his legs shaking uncontrollably. He grabbed Mickey's tie and pulled him to his feet. "You always were the stupid little brother, Mickey."

He swung a punch. Mickey ducked under it, caught the arm and twisted it into a lock behind Marcus's back. He forced his brother down to his knees.

"You're breaking my arm!" he shouted.

"You're lucky I'm not breaking your neck," Mickey shouted.

Sinclair jumped down from the bar and ran over. "Hey! What's going on?"

"Nothing for you to worry about," said Mickey.

"Doesn't look like nothing to me," Sinclair said as he separated the two.

Marcus got up from the floor and brushed some sawdust off his trousers. "Have it your way then, Mickey. But you've just made the biggest mistake of your life."

82

"I still don't get it," Eddie said again. "Why would anyone just walk away from twenty million quid?"

It had been practically the only topic of conversation in the incident room that morning. Along with ideas for what a person could buy with twenty million.

"There's one possible explanation," said Hunt. "Mickey knows he can't get away with this. He knows we've got him and we're going to charge him for five murders, so he's started work on his defence. He'll claim he passed up the money because he felt too bad about taking money off his dead friends. His defence will then argue that without the money there is no motive."

Frank chewed the end of a pen until it cracked. The pen wasn't the only thing showing the strain. Frank hadn't slept properly for he didn't know how long. "So what was this fight with the brother all about?"

"That's easy," said Hunt. "Mickey was going to use some of his lock-in to save his brother's business. No wonder the brother threw a wobbly when he told him he'd left it on the table. Poor bloke's whole business is going under."

"Poor bloke!" scoffed Frank. He dropped the chewed pen in the bin. "There's no such thing as a poor banker."

"Still, I feel sorry for him," said Hunt.

"Do you?" said Frank. "Well I feel like getting some surveillance on him."

"On the brother? Why?"

"He stood to be a major beneficiary of the proceeds of five murders. He helped Mickey with false alibis. He bought the car that we believe was used in the hit-and-run. Take your pick."

83

When Mickey saw the receptionist emptying her personal belongings into a bin liner, it became clear why no-one had been answering the phones at Summer Securities. She didn't even look at him as he walked into the building.

A security guard blocked his entrance to the trading floor. "Are you an employee?"

"I'm the brother of the owner."

"The firm's gone into receivership," explained the guard. "We're clearing the premises."

"I need to find my brother."

"I'm only supposed to let staff in," the guard said.

Mickey showed him his driving license. "My name's Summer. The sign outside says Summer Securities. I have to find my brother."

The guard stood to one side. "I don't think he's in, but you can go check."

Mickey walked into the room where people were clearing their desks. A man Mickey half-recognised looked up from his pile. "If you're looking for your brother he's not here."

"Any idea where he is?"

"Wherever rats go when they desert a sinking ship. Gave us all notice by email then walked out without saying a word. Coward."

"I'm sorry, mate," said Mickey.

"Not sorry enough to have invested in the business though. I heard you pulled the plug on us at the last minute."

Mickey didn't know what to say. He hadn't slept a wink overnight, worrying if he'd done the right thing.

"It's more complicated than that," he said eventually.

The man grunted then turned back to his piles.

"Don't mind him, Mickey," a voice called from another desk. "We all knew the risks of coming here. Tell me though, is it true you quit Royal Shire just before you got your lock-in? Why on earth did you do that?"

Mickey recognised the man from the early days at Shire. "Long, long story Tim. Bottom line is: I didn't want the money."

Tim shook his head in disbelief. "I'd have taken it for you. Just to be helpful like."

"Not if you knew the whole story," Mickey said quietly, as he continued to Marcus' office.

Michelle finished her phone call as she saw him approach. She dabbed her eyes with her blouse sleeve. "Marcus isn't here."

"Any idea where he is?"

"No. He's turned off his mobile."

"How are you?"

"I know I shouldn't be shocked because we've known we were in trouble for a long time." She sniffed. "But I thought Marcus would pull us out of it somehow. I thought you were going to help. But Marcus says you changed your mind at the last minute."

"It's a long story, but the bottom line is I didn't have the money to invest in the end. I'm sorry."

She shrugged her shoulders. "Do you need a good PA by any chance?"

"I haven't got a job," said Mickey.

His phone rang and he turned away to take the call.

"Is that you, Mickey?"

"Marcus. Where the hell are you?"

"Never mind. Has this number come up on your phone?"

Mickey checked. "Yes."

"Ring me back on it from another phone."

Mickey stored the number and then dialled it from a nearby desk. "Are you all right, Marcus?"

"We need to talk," said his brother. "But alone. You need to get rid of your police tail."

"Sinclair and his man ain't with me no more. I've got Karim just to be on the safe side, but I told the police I don't need extra protection now the lock-in has been paid."

"Except of course your lock-in wasn't paid was it?"

"You know what I mean."

"I do know what you mean," said Marcus. "Anyway, the police still have you under surveillance. Lose them. And lose Karim as well. Then make your way to St Paul's. Get a new throwaway and ring me back on this number."

84

The incident room was lit up by the entrance of a lanky courier in a luminescent jacket and leggings.

"Special delivery for DI Brighouse," he bellowed.

"Over here," said Frank, waving an arm.

Frank signed for the small package. Inside were a type-written note and two keys.

Detective Inspector Brighouse.

I confess to killing Daniel Goldcup, Vanni Gamberoni, Benaifa Bendhiri, Percival Hetherington and Ben Stein.

I guess you want to know why? Why does anyone do anything in the City? For the money of course. It's a jungle. Survival of the fittest and all that. Killing for money is just taking it one step further.

Only problem is thanks to my double-crossing brother all my hard-earned money was going to be pissed away in his useless business. But I put a stop to that. Cost me the lot of course. But that's not your problem. That's his.

So well done Frank. You were right all along that it was me. And you got there in the end. Sorry I won't be there to witness your glory. And neither will my brother.

Cheers,

Mickey Summer

PS. Enclosed keys are for a lock-up in Selby Road, Leyton, and the Golf that you'll find inside it.

85

Mickey walked casually up Cheapside to the nearest phone shop and picked up a new throwaway. Out the corner of his eye he saw a chubby little man hanging around aimlessly in the street. But in the City nobody hangs around aimlessly, not even the beggars.

Marcus was right, he was still being followed. Leaving the shop, he walked down the narrow cobbled streets to a pub he used to go to in the early days of Shire.

"Pint of Guinness," he said to the barman. Karim declined the offer and took up a position near the door.

Through the open doorway Mickey saw the chubby bloke glance in as he walked by the pub. He was definitely following him. Time for another disappearing act. He was happy enough to lose the police but he was uncomfortable going about without Karim. He could handle himself against Marcus if he wanted another round of fisticuffs, but the police still didn't know whether or not it was one of the lock-in group behind the killings. It might still turn out to be some deranged anti-capitalist who couldn't care less that the money had now been paid. And although the crusties had long since been kicked out of their camp in St Paul's, they still hung around there during the day. Mickey could be walking into the lions' lair. Too late to worry about that now. He stood a ten pound note on the counter.

"I'm desperate for a whizz," he explained to the barman.

The toilet was halfway down a corridor. Mickey walked past and on to the fire exit that led to the back alley, where he'd had many a cough and drag in the days he used to smoke. Shit. It was fastened with a heavy chain and padlock. Health and Safety wouldn't be too impressed.

He hurried back to the gents. The windows were all above head height. He climbed up on a sink and pulled up a rusty metal lever. He pushed the window open as wide as it would go and wriggled through head first. He wished he hadn't eaten and drunk so much over the holiday as he struggled to get through. He pushed extra hard on the sill and felt himself falling.

"Urgh!" he said as he found himself on top of the pub's bin bags. A rat scuttled off down the alley. Mickey followed.

86

Frank turned the key in the lock. A click and then the garage door swung open on a black Golf. Frank checked the registration. It was Mrs Summer's alright.

Clearly distinguishable on the bonnet was a dent where the car had struck something. No doubt that something had been Vanni Gamberoni. Forensics would prove that soon enough.

"We've got him now," said Eddie.

Frank pulled on some rubber gloves, squeezed down the side of the garage and opened the driver's door as wide as it would go. He looked inside.

Empty.

He walked round the back and opened the boot. He pulled out a blue sports bag, took it back outside into the daylight and opened it.

Sifting through the contents he called out what he found while Eddie took notes. "One pair of size-nine Aesics running shoes. One Star of David. One bag of green leaves, we can safely assume is the Queen of poisons. One pill box containing white powder, we can assume is dodgy cocaine."

"Looks like game, set and match," said DI Hunt, grinning madly. "Come in Mickey Summer, your time is up."

Frank zipped the bag up, placed it on the passenger seat inside the car and then called the control room. "Control, this is DI Brig-house. Can you arrange a full lift for a VW Golf from Leyton lock-ups in Selby road. And can I have an ETA."

"Roger, full recovery, will contact next on list."

"And," said Frank, "Can you tell me where the Summer brothers are now?"

There was a short pause while control checked. *"Surveillance hasn't yet tracked down Marcus Summer. Mickey is at the Dog and Duck off Cheapside, EC1."*

"Tell the team I'm on my way to join them."

87

Mickey hid behind a newspaper as he passed CCTV cameras on his way out of St Paul's tube station. On the stairs up to street level he dialled Marcus. "I'm at St Paul's tube. Where are you?"

"Inside the Cathedral. On top of the dome."

"On top of the dome," repeated Mickey. "What the hell are you doing up there?"

"Enjoying the view. Come on up."

"You know I hate heights," said Mickey.

"Don't look down then."

Mickey reluctantly agreed. He walked on but stopped at the entrance to St Paul's Churchyard. This time of year it was normally empty but now it was full of an eclectic mob of anti-capitalist protestors, many of them wearing the Guy Fawkes Vendetta masks that had become the face of the protest. If any of them recognised his own face from the newspaper photo, things might turn nasty. He wished now that he hadn't left Karim behind. He took a deep breath and plunged in.

Fortunately nobody so much as looked at him. In a moment he was passing through the entrance. He'd never actually been inside the cathedral before and couldn't fail to be impressed. The golden dome echoed with hundreds of footsteps and was big enough to house the Stock Exchange and the Bank of England and still have room for a couple of trading floors. In this age of technology,

Mickey was amazed to think it had been built by hand, with ladders and ropes, hammers and chisels.

He was less impressed by the lack of a lift to the top and the thirty minutes of endless steps before he finally emerged into a cold fog on the outside walkway on top of the dome. Mickey didn't dare look down. He told himself that the dome was just a few feet off the ground, as he hugged the inside wall on the walkway.

He found his brother sitting in a stone recess, his coat collar pulled up and gloved hands stuffed in pockets.

"You took your time," Marcus said.

"I left the chopper at home," said Mickey. "What are you doing up 'ere anyway?"

"I thought you would appreciate the setting," said Marcus. "Since you decided to play God."

"Play God?"

"Isn't that what you were doing by throwing away my money? Delivering divine retribution on me."

"Retribution?" Mickey was confused. "I didn't like being lied to and tricked, that's all. Besides which it was my money, Marcus, and I wasn't feeling too great about it in any case. I decided to give it away. My choice."

The fog suddenly lifted and out of the corner of his eye Mickey saw tall buildings rising up around them. He could no longer pretend they were just a few feet above the ground. He grabbed hold of the stone railing to steady himself.

Marcus stepped beside him and pointed to the distance.

"There's Lloyds," he said. "And over there is the NatWest Tower."

"It's been Tower Forty Two for years," corrected Mickey, while forcing his gaze on the stone floor at his feet. "Not that it matters."

"Not that any of it matters," echoed Marcus. "I've worked in the City for twenty-five years. Can you imagine over that time, just how many fortunes have been made down there?"

"And lost," said Mickey, uncertain where the conversation was leading.

"Thousands have found those streets paved with gold, Mickey. Maybe even hundreds of thousands. Young men have made a name for themselves, left their mark and are already enjoying a comfortable retirement." He turned to look at Mickey. "But I won't be, will I? Thanks to you, little brother, I'm ruined."

"I'm sure you'll find a way to come back. You always do."

"Not this time, Mickey. Summer Research was my last hurrah. Now it's gone, thanks to you."

In spite of all his trickery, Mickey did genuinely feel sorry for his brother. He looked small and broken. "I'm sorry it didn't work out."

"Didn't work out? But it *was* working, Mickey. You killed it."

"You lied to me, Marcus. And you tricked me out of a promotion. In any case I couldn't take that money. It wouldn't have been right. It was blood money."

"It was blood money the moment they signed the lock-in contracts and put the final nail in the coffin of the old City," said Marcus.

"You don't mean that," said Mickey. "It sounds like you think they deserved to be killed."

"They all had it coming," said Marcus. "Thirty pieces of silver for betraying five-hundred years of tradition."

Mickey thought back to the boardroom vote on the acquisition. He couldn't be sure, but he seemed to recall that all five who were now dead had voted to allow State Financial to take its stake in Royal Shire.

"That's not a reason for someone to kill them."

"Good enough reason in my book."

"Are you saying you think that's why they died?"

"That's one of the reasons. Though …" Marcus was interrupted by some Japanese school kids spilling onto the walkway. They peered over the railing, laughing and giggling before disappearing round the dome. Marcus followed.

Mickey walked after him and found him padlocking a chain that he had fastened around the railing and the door that led back inside the Cathedral.

"What the hell are you doing?"

"We need to be alone," said Marcus.

"We definitely don't."

Mickey pulled the chain. It slid an inch on the stone but gave no slack. He tried the door, but it wouldn't budge.

The guard banged on the door from the inside. "Open this up!"

"I'm trying, mate!" Mickey yelled back. "Give us some help here!"

Mickey pulled again but there was nothing giving. He hurried round the walkway to the entrance, but Marcus had also padlocked that door.

"How do you know that was one of the reasons they died?" asked Mickey, although a terrible fear was growing that he knew the answer. He grabbed Marcus on both shoulders and shook him. "How do you know?"

Marcus stepped back. His right hand held a gun. "How do you think I know, Mickey?"

88

Frank and Eddie drove back to the City in silence. Frank was fully occupied trying to figure out whether the confessional letter, the car and its contents supported his theory or blew it apart. It could work either way. But his gut instinct was strong. Mad, bad or telling the truth. He reckoned he now knew which applied to Mickey Summer.

His thoughts were interrupted by the ring of his phone.

It was Sinclair. "Sir, we've lost Mickey Summer."

Frank slapped a hand on the dashboard. "How?"

"He went into a pub. Went for a pee and jumped out the toilet window."

"Oldest trick in the book," said Frank.

"Sorry, Sir. If I'd had more men I'd have put someone round the back."

Frank knew that Sinclair had put in a request for support but had got no joy. "You need to put out an urgent observations."

"Will do," said Sinclair. "Shall I alert London airports as well?"

"Do it," said Frank.

"Shall we head to the airport?" asked Eddie.

"I don't think Mickey's doing a runner," said Frank. "My guess is he's meeting his brother somewhere."

"In that case we need to get to the brother before Mickey does."

89

"So, how do you know?" Mickey asked again.

"You know how I know," said Marcus, smiling.

Mickey's mouth had run dry and he could barely speak. "You killed them."

"Not all of them," said Marcus. "Ben was a genuine heart attack, although to be fair it was probably brought on by the sight of the knife in my hand. So let's not quibble."

Mickey's legs felt weak. He steadied himself on the railing and tried to comprehend. "Why did you do it? Surely you didn't kill them just because they voted for the merger?"

"They sold the last bastion of British investment banking," said Marcus. "But you're right. That was only part of it. The real reason was I needed the money and I realised it would create the windfall you needed to be able to invest in Summer Securities. Only you messed it all up, little brother."

So it was true. Marcus was admitting it. Mickey fought the urge to grab his brother by the throat and smash his head into the wall. The fact that Marcus had a gun also stopped him. He needed to keep calm. He needed to keep Marcus talking. Sooner or later the guards would break the doors down and they'd be able to tackle the madman together. Mad? That was the least of it. He was a killer. Mickey still couldn't quite believe it. His own brother.

"How could you do it, Marcus?"

"It was simply a question of careful planning and good execution," said Marcus. "If you'll excuse the pun."

"But you can't possibly get away with it," said Mickey.

"Oh, but I can," said Marcus. "You see, I arranged everything so that you were implicated in each murder. I did that as an insurance policy because I thought you might just be clever enough to work out what was happening and so I was going to use this to keep you silent. But I overestimated you, Mickey. Not only were you not clever enough to work out what was going on, you were stupid enough to throw away the money. So now I'll use my insurance policy to exact my revenge on you instead."

"So do you plan to kill me as well?" asked Mickey.

"Better than that," said Marcus smiling. "I've sent DI Brighouse a letter from you confessing to the killings."

"I'll deny it."

"I've also sent him the keys to a lock-up where I hid Mum's car. They'll discover a big dent where the car hit Vanni."

"I'll just explain it was you driving."

"Of course you will. And I'll deny it. Then they'll examine the car. You see the thing is, Mickey, I was very careful not to leave any prints. Yours, on the other hand, will be all over it from the time you drove it round to Mum's."

"It'll be your word against mine then."

"In a bag in the boot of the car," continued Marcus, "Are a number of items that will interest the police. Your Aesics running shoes which I wore round at Ben's house, although I had surgical shoes on at the time so again, there will be no trace to me. They will of course be stuffed full of forensic evidence linking them to you."

"I'll explain that. The Old Bill ain't stupid …"

"The Gold Star of David is in the car as well, wrapped in a pillow case from off your bed. Then there are the poisonous leaves Benaifa ate, which are wrapped in a plastic bag I took from your house. Finally, there is a batch of the bad cocaine I gave Percy, which is stored in a plastic pill box I took from your medicine cabinet. So all in all, there should be plenty of forensic evidence to link these items directly to you."

"I'll take my chances," said Mickey. "My word against yours."

"Que sera, sera."

"And you can cut out the Latin."

"That was Spanish actually," said Marcus. "But in any case Mickey, there's more to my plan than a game of chance."

Mickey didn't see Marcus' fist until late. It caught him straight between the eyes and knocked him back on his feet.

"Feel better for that do you?"

Marcus said nothing. He pointed the gun at Mickey and began to slowly pull back the trigger. Mickey lunged forward and locked both hands on Marcus' gun hand. The two men wrestled on the walkway, moving back and forth until they came to a halt, both leaning out precariously over the railing. Far below Mickey could see toy-town cranes and diggers. His head started to spin. He was going to faint.

Still holding his brother's gun hand, Mickey twisted and turned away from the edge.

Then the gun exploded.

Mickey and Marcus both fell to the ground. The two men lay still for a moment. When Mickey recovered, he realised Marcus was curled up, clutching his stomach. A red stain was forming on his white shirt.

"Oh my God," said Mickey, who now had a hold of the gun. "You've been shot."

Marcus pulled himself up on one elbow and looked down at the blood.

"Keep the pressure on the wound," said Mickey.

He took off his jacket and pressed it against his brother.

But Marcus only laughed and pushed Mickey away. He pulled himself back on to his feet

"Marcus, sit down. You're bleeding badly."

"Of course I am."

Marcus tried to throw another punch but stumbled. He turned back to Mickey.

"Stay back," said Mickey, pointing the gun at Marcus, his hands shaking. "And sit down. For your own good, sit down."

Marcus sat down, propped up against the railing. "You really are following the script, Mickey. You see, when the police find me dead, from a bullet from that gun, it will have only your finger-prints on."

He held up a gloved hand and smiled.

90

"We're looking for a needle in a haystack," said Eddie as he swept his eyes along the pavements.

"It's all we've got," said Frank.

"I hope we can find Mickey before he finds his brother," said Eddie. "We can't let him kill again."

"I'm not so sure Mickey has killed anyone," said Frank.

"We've got a confession."

"Did Mickey write that letter?" asked Frank. "Could be another set up job."

"Don't start on this again," said Eddie. "We've got hard evidence now. The car and the shoes and all the other stuff in that bag. I'll bet my pension Mickey's prints are all over them."

"No doubt," said Frank. "But that still doesn't necessarily make him the killer."

"So who is the killer then?" asked Eddie.

"Could be the brother."

"The brother?" asked Eddie. "Why?"

"Money," said Frank. "And because he could be a psychopath."

"How do you work that out?"

"Remember the homicidal triad? Marcus Summer set fire to Woodhouse School. And it was probably him, not Mickey, who burnt Mrs Sidnall's cat. And it was him, not Mickey, who wet his bed. More importantly we've since found out it was Marcus who suffered abuse. Marcus could be the psychopath. Maybe we've had the wrong brother all along."

As they turned passed St Bart's hospital a message came in from control.

"*All patrols. All patrols. We have a report of a firearm incident at St Paul's Cathedral. ARVs have been dispatched.*"

Frank picked up the handset. "Control, this is DI Brighouse. Any more detail on that report?"

"*Two men have padlocked themselves behind the doors on the dome of the Cathedral. One of them has a gun. And we have reports of a discharge.*"

"Control this is DI Brighouse. Show me in attendance."

"*Do not approach,*" said control. "*ARVs have been dispatched. Repeat.*

Do not approach."

Frank hung up without replying.

He turned to Eddie. "What are you waiting for? Let's go."

"You heard control," said Eddie. "Do not approach."

"I'm going deaf. Get us round there."

"I'm not disobeying a direct order, Sir."

"Drop me here then," said Frank. "I'll be quicker running anyway."

Eddie pulled up. "Are you sure we should be doing this?"

"You stay out of it."

Frank sprinted through Paternoster Square and into St Paul's Churchyard. As he came to the protesters milling around the front of the Cathedral, he saw the armed response units pulling up with lights flashing but sirens off. Guns shouldered, they marched quickly through the protestors who jumped aside, clearly worried that they had arrived to move them on. Frank knew he had to get to Mickey before the armed police did.

He ran up the front steps two at a time. Inside he slowed to a respectful jog down the main aisle but his heels still clicked loudly on the ancient tiles. He found himself apologising under his breath.

The security guard at the bottom of the steps to the dome confirmed that his colleagues at the top had been locked out of the highest walkway. They had radioed down for bolt cutters.

Frank started up the steps, noting a sign warning there was no turning back before completing the hundred and sixty steps up to the Whispering Gallery. Frank had no intention of turning back. He made it up a hundred steps before getting stuck behind an American family.

"Remember kids we're taking this real slow," said the mom, who didn't look in any shape to take it otherwise.

"Let me through," shouted Frank. "I'm a police officer."

"Is there a problem?" asked the mom.

"Nothing for you to worry about, but you should go back. Now, I need to get past."

He squeezed by the rather plump group, apologising again, and continued on up. His heart was pounding by the time he came out onto the dome's inner walkway. He hurried round the circle to where a guard was sitting on a stool outside a small door.

"How much further to the top?" asked Frank.

"The top is closed," said the guard. "I have to ask you to make your way back down again."

Frank flashed his badge. "I need to get up there." He took a deep breath, ducked through the doorway and started up the spiral stairway. His natural athleticism kicked in, as well as adrenalin, as he raced on up. He soon caught up with the guard taking up the bolt cutters; wheezing as he took each step.

"I'm police," said Frank. "I'll take those."

The guard didn't argue, grateful for some respite.

Frank climbed on, and although his breathing became harder as the handrail grew colder, he kept his speed up.

At the stone gallery, an anxious looking guard waved him on up the final flight to the Golden Gallery.

91

Marcus had sunk into a monologue about the death of British merchant banking; the old City names that one-by-one had been taken over by foreign banks and gone to ruin.

Mickey let him talk. Eventually the guards would have the doors down and then they could get Marcus off to hospital. He looked to be losing a lot of blood, though a part of Mickey didn't really care.

"What I don't get, Marcus, is how you're so nostalgic for the old merchant banking days yet you don't appear to feel sorry for killing five innocent people."

"Daniel, Vanni, Ben, Percy, Benaifa." Marcus reeled off the names proudly. "They got what they deserved. They knew that Royal Shire was the City's last stand. It was a family. The only real family I ever had. They said they understood our values. But then, when the money was put in front of them they sold out."

"That was never reason to kill," said Mickey. "What happened to you, Marcus? What on earth turned you into a killer?"

"You really want to know?" Marcus' eyes narrowed. "You

thought I was the lucky one winning that scholarship, didn't you. But you don't know what happened to me when I got there, do you?"

"I know about the bullying by Ranger, if that's what you're talking about. So that turned you anti-American did it? That's no reason to kill the others, just because they sided with the Americans."

"Bullying!" shouted Marcus. "Is that the euphemism they used?"

"What did happen then?" asked Mickey, fearing the worst, but needing to know once and for all.

Marcus said nothing for a while. Eventually he spoke, almost in a whisper. "He would come into my room at night. He had his own key you see. Then he would lock the door behind him." Marcus bit his lip and looked away. "So it was a bit more than bullying, you see."

"I'm sorry," Mickey whispered back. It seemed such a useless response, but he couldn't think of anything else to say.

"Ranger said I'd be sent to prison if I told anyone," Marcus continued. "But I did eventually tell Dad. And we all know what happened then. It was him who went to prison. So you see, that was my fault."

"That wasn't your fault," said Mickey. He was innocent of that at least. However, Marcus had known what he was doing was wrong when he'd pushed Daniel into the river, run over Vanni and poisoned Benaifa and Percy.

Mickey couldn't forgive Marcus for what he'd done, but at least he was starting to understand.

"It's maybe not surprising you got messed up," said Mickey. "Maybe the courts will go easy on you."

"I won't be going to any court, Mickey."

"We'll see. First we need to get you to hospital before you bleed to death."

"It's too late for that." Marcus pulled himself back onto his feet. Then he put a foot on a ridge in the alcove and stepped up onto the railing.

"Careful!" shouted Mickey.

Frank's lungs were bursting as he reached the last step. He sank to his knees and took five sharp recovery breaths before showing the guard his badge.

"Leave this to me."

As he worked the cutters through the gap in the door he could hear the Summer brothers arguing on the other side. He strained to catch some of their conversation but was forced to concentrate on the chain links, which were a full half-inch thick and weren't giving in without a fight. Frank pressed one cutter arm against his tensed stomach and pulled the other with all the strength he could muster.

The chain finally broke. He pulled it free of the lock, pushed the door open and ran outside to find Marcus Summer standing precariously on the stone railing.

"Thank God you've got here, Inspector! My brother's gone mad. He shot me and now he's making me jump over the side."

Suddenly a helicopter buzzed in from the other side of the dome and hovered overhead. The downdraft buffeted Marcus, almost knocking him off the railing. "Put your hands on your head!" someone called on a loudspeaker.

"Back off! Back off!" Frank shouted, waving the pilot away.

It moved fifty metres, but as it did so a door slid open and a marksman leant out, aiming his rifle at Mickey.

"Drop the weapon!" someone called on a loudspeaker.

Mickey had forgotten he still had the gun in his hand.

"It went off by accident," he said.

"Drop it!" Frank shouted.

The gun clattered to the stone floor.

"I'm Police! Back off!" Frank screamed at the marksman. He jumped in front of Mickey and slowly the marksman lowered his weapon. Frank stepped over to Marcus and held out a hand. "You can come down now. Come on. I'll look after you."

Marcus stretched out a hand but then snatched it back. As he did so he lost his balance and toppled backwards. Frank jumped in and flung an arm over the railing. But he caught thin air.

Marcus landed on his side on the shallow gradient at the top of the dome. He rolled onto his feet and held steady for a moment, stretching for a hold on a lightening conductor.

"Hang on!" Frank whipped off his jacket and lowered it over the railing.

Marcus reached out a hand but his foot slipped and he slid further down.

"Hang on!" called Mickey. He took the jacket off Frank and climbed over the railing. "Grab hold of my legs."

"It's too dangerous," said Frank.

But Mickey was already over the side and Frank had no choice but to grab hold of Mickey's ankles as he reached down for his brother.

Mickey tried hard to pretend he wasn't hundreds of feet above ground. He stretched out and lowered the jacket within inches of Marcus. His brother reached up for it but missed and slid down further.

Frank screamed at the helicopter. "For God's sake help us! We need a rope."

Marcus tried to climb up again, but lost his footing.

And then he was gone.

Over the side, falling to whatever lay waiting for him hundreds of feet below.

Mickey shut his eyes. His body went limp.

"I've got you!" Frank shouted.

He pulled Mickey up and back over the railing.

They sank together to the stone floor.

"It was an accident," said Mickey. "Marcus set it up so it looked like I was trying to kill him. Just like he set up …"

Mickey stopped. There was no point trying to explain. Who was going to believe him now?

* * *

"Hands up! Up!" screamed the head of the armed response unit, his gun readied. Behind him on the narrow staircase the rest of his team were breathing heavily from the climb.

"Keep your hat on," said Frank. "I'm police. The situation is under control." He showed his badge.

"There were reports of a gun discharge."

"I've got the gun," said Frank.

"I'll take that."

Frank handed it over.

The man frisked Frank and Mickey. "Where's the third man?"

"He went over the side," explained Frank.

The officer lowered his weapon. They descended slowly, in a silence that was only broken by the occasional clatter of weapons against the stone wall. When they emerged onto the floor of the Cathedral, all hell broke loose.

"Is that Mickey Summer you have under arrest?" asked someone.

"Has he been charged with murder?" asked another.

The questions flashed as quickly as the cameras.

"Has he killed another banker?"

"Can you confirm he's the Royal Shire Killer?"

Frank threw his jacket over Mickey's head and hurried him away down the aisle and out of the Cathedral. As they appeared on the outside steps, the anti-capitalist protestors jeered and whistled, though it wasn't clear to Frank whether that was at the sight of a killer apprehended or just a banker in handcuffs.

"Out of the way!" he shouted, as he forced a path through to the line of police cars. He spotted Eddie waiting with the rear passenger door open and bundled Mickey in.

"Snow Hill?" asked Eddie.

Without waiting for an answer he pulled out into traffic, light flashing but siren off, and they were soon racing up Farringdon Road. Frank looked out the back to see a couple of press motorcycles following close.

"Do you want me to lose the press?" asked Eddie.

"No need," said Frank. "And slow it down. There's no emergency now."

With a look of mild disappointment, Eddie eased his foot off the accelerator.

262

92

They waited in silence for Veronica and Armstrong to arrive, and then Frank gave Mickey the all clear to talk.

"I guess you're probably not going to believe any of this, but it was my brother behind the killings all along. Marcus needed the money to save his business and he knew how the moat pool worked. So he killed them so that I got a windfall that I wouldn't mind investing in something speculative, like his business. At the same time, he framed me for the murders, so if I found out what he'd done he could blackmail me to stop me going to the police. So he ran over Vanni in my Mum's car, which had my prints on it but none of …"

Mickey stopped and shook his head. "What's the point?"

"Don't stop," said Frank.

"You don't believe me," said Mickey. "You never have."

"Try me."

Mickey sighed. "Marcus also wore a pair of my old shoes round to Ben Stein's house and made sure he left footprints to frame me. He wore surgical shoes inside the trainers so there was no trace of him. He stored the poison he used on Benaifa and the bad drugs he used on Percy in containers he got from my house. So again they had my prints on but not his. The gambling debts, the payments to Dave Casey, the false alibis, they were all Marcus' tricks designed to make you suspicious of me, but not enough to give you reason to arrest me. He was very clever."

"Too clever," said Frank.

"How do you mean?"

"A serial killer plans meticulously. He doesn't push someone off a bridge minutes after having an argument. He doesn't run someone over in his mum's car, traipse muddy shoes over a white carpet or leave poison wrapped up neatly in his own toiletry bags. It was obvious you were being set up."

"So, are you saying, you think I'm telling the truth?" asked Mickey.

"I do," said Frank.

Armstrong didn't look so sure. "Let's step outside a minute,

Frank." They left the interview room and moved a few metres down the corridor. "You're just going to take his word for it?"

"We'll check it all out," said Frank. "But I'm sure he's telling the truth."

"Don't you want to at least question him about what went on up at St Paul's?" asked Armstrong.

"I was there," said Frank. "It's as Mickey said. The brother threw himself off, trying to frame Mickey for yet another murder. Only he didn't count on me getting there in time to see it."

"What about the gun shot?" asked Armstrong.

"It was Marcus' gun. Shouldn't be difficult to prove that. It went off by accident when Mickey tried to disarm his brother."

"You saw all this?"

"Not as such."

"How do you know then?"

"Gut instinct, Sir. Besides, why would Mickey shoot his brother on the top of St Paul's from where there is no escape? It doesn't stack up."

"And the confessional letter?"

"Another trick. Marcus wrote it."

Armstrong looked to Mickey. "Are you sure about this, Frank?"

"Like I say, we'll check it all out. But I'm sure."

* * *

"So is Mickey free to go then?" asked Veronica, once they had returned to the room

"For now," said Frank.

"That is, we aren't pressing any charges for now," Armstrong added quickly.

"What do you mean 'for now'?" asked Mickey.

"Assuming the rest of our enquiries corroborate your version of events, then you have nothing to worry about."

"I'm not sure I like the sound of that," said Mickey.

"It is what it is," said Armstrong. "And for sure we'll need to talk to you again, to clear up certain matters. But we can leave that until another day. You've had a rough time. Probably need time to think."

Mickey turned to Veronica. She looked comfortable with what Armstrong had said, so he relaxed a little. The end of this hell was in sight. Not that it would ever be over totally. He was slowly coming to terms with the fact his brother had killed his friends, and was now himself dead. But he didn't believe it would ever really make sense.

"Well, I'd better go feed the press something," said Armstrong. "I'd like to see you straight after, Frank."

He left the room and Veronica then turned to Frank.

"Let me know when you want Mickey to come in again," she said. "I appreciate it's only to clear up loose ends, but he'll still need a lawyer."

"Thanks, but there's no need," interrupted Mickey.

"Are you sure?"

"Sure I'm sure. Me and DI Brighouse understand each other now. Don't we?"

"I think we do," said Frank. "I'm sorry it took me so long."

"You got there in the end," said Mickey.

Veronica nodded. "Well, Mickey, if you don't need me any longer, I'll say goodbye."

She shook his hand but he couldn't stop himself giving her a peck on the cheek. She turned and walked away.

Another time, another place, thought Mickey. He and Frank were left alone in the room.

"One thing I still don't get," said Frank. "That twenty million pounds you left on the table …"

"You're too late," said Mickey. "The cleaners will have pocketed that by now."

"But you worked hard for it," continued Frank. "And you fought to keep the money when others wanted to take it from you. But in the end you just walked away from it, as if it didn't matter after all."

Mickey had surprised himself on that as well. "I did it because I wanted to punish Marcus for lying to me. And I also never did feel right taking the money off the dead. And that was before I realised that my own brother had killed them."

"So it was just to get back at your brother then?"

"I guess I had also started to realise I'd been in denial."

"Denial?"

"Not de river in Egypt," said Mickey. "Denial about the lock-ins, the bonuses, the whole system. I ain't turned into an anti-capitalist or anything but, well, something's wrong ain't it, when one person can walk off with enough money to run a hospital?"

"I wouldn't be so hard on yourself," said Frank. "Like me, you got there in the end."

Mickey nodded. "I thought Marcus had really done for me up there on St Paul's. Thanks."

"Don't thank me," said Frank. "I should have worked it out sooner. Might have stopped the killings earlier. I'll have to take my share of the blame for that."

"Don't," said Mickey. "There's only one person to blame. Though I still can't really believe my own brother killed them. How could he do that?"

"The Marcus Summer who did this wasn't the same Marcus Summer that you remember as your brother," said Frank. "He was a psychopath. Damaged by what happened to him at that school."

"So are you saying it wasn't his fault?" asked Mickey. Somehow he really wanted to hear that.

"The law says psychopaths are responsible for their actions," said Frank. "That's why they go to jail."

"But what do you think?" asked Mickey. "Can we really blame him, after what happened to him?"

"God will be the judge of that."

93

Frank's spikes clattered across the gritted car park, then crunched over the frosted field as he jogged towards the race start. The thought of footwear reminded him of what MacIntyre had said. He was now a 'shoe in' for Chief Inspector when the next vacancy arose. Funny thing was, now that it was on offer he was no longer so sure he wanted promotion to a desk job.

He checked his watch and realised he needed to get a shift on. He picked up his knees and sprinted through a gate into the next field where hundreds of runners, in vests of every colour, were rubbing hands, jumping up and down to keep warm, stretching, checking watches and tightening shoelaces. Frank spotted some clubmates and ran over to join them, just before the crack of the gun started a stampede up the first hill.

As his feet slipped on the icier patches, Frank realised he should have worn longer spikes. The run would be a lot harder without them. There again, that suited him fine. He wasn't here to win prizes. He gritted his teeth and pressed on.

Forty minutes later the finishing line came into view. Two hundred metres to go ... one hundred ... fifty ...

He made it, and somehow he didn't feel as knackered as usual. He wandered down the rope funnel and picked up his place disc. Sixty-first. He had to double check. Best finish ever. He handed his disc to the team captain, who was suitably impressed.

"Well run, Frank. Those grey hairs of yours are deceptive."

"What grey?" said Frank. "That's quicksilver, son."

94

It had been an honourable defeat for the Hammers against the Premiership leaders, and Mickey had thoroughly enjoyed an afternoon singing his voice hoarse and being anonymous in a crowd of forty thousand. The first flecks of snow were falling as he disappeared into the underground station.

By the time he resurfaced in Royal Docks he was struggling through a whiteout. And so he didn't at first notice the person sitting on the bench near his house, until she called out.

"Mickey?"

He wiped away a snowflake that had fallen in his eyelash. "Helen? What are you doing out here?"

"Waiting for you."

"But you've got a key."

"I didn't want to presume," she said.

"Come on in, you must be freezing."

Mickey took her arm and led her into the flat. He shook the snow off their coats and hung them up to dry. Then he made hot drinks.

"This global warming is getting serious," he said, as they pulled two chairs up close to the fire. "Anyhow, it's great to see you."

"And you," she said quietly.

She seemed lost for words, and for once, so was Mickey. They sat in silence a while.

"I've had a change of mind, Mickey," she said eventually.

"Brain surgeons can do anything nowadays can't they?"

"I mean about your proposal," she said. "That is, if you still feel the same. If it isn't too late."

Mickey set his drink down on the carpet. "I'm afraid it is too late, Helen. There's a lot happened since we last met. I don't really know where to start. They say start at the beginning don't they, but I need to start at the end. This is going to come as a shock, but it turns out Marcus killed them all."

"I know," she said. "It was in the papers."

"I've been avoiding them," said Mickey. "And Marcus set it all up so it looked like I done it. That's why the police were all over me like a squirrel at a jar of Nutella. But that DI Brighouse turned up trumps in the end and realised I was innocent."

"I never doubted that for one moment."

"Thanks," said Mickey. "But the thing is that, although I didn't realise what Marcus was up to, I did realise he'd tricked me into putting the extra lock-in money into his business. And that got me mad. So I resigned and forfeited the money."

"I know, Manita told me."

"I mean all of it, Helen. Twenty million squid up in smoke. And then all the savings I did have. The million quid nest-egg. Well I went and give that away to Manita's charity in Nepal. I'd sort of promised it her. Couldn't let her down."

"She told me that as well," said Helen.

"So you see, it's too late. I can't buy Whitwell farm now. Don't have the money."

"I'm not bothered about the farm," said Helen. "Giving up the money's why I'm here."

"Really?"

"Yes. It proves what you said all along. That it isn't really about the money. And now I have to prove what I've been saying all along. That you weren't the problem in our relationship. And there's only one way I can do that, isn't there?"

She edged closer.

They kissed.

"Welcome home."

About the author

Michael Crawshaw grew up in Leeds. He studied Chemistry at Manchester University and passed up the opportunity to spend his life researching metal benzoate compounds in favour of a spell in the City. He decided to give it two years. Sixteen years later he got out, having worked for several of the world's leading investment banks.

When he is not writing, Mike devotes his time to the charity *Hands Together – Tiplyang Project*, **www.handstogether.org.uk**

Acknowledgements

Support and advisory: Dave Stacey, Helen Wilkinson, Penelope Overton, Hamish Thompson, Carolyn Boyes and, of course, my family.

Editorial: All the above, Michael Roscoe and the inspirational Lynne McCallister, plus Benjamin Sharkey for the cover design concept.

Police procedural: Mark Peterson-Johansson, Mike White, Tim Stevens (all mistakes are mine).

Finance: This is a work of fiction. But clearly a little part of many people has inevitably, sometimes subconsciously, been absorbed into characters and settings. You know who you are!